Rural Route 8

Rural Route 8

E. Raye Turonek

URBAN
Renaissance

www.urbanbooks.net

Urban Books, LLC
300 Farmingdale Road, NY-Route 109
Farmingdale, NY 11735

ISBN 13: 978-1-64556-462-1
ISBN 10: 1-64556-462-2

First Mass Market Printing June 2023
First Trade Paperback Printing August 2022
Printed in the United States of America

10 9 8 7 6 5 4 3 2 1

This is a work of fiction. Any references or similarities to actual events, real people, living or dead, or to real locales are intended to give the novel a sense of reality. Any similarity in other names, characters, places, and incidents is entirely coincidental.

Distributed by Kensington Publishing Corp.
Submit Orders to:
Customer Service
400 Hahn Road
Westminster, MD 21157-4627
Phone: 1-800-733-3000
Fax: 1-800-659-2436

Rural Route 8

by

E. Raye Turonek

A Message from the Author

First and foremost, I give thanks to God, my angels, ancestors, and spirit guides for supporting me through this process. This book is dedicated to my late sister Margaret Buckman, my grandmother Maggie Hatcher, and my grandfather Charles Richard. Without them this would not be possible. You are loved and will be forever missed.

To N'TYSE aka Shawanda Williams of Black Odyssey Film & Media, I owe you a debt of gratitude. Thank you for being you! You have been a blessing to me since the day we connected. I wish you all the success in the world, Queen.

Kevin Dwyer, your input has been invaluable. Thank you!

Generational curses are meant to be broken.

Prologue

The Beginning

Semper Fi

Kuwait, Camp Joe Foss

Vengeance disguised as patriotism drove their boots across desert sand into a senseless battle fueled by what in the end proved to be a nation's greed. Still, the evil that men do is not confined to the coveting of another's money. In fact, it is the flesh that reigns over all trappings of man.

"When the fuck are we gonna get out of here?" Lance Corporal Jackson Pierce whispered as he stood at the entryway of the tent that housed his platoon. He glared out at an almost-golden, glowing sky over a wall of sand the soldiers called a berm. That was what it looked like anyway, a glowing sky. In actuality there was a fire ablaze about fifty miles northwest of their location. At length, the oil the Iraqis had ignited spanned about two miles. It was indeed oil that kept them stationed there in that hellish place. During daylight, the heat was like nothing they had ever felt in the States. Every day, the soldiers looked forward to the sun's descent.

That night, Lance Corporal Pierce noticed the line dwindle to about forty marines, all waiting in line for their opportunity to call home. This was a once-per-month opportunity with only one phone available in the bunker to dial out. The process was a daunting one, but a chance to speak with their loved ones for even a second was worth the feeling of immense joy it granted the homesick marines. A second, most times, was all they were granted. Once a soldier finally held the big green bulky military phone in hand, they would have to be transferred to Al Jaber, a main base in Kuwait, before being transferred to the closest base to their home in the States. From there they'd be connected to the person they waited nearly three hours to speak to. And, like I said before, most times they would merely get a second to belt out a "Hey, baby" before the line would disconnect. At which point, the five-minute process would have to be endured once more, with hopes of making a successful connection.

Lance Corporal Pierce rushed to take his place in line, joining the others. Well, as fast as he could, trekking through sand. The other marines kept themselves busy as they waited, sitting on crates playing spades, euchre, or whatever game they could think of using a deck of cards. The tall, bald caramel-complected 30-something African American took his place in line behind Lance Corporal Flynn. He too stood about six feet four inches tall. Lance Corporal Flynn's energy was like no other. When he spoke, he would wave his hands to and fro, explaining his stories with great exaggeration. His gleaming gray eyes would bulge, encouraging you to feel the full weight of his enter-taining tales. Although Lance Corporal Flynn was a ginger fellow and Lance Corporal Jackson Pierce was as chocolate as a Hershey bar, they were like brothers, two peas in a pod, bound by their oath to serve the United States of America. They had grown closer over their eighty days stationed at Camp Joe Foss. Flynn was really the only person he spoke with frankly.

"I thought you were sleeping, soldier," Flynn called out to Lance Corporal Jackson Pierce as he approached.

"It's not often the line gets this low. I figure I'd better take my opportunity now."

"I can imagine you're super stoked to call your wife and tell her you'll be home in a few weeks."

"I'll be even more excited when I can tell her I'm coming home for good," Lance Corporal Pierce countered.

Lance Corporal Flynn broke out into song. "'Cause, Mama! Mama, I'm coming hooooome!'" He'd even imitated Ozzy Osbourne's singing voice as best he could while belting out a rendition of the classic.

"Exactly! Mama, I'm coming home!" Lance Corporal Pierce enthusiastically agreed. "I can't wait to see my kid. She's three years old, and I've already been absent more than a third of her life because of this bullshit. Is it ever going to end, or are we going to be fighting this senseless war for the rest of our lives? I can't help but feel like we're stuck here, and no one really cares."

"'Stuck in the middle with youuuu,'" Lance Corporal Flynn responded in song once more, that time performing his rendition of the *Reservoir Dogs* classic. He danced around, clapping his hands twice above is head, first to the left then to the right, considering the beat and melody of the song as he put on a show. He had gotten the rest of the soldiers so amped up that one of them turned on the radio playing that exact tune.

Most joined in, pointing at one another as they repeated the chorus in unison, "'Stuck in the middle with you!'"

"And that's why you're my buddy. You always know how to bring light to the darkest of moods."

"Hey. We've got to stay sane out here. Depression is real. I'm just doing my part to make sure my fellow man is in the right frame of mind to watch my six."

"Aww, man, you know I've got your back, like four flats on a Cadillac," Lance Corporal Pierce responded.

"Now see, that's where you lost me. What does that even mean? What does having my back have to do with four flat tires on a car? I mean, really, I don't understand. Is it because I'm white?" The latter part of his statement being a joke . . .

"Listen up, my ginger brother from another mother. When you've got four flats, you're all the way down. So, when I say I've got your back like four flats on a Cadillac, it means I'm down for you. In other words, you can count on me."

"I see. Well in that case, likewise, my brother," Lance Corporal Flynn shot his fellow soldier in arms a salute.

Just then a ruckus caught their attention. "Get him, soldier! You can't get him?" one of the marines waiting in line shouted at another who was busy wrestling with their gunner sergeant. At six feet six inches tall and weighing well over 290 pounds, many had tried and failed miserably to take down Gunner Sergeant Anthony Taylor.

"I bet I can take him down," Lance Corporal Pierce remarked as he sized up his superior.

"I know I agreed to having your back like four flats on a Cadillac as well, but I think I'm gonna sit back and enjoy the show this time."

His hands sounded like sandpaper when he rubbed his rough palms together. "Watch and learn, Corporal. Watch and learn." For some reason, Lance Corporal Pierce's testosterone levels were at an all-time high, or maybe it was just the fact that Gunner Sergeant Taylor was already preoccupied wrestling with one of the others, making him an easy target, or so Pierce thought. The latter was most likely the case. Lance Corporal Pierce moved to sneak up behind him. It must have been the eyes of the other soldiers that clued Taylor in on the incoming attack, because he turned just as Lance Corporal Pierce leaped into the air to pounce on his back, catching him midair in a bear hug that nearly took his breath away. Gunner Sergeant Taylor flung him around like a Raggedy Ann doll.

Holy shit. What have I gotten myself into? He questioned his decision a little too late. The sergeant forced Jackson back down toward the sand, but as opposed to his boots touching ground, he bent his knees figuring he could use his weight at a lower level to gain the upper hand before his sergeant would lift him back up again. It was no doubt a prelude to body-slamming him backward onto the sand. Unfortunately, when his knees touched down instead of his feet, Gunner Sergeant Taylor toppled over him, smashing his body down but in the opposite direction. The back of Lance Corporal Pierce's head nearly met his feet, and a loud popping sound that erupted from his back halted all horseplay at once.

"Ahhhh! What the fuck? Ahhhh! I think you broke my back!"

Gunner Sergeant Taylor held his hands on either side of his tapered head. "Are you okay?" he inquired. His big brown eyes filled with regret. He'd heard that popping sound as well, yet he'd hoped it was merely a fluke. "Get up, Corporal! Stop goofing around!"

"I'm fucking serious, Sergeant. I can't feel my fucking legs!"

Oh, my God. He didn't actually say it out loud, but the look in his eyes more than expressed the sheer panic that had shot through his body. He bolted off toward his tent. Within seconds other troops had gathered around to strap Lance Corporal Pierce down on a green cloth gurney with wooden sides. A convoy truck pulled up nearby. Several soldiers helped to load Jackson Pierce onto its rear with medical support riding along with him. The convoy sped across the desert, attempting to make it to their main post deeper into Kuwait as quickly as possible. Every bump they hit he could feel what felt like crunching in his back.

"Ahhh! Slow the fuck down!" he yelled at the soldier behind the wheel.

The medical staff corporal on board commenced to poking his lower extremities with a sharp metal object. He moved to Jackson's feet, poking and prodding their soles until he was jamming the object hard enough to pierce through his skin.

"Can you feel that?" the soldier asked.

"Feel what? What the hell are you doing down there?"

The soldier lifted Jackson's foot so that he could see. Blood leaked from its sole, soaking into the cloth gurney.

"No, I can't feel it, so stop fucking stabbing me!"

By the time they made it to the main base deeper into Kuwait, which took a grueling forty-five minutes, others were already standing outside the medical tent waiting to assist.

"How did this happen, Corporal?" Even though Lance Corporal Pierce was in a severe amount of pain, he still had his wits about him. The last thing he wanted was to get his sergeant into trouble, so of course he did the only other thing he could do: lie.

"I was cleaning the gun turret when I fell off of the tanker. I don't know what happened. I just felt dizzy, and then I fell."

"So that's the story you're going with? Are you sure that's what happened?" another sergeant asked with a warning note in his voice.

"What do you mean the story that I'm going with? That's what happened." Jackson stuck to his guns. He was a loyal friend indeed.

They all paused for a few seconds waiting for him to change his story to a truth that never came. Once they got him onto a bed inside of the infirmary, the doctor came inside. Dr. Annette Thomas was tall, blond, beautiful, and very assertive. "Do you have an erection?" she asked.

"What do you mean? Why are you asking me that?" Secretly he hoped he did have one just so that she could see the full extent of what he was working with. "I don't think so," he replied.

"Cut off his pants," she instructed. A medical assistant cut his combat trousers from the ankles to the waist at both legs, ripping the pants off Lance Corporal Pierce faster than he had put them on. To Annette's relief, there was no erection. She touched her hands to his bloody toes. "You can't feel that at all?"

"No. I can't feel it. I keep telling you guys, I can't feel anything except the pain in my back."

About an hour later, as they stood just outside the tent trying to make a decision on what they should do about his pinched nerve, medical staff could hear a giggling sound coming from inside the tent. With the others not far behind, Annette rushed in to see what was going on. *Oh no, he's gone mad,* she thought upon seeing Lance Corporal Pierce lying there in a fit of laughter.

"What's going on? Why are you laughing?"

"My legs are tingling," he happily admitted.

"Get him up!" Two soldiers lifted him from the bed. Annette immediately stuck a shot of morphine into his buttocks underneath his tighty whities. "Try to move your legs. You need to try to walk immediately, while you have sensation."

His body was limp to say the least. Following orders, Jackson tried his best to stand. The sensation returning began in his toes with a subtle yet painful tingling, traveling up his weak extremities. You know how it feels when you sit in a position for too long that makes your leg go numb, then when you get up all the blood comes rushing back? That was how it felt. The relief it brought his mind to feel again granted him a feeling of relief he had never experienced until that moment. They were all relieved to see his toes wiggling in the sand. They released their hold on him once his wobbling legs began to straighten. After his brush with possible paralysis, Lance Corporal Pierce was exhausted. Within ten minutes the soldier was counting sheep. He managed to sleep the entire trip back to Camp Joe Foss.

Chapter 1

Mama, I'm Coming Home

When he opened his eyes the next morning as a horn called for reveille, his pain rushed back instantly. "Ouch." He moaned and groaned, trying to adjust his position on the uncomfortable cot back at his tent. It was no use. The morphine had worn off completely. Lance Corporal Pierce closed his eyes. *There is no way I can get up to do anything today,* he concluded. His injuries were not detrimental, nor did they require further medical care, so he was sent back to camp. Their medical unit had no room to house one whose injuries weren't deemed serious. The Marines was no place for crybabies. Unless you were paralyzed or had a limb blown off, you were expected to report to duty.

The other dozen or so marines in his tent had already hopped out of bed and were busy rushing to get dressed in trousers and T-shirts to make it to formation within the allotted time.

"Come on, soldier. Lazy time is over," Lance Corporal Flynn instructed, tapping the side of Jackson's leg.

Jackson opened his eyes but kept silent.

"What's up with your fancy pants, trader?"

"They cut up my Marine-issue trousers."

"So, you left a marine and came back an army soldier?"

"I'll always be Semper Fi." He held up his closed fist for a fist bump. Lance Corporal Flynn gladly reciprocated.

"Ooh rah," Flynn remarked.

"Ooh rah," Jackson repeated with less enthusiasm. The aching he felt had taken its toll on him, keeping the marine in him from giving his all.

Lance Corporal Flynn could see plainly the pain his dear friend was still experiencing. "What are you gonna do? It's time for reveille. Can you walk yet?"

"There's no way I can get up. There's just no way. Can you get Gunner Sergeant? Tell him I need to see him."

"Sure thing, soldier," he agreed before ducking out of the tent.

Within a few minutes Gunner Sergeant Anthony Taylor ducked his head inside. "How you feelin', Lance Corporal Pierce?"

"Sergeant, there's no way I can walk. I just can't," he admitted with sincerity in his eyes.

"I know. The doctor already informed me that you would be out of commission for a few days. But don't worry. I've got your back like four flats on a Cadillac."

Lance Corporal Pierce snickered lightly at the reference.

"You know I really appreciate what you did for me."

"You're my sergeant. I'd never throw you under the bus," Pierce replied.

"The thing is, I'd already told them the truth of the matter, but you stuck to your guns, and for that I truly appreciate you. That being said, I've got something for you."

Gunner Sergeant Taylor lifted him from the cot as if carrying a bride over the threshold, taking Lance Corporal Pierce to his personal tent. Cool air blowing from an air conditioner made the temperature in the tent perfectly relaxing. Gunner Sergeant Taylor had everything a marine could ask for packed inside his pop-up abode. He laid Jackson on top of the queen-size air mattress that sat atop two cots pushed together. Sergeant Taylor moved over to the television, grabbing a remote from the top of the digital versatile disc player. There was a stack of at least a hundred DVDs in a large green crate next to the television.

"Anytime you want me to change the movie, hit me on the radio. If you need to get up, hit me on the radio. Anything you need, I'm a button away. You looked out for me. Now I'm going to look out for you." He handed the remote over to Lance Corporal Pierce, then removed a walkie talkie clipped at his waist, handing it over as well.

Now this is pimp, he thought as he graciously accepted the grand gesture. Gunner Sergeant Taylor walked out of his tent, but just as he promised, every time Jackson pushed that button, either Gunner Sergeant Taylor or another marine would come to assist him. They changed the movie for him, helped him to the restroom, and even brought him his chow or a meal ready to eat, MRE, of his choice at mealtime. Every night Sergeant Taylor would carry Lance Corporal Pierce back to his cot, and like clockwork, every morning he would carry him from his cot back to the queen-size air mattress in his own tent. After three days of wallowing in a lap of luxury, or as luxurious as it could get in a pop-up tent in the middle of the desert, Jackson was ready to walk without any assistance at all. Fortunately for Jackson, Gunner Sergeant Taylor had one more surprise in store for him.

Preparing himself for a full day's work, Jackson gathered his thoughts. The other marines had already vacated for reveille. Yet, Jackson sat at the edge of his cot, pushing his feet around deep in the sand, allowing it to cover his toes completely.

It was how he grounded himself whenever he felt uneasy.

"Are you ready to go home, Corporal?" Gunner Sergeant Taylor asked upon walking into the tent on his fourth day of rest.

"Seventeen days and I'm homeward bound," Jackson replied as he lifted his head to address Sergeant Taylor.

"More like ninety minutes. Well, two hours at most," he happily delivered the news.

"What are you talking about? I'm not set to leave for at least another couple of weeks."

"I took care of it. Pulled a few strings and got you in for a left-advance party."

"Seriously? You're not pulling my leg? You know they can't take much more."

"Aww, man, I just wanted to show my appreciation for what you did. I'm glad you are okay. Now it's time to go home and see your kid. Put it to the wife so you can relieve that stress without digging your feet into hot sand."

"I can definitely dig that." They furnished one another a fist bump.

By the time the C130 cargo plane landed at their main base in Al Jaber, Lance Corporal Pierce was waiting nearby with another twenty-one soldiers scheduled to head home. With his green duffle bag strapped over his shoulder, he loaded the plane, eager to make it to Jacksonville, North Carolina.

Jacksonville, North Carolina

"Woooo! I'm so happy to smell the Jacksonville air! I'm home!" Lance Corporal Jackson Pierce declared, yelling from his vehicle's window as he cruised up Main Street in his 2001 white Ford Bronco. The breeze blowing in felt exhilarating on his skin. He had his window down, allowing rays of sun to beam onto his bald head. It was a different kind of heat, much gentler than temperatures he'd braved in the Middle East. Jackson turned up the volume on the radio, then glanced over at his passenger, Lance Corporal Flynn, inciting his enthusiasm.

"'I want to love you! PYT! Pretty young thang,'" Jackson sang, tapping his hands on the steering wheel. His passenger smiled before commencing to groove along with the rhythm of the beat like his comrade.

"What's the first thing you're going to do when you get home, Flynn?"

"Awww, man, I've got a date with a little hottie. I may not have a wife, but I do my thing. Quite frankly, they love me, man. I can't keep 'em off," he boasted.

"King Ding-a-ling, huh?"

"Nah. I'm coming in at about four inches, but four inches pumping at one hundred miles an hour can do some damage, if you know what I mean."

The two of them laughed at the crude truth masked as a joke they were genuinely amused by.

Just then, Jackson turned his head, something to the left of him piquing his interest. "What the hell?" He yanked the steering wheel to the left. Screeching tires painted the asphalt as he pulled into the parking lot of a Motel 8.

Lance Corporal Flynn grabbed tight to the seat belt strapped across his chest. "What's wrong, man?" Flynn inquired.

"That's my wife's car," he admitted, voice reeking with devastation. His body burned with anger while his heart pounded in fear of what he was about to discover. Jackson felt sick to his stomach, yet rage wouldn't allow the feeble release.

A gray Honda Accord was parked between two motel doors, one ajar.

"Naw, man. That's not her car. Don't jump to conclusions."

"It's her car," he assured Flynn. Jackson could tell by the I SUPPORT THE U.S. TROOPS bumper sticker pasted to her rear window. Not to mention, the numbers and letters on the license plate were a perfect match.

Without another word, Jackson parked next to her car, hopped out of his truck, then headed straight for a slightly open motel room door with a number 8 attached on its front. The three marines standing there in uniform were surprised to see him busting into their room, yet none of them said a word. Like Jackson, they knew he was of superior ranking. His uniform and patches told them so. They, on the other hand, were wet behind the ears in terms of service to the country. Each of them were no older than the age of 20. Even so, he had to be sure they were aware of his authority.

"Where's the Asian bitch in the gray Honda?"

"She's next door with my boy," one of them spoke up.

"Do you know who I am?"

"No," the same marine replied.

"I'm Lance Corporal Jackson Pierce, and that's my wife, so you need to stay out of this."

"Yes, sir," the soldier agreed, while the rest of them nodded in agreement.

Jackson turned, bolting from the room. He stood in front of the motel door with the brass metal number 9 screwed into it. Deep breaths he took did nothing to calm him. He reached for the knob to open the door, then turned it. To his dismay, it was secured. But Jackson had an advantage. His height allowed him to see through the high windows. When he stepped to the side to look inside, he could see the petite Asian American woman with the straight black hair, who had vowed to spend the rest of her life with him, slowly riding the stiffened member of a younger soldier and loving it. She had her head thrown back, long hair brushing across the top of her buttocks. The young marine's hands squeezed her perky B-cup breasts. Jackson's perky B-cup breasts.

A fuming Jackson's eyes bulged from their sockets. "You bitch! Open this fucking door!" he screamed at the top of his lungs.

Lance Corporal Flynn watched from the passenger seat, in shock at the entire scene.

Sue, his wife, hopped off the startled marine, scooped up her short red dress, then ran to the bathroom to dress herself. Her companion had no idea what was going on. She had neglected to inform him of her marriage and child.

He hopped out of bed, then slid on his boxer briefs. "What the hell is going on here, Sue?"

His inquiry received no reply. Shattered pieces of glass from the upper window shot into the room once Jackson laid his fist into it. The smell of must and sex filled his nostrils.

"Open this fucking door, or I swear I'm going to kill you!" he demanded once more of the frightened marine backed against the wall.

The young marine hesitated, stepping forward. In a frozen panic, his eyes darted around the room as if questioning what to do. Beads of sweat formed across his brow. As far as Lance Corporal Pierce was concerned, his subordinate's future was bleak. Standing at six foot three inches, furious and yelling through the window at the top of his lungs, he knew how intimidating his presence could be.

Jackson's patience was no more. He forced his fist through the other window, shattering it as well, then commenced to ripping at a wooden plank that separated the two. There was nothing left to do but try to climb inside, which he most certainly did.

Color drained from the younger marine's face. You'd think as pale as he'd become, he'd seen a ghost. It was more like his life flashing before his very own eyes. That in itself incited his approach toward the door. He was sure the enraged marine would get in somehow. But Jackson's large frame wouldn't allow it.

Once Jackson saw the soldier coming toward him, he moved over to the door. As soon as it opened in the slightest, he snapped his foot back, then launched it forward, smashing the heel of his combat boot to the door. The edge of it cracked the young soldier in his head, square between the eyes. Jackson came at him with full force, landing blows to his face as he staggered back farther into the room. As soon as he hit the floor, Jackson was on top of him, with his knees pressed firmly into the undersides of his biceps. Blow after blow crashed down on his face. Blood leaked from his mouth and nose. Jackson whaled on him until his arms felt like wet noodles.

His frightened and embarrassed adulterous wife came out of her hiding spot, attempting to sneak by them. Jackson could smell her stench. She'd even worn her favorite perfume for the now-battered stranger. Jackson sprung up, instantly grabbing her by the throat. Her almond-shaped eyes opened as wide as they could stretch as her body was lifted into the air then slammed down onto the bed. The choke slam sent her small frame bouncing off the double-sized mattress, then into the wall above the headboard. Her head left a dent in the wall, tearing through cheap orange and yellow striped wallpaper that covered it. It was the first time he had ever touched a woman out of anger. Fear of it not being the last prompted him to leave. Before he walked out, he lifted the thirty-two-inch television from the dresser, dropping it on the head of her lover.

It was the last time Jackson Pierce ever served in the Marines. That violent occurrence caused him to be discharged from duty. A fact that crushed him to his very core. His only victory was the dishonorable discharging of his wife's lover for his part in the destruction of Jackson's marriage.

Chapter 2

Medicated

One Month Later

Jackson Pierce stood over the sink, staring at his reflection in the bathroom mirror. He straightened the knot in his royal blue tie before smoothing it down, then took in a deep breath, buttoning the jacket of his black suit. He breathed deep, not because it was a tight fit but because he was nervous about an interview scheduled that day at the United States Postal Service. The sigh of relief he let out was long. He had moved on from his cheating wife, starting a new life in the small yuppie-filled town of Clarkston, Michigan. Unfortunately, his child was left to bear the brunt of his absence, the betrayal being something he had yet to allow himself to overcome. Jackson thought about his daughter every day. Yet, memories weren't enough to force him back into her presence. Resentment and bitterness kept him from facing his adulterous wife. Besides, he couldn't bear seeing her living with another man. He never wanted to see Sue's face again. It was the same face he recognized when looking at his daughter. He wanted to fight for his child, but hate wouldn't allow it. Even if he forced himself to get over it, he hadn't the means to take care of his daughter alone. He was a soldier, not a single father. Jackson had been reduced to shoving a pill down his throat every day to balance his mood swings and PTSD.

He recalled the old Southern doctor addressing him as if he were a wild teenager when he handed him the prescription back in North Carolina.

"Now, son, it's imperative that you mind that temper of yours. You remember what happened before. That's why it's important you take this medicine to keep you right. It's not uncommon to have these issues, being a product of war and tragedy, among other things. Just do as I've instructed, and you'll be fine. Just fine." The old Southern doctor furnished him with a pat on the back, then sent him on his way.

His cordless phone rang, tearing him from the recollection. Jackson didn't budge, allowing an answering machine to take the call. He refused to answer. Nothing was of more importance than his upcoming interview. He needed that job, or more so the insurance.

"You've reached the residence of Lance Corporal Pierce. I'm unavailable at the moment. Please leave a message, and I'll be sure to return your call." The answering machine beeped once his message ended, then a soft voice came through.

"Mr. Pierce, my name is Hilary Osborne, postmaster over at the Clarkston post office."

Before she could conclude her reason for calling, Jackson snatched up the phone receiver sitting on a mahogany nightstand next to his queen-size bed, interrupting her message. "Hello. I'm here. Sorry, I almost missed your call."

"Oh, hello. No worries," she replied. "I just wanted to confirm your attendance for your interview at eleven."

"Yes, ma'am. I'll definitely be in attendance. I appreciate the opportunity to interview with you and look forward to it."

"Well, that's good to hear. I look forward to interviewing you. I'll see you at eleven."

"Wonderful. I'll see you in about an hour. Good day, ma'am." Jackson disconnected the call, then placed the receiver back atop its base.

Confidence overwhelmed him. *I've got this job in the bag,* he thought, knowing all too well his capabilities of charming women. Jackson wasn't above using his good looks to get ahead if the situation warranted it. He looked around his small studio apartment, everything neatly in its place. Even his bed had already been made. Every morning he woke up, the first thing he'd do was fix his white sheets and camouflage green comforter. The structure he'd learned in the military was still at play, regardless of the chaos that brought his seemingly perfect life crashing down.

The discharged marine headed for the kitchen. It was time for his morning cup of joe, black, no sugar, no cream. He grabbed a coffee pot from its base, filled a small white mug nearly to the top, then placed the coffee pot back on its base. Jackson's steady hands lifted the mug to his lips, taking small sips as he moved over to a window in the living room. He pulled at a string, lifting the white venetian blinds to stare out at pedestrians traveling Main Street. *This is just the fresh start I need,* he reassured himself. The town seemed pleasant, quiet, clean, and classy. Jackson was eager to establish new roots there in Clarkston, Michigan.

He grinned, happy to see a group of preschoolers marching down the sidewalk in a straight line, led by their teacher. His daughter, Mya, crossed his mind. Suddenly, a cloak of sadness washed over Jackson, prompting him to rush back to the bathroom. He placed his coffee mug down on the sink, opened the medicine cabinet, grabbed a bottle of pills labeled fluoxetine, a more common name being Prozac. When Jackson twisted off the cap, he peered inside. His antidepressant pills were dwindling, a fact that worried him terribly. Obtaining a position at the post office was imperative to his mental health. Veterans Affairs often did little to help those returning from battle. He needed the federal health insurance the post office would supply in order to see a primary care physician. The doctor he was seeing before discharge was something mandatory to assess his state of mind, or more so his aptness for the Marines. Unfortunately, their findings gave him the boot along with a bottle of medicine, as if to say good luck but good riddance. Jackson popped one of the blue and yellow capsules into his mouth, swallowing it without a sip of coffee. Instead of putting the bottle back inside the medicine cabinet, he recapped it, then shoved it into the pocket of his black dress pants.

Jackson pushed the mirror back into place, coaching himself. "You've got this. Everything is going to be just fine, Lance Corporal Pierce."

At approximately 1100 hours, he was buzzing for assistance at the customer desk of Clarkston Post Office annex building, where interviews were held.

"Can I help you?" the statuesque chocolate 30-something woman with the naturally curly hair inquired.

Jackson thought she was beautiful to say the least. When she smiled, her teeth gleamed so bright he assumed they were fake. "What a beautiful smile you have," he replied.

"Thank you! It's in the genes. So, what can I help you with on this wonderful Wednesday morning, sir?"

"I'm scheduled for an interview with Hilary Osborne at eleven."

She looked up at a clock above his head on the wall behind him. "Looks like you're right on time, Mr. . . ." She waited for him to give his name.

"Pierce. I'm Lance Cor . . ." He paused, remembering he was no longer a soldier. My name is Jackson Pierce."

"Hey, Jackson Pierce, I'm Evelyn. I'll take you back to our postmaster's office." Evelyn walked around the counter, then pushed open the door, allowing him to walk through.

"Follow me," she instructed.

You could tell she was a diligent worker. She walked fast and with purpose, leading him to a big office in the back of the building. Other clerks gawked at them, whispering among one another. "Is that a new clerk?" they wondered. They were all eager to gain a new employee. A shorthanded staff and increasing workload weighed heavily on them. The pressure to get the mail up in time, then over to the mail carriers, had become a daily daunting task. Clarkston Post Office didn't have fancy machines to sort mail. Everything was done manually. So, the sight of Jackson was a welcome one.

She stopped in the hall between two doors, one being a training room, the other the postmaster's office. "Have a seat, Jackson. Sign in on the clipboard on the table, and Hilary will be with you shortly." Evelyn pointed him toward the training room.

"Thank you, Evelyn. Hopefully, you'll be seeing me again soon."

"I certainly hope so, Jackson. Good luck with your interview," she replied before leaving his presence.

As Evelyn made her way out onto the workroom floor, Jackson stood in the doorway, peering out at operations. Evelyn was approached by another mail clerk, Elise, a petite 30-something strawberry blonde. Elise was determined to move up in the ranks at Clarkston Post Office. She made it her business to know everyone and everything that could possibly stand in her way. Although she would be superior in ranking as far as clerks went if Jackson were hired, she made it her business to know exactly what she was up against.

"So, who's that?"

"His name is Jackson Pierce. Lance Corporal Jackson Pierce," Evelyn responded with raised brows.

"He's military? Oh, he's got this position in the bag. You know military gets preference over civilians."

"And they should. I'm sure what he's experienced wasn't easy," Evelyn admitted.

The two of them glared at Jackson as Hilary led him into her office.

"Is he interviewing for the clerk position?"

"Nah, he's interviewing to be the new rural carrier assistant on Route 8."

"What are you two gawking at? Those packages aren't going to throw themselves!" the rural delivery supervisor yelled from one of two desks at the center of the floor.

"Why don't you worry about getting next week's schedule done? Because if it's not out by the time I'm off today, I'll be filing a grievance!"

Elise's counter shut Deborah up in an instant, knowing all too well their schedule had to be up by the end of day, Wednesday. If not, it warranted a grievance. Deborah didn't feel the need to argue. Besides, she wasn't one for going back and forth with the employees. She preferred her payback to be dealt out in a more subtle, underhanded fashion. Although Clarkston Post Office had two supervisors and a postmaster, it was the clerks who ran the operation. Everything went through them. They had the ability to control the mail flow, which gave them all the power that was to be had.

The look on their supervisor's face turned sour. She tried to be as pleasant as possible, which never really worked. Deborah hated almost everyone, and the resting bitch face she often possessed spoke of her misery. She was divorced, and in her early fifties, but open to finding love again. Unfortunately, many suitors used her naivete to their advantage.

Evelyn snickered, amused by Elise's snappy comeback. Even though she and Deborah had a pretty good relationship, Evelyn enjoyed the light bickering that went on between the clerks and supervisors. It was their only form of entertainment, and there was plenty of it going around. Jackson Pierce had no idea the mess he was walking into, but he would soon find out.

Hilary stood, pushing her brown bobbed hair behind her ears. "Welcome to the team, Mr. Pierce. Our new pay period begins on Saturday, which will be your first day of work. You are to report here at eight a.m. Can I count on you?" Hilary glared at him with intent in her crystal blue eyes. It was her subtle form of intimidation, which worked on no one. Yet, she continued to delude herself, believing it was so.

"Yes, ma'am. Thank you so much for the opportunity. I won't let you down," Jackson eagerly replied.

His interview had gone well. He was elated to be of service to the people of his country again, although in a less official position.

"I've enjoyed interviewing you, but I have other work I must attend to. Can you see yourself out?"

Jackson stood from his seat. "I can. Have a good day, Mrs. Osborne."

"Please, call me Hilary."

"I'll see you Saturday, Hilary."

"Actually, I don't work on weekends. When you get here, you'll report to Deborah. She's the rural carrier supervisor and will be the one helping you. If she's not here, then you'll report to Evelyn."

"I've met Evelyn. She seems very nice."

"Huh. Does she? Well, good for her," Hilary replied.

Jackson's eyebrows wrinkled a little. He tried to control the look on his face, though he wondered what it was she meant by the question she'd posed but didn't really expect an answer for. In the grand scheme of things, it really didn't matter. He had successfully obtained the position. Ruffling feathers would have been counterproductive at that point.

"I'll leave you to your work. Good day, Hilary."

He mashed his lips together into a mirthless grin before turning to leave her office. Jackson traveled the pathway behind the city carriers' cases to get to the front. Just then, Evelyn came zooming around the corner to clock out for the day.

"I guess I'll be seeing you on Saturday," he proudly admitted.

"Congratulations. You got the job. Good for you. Be sure to get some good rest. You're gonna need it." She smiled.

"That smile alone is worth the hard work I'm going to put in."

Evelyn's smile fleeted. *I know he's not hitting on me already,* she thought. "Well, I'm off. So, I'd better get home." The moment the clock flashed 1150 military time, Evelyn swiped her card to end her tour for the day.

Jackson followed behind her as she pushed through double doors that led to the parking lot. "So, are you married, Jackson?" She was fishing to determine how much of a creep he could potentially be.

"I am. I have a beautiful wife and a three-year-old daughter," he replied. He wasn't ready to admit the fact that he was in the middle of a divorce. The embarrassment would be too much to bear.

"Awesome. Well, I'm sure your wife will be happy to hear you've got the job."

"She'll be elated," he said, adding the words, "to collect the child support," under his breath. He knew taking a chunk of his check would be the first thing Sue would do.

"Well, I'll see you Saturday, Jackson." Evelyn continued to her vehicle.

"See ya." He bid her farewell with a wave, then strolled up the walkway feeling as light as a feather. Jackson breathed a sigh of relief, sure that he was piecing his life back together.

Chapter 3

Training Day

That night, Jackson lounged on the sofa in front of his large floor-model television, trying his damnedest not to drift off to sleep. Once he was under, nightmares of his wife cheating and that dreaded judgment that concluded his service in the United States Marines were sure to come flooding back. A rerun episode of *Law & Order* on the television was quickly losing its appeal. So much so that he had begun focusing on the water ring on a glass coffee table out in front of him. He lifted a bottle of beer to his lips and took a sip. He'd nearly finished an entire six-pack, the bottle in his hands being the last of them. The rest sat empty, scattered across his coffee table. Jackson's eyelids felt heavy. He blinked lethargically. The pace of his breathing slowed, along with his heart rate. His eyes closed and head fell off to the side. The bottle of beer he held in his hand that sat atop his knee dropped to the floor. The remainder of the liquid spilled out onto the wood.

The moment he drifted off to sleep, he was back in Kuwait.

Traveling what they called the chow run was one of his duties, his and Lance Corporal Flynn's. They were to take the Hummer from Camp Joe Foss forty-five minutes across the desert into their main base at Al Jaber. There, they would pick up hot meals for the other marines at their base to eat. The job was a welcomed one. The MREs they normally scarfed down left much to be desired. They'd already packed the green plastic containers into the Hummer at Al Jaber and were on their way back to the base with food, dishes, and eating utensils.

"Man, I can't wait to sink my teeth into some hot meatloaf and mashed potatoes with some brown gravy. Mmm-mmm, I can taste it now."

"I'm actually full from the beef stew MRE I had for lunch. It was pretty good," Lance Corporal Flynn admitted.

"I had the chicken and salsa, and it tasted like shit."

"Those always taste like shit. You know that."

"Yeah, well, I've been waiting on this one. Meatloaf is my favorite," Flynn replied.

Just then they could hear the soaring sound of the SCUD missile being shot from Iraq coming their way as it soared through the air.

"Watch out!" Flynn blurted, pointing at the giant dub dub lizard crossing their path ahead.

Lance Corporal Pierce jerked the wheel, swerving to avoid the reptile. Suddenly, the Jeep lifted several feet from the sand before slamming back down onto the ground. Ringing he heard in his ears was loud. At first, he thought they'd nearly been hit by the SCUD missile, but it had flown overhead, being directed at the main base. It was an IED, improvised explosive device, hidden in the sand that exploded beneath them. Thankfully, the sandbags covering the floor of their Hummer saved them from the blast being fatal. Still, Lance Corporal Flynn was unconscious with blood leaking from his nostrils and earlobe. Once the ringing stopped, Lance Corporal Pierce glanced over at Flynn, noticing the terrible shape he was in. "Flynn! Flynn! Wake up, Flynn!" He nudged his shoulder, trying desperately to bring him back to consciousness.

Saturday morning had finally come. At 0800 hours, Jackson Pierce stood at the customer desk at Clarkston Post Office's annex, dressed in plain clothes just as the postmaster had requested. A pair of tan cargo shorts and a black V-neck T-shirt perfectly showcased his chiseled physique. Jackson rang the buzzer.

"How can I help you?" Elise inquired as she approached the counter.

"I'm Jackson Pierce, the new RCA. I'm here to report for duty."

"Good morning, Jackson. I'm Elise, one of the clerks. It's great to finally meet you. I've heard a lot about you. You must have really impressed the boss."

"Nice to meet you, Elise. I'm glad to hear I made a good impression," he replied.

"I'll come around and let you in. Give me a second." Elise walked around to the other side of the wall to allow him entry. "Deborah isn't here just yet, but I believe Evelyn has your identification. I'll take you back to her. Follow me," she said as she held open the door for him.

"I appreciate that." Jackson followed her past some of the carrier cases to get to the back. He glanced left then right, up and down, taking in the scenery. The post office had an open floor plan, so he could see most of the other clerks and carriers working there that morning. There were several training rooms with a men's and women's bathroom station along the borders. It was clean and well organized, due to most clerks having a mild case of obsessive-compulsive disorder. Jackson would fit in well there. When they made it back to the letter cases, Evelyn was just finishing the last of her letters. She had already sorted 400 inches that morning, all of which had to be passed to routes, so there was no time to waste.

"Evelyn, I've got someone here who needs to see you," Elise announced.

When Evelyn looked up, she recognized him. "Hey, Jackson. You made it," she replied before turning to Elise. "Thanks, E. I'll take it from here." Evelyn addressed many of her coworkers with a nickname. Of course, she'd yet to make up one for Jackson. "So, you ready to get started?"

"I'm ready to work," he eagerly replied.

"Let me get your identification, and then I'll take you over to your trainer, who will be Randy."

"Sounds good." Jackson followed her over to Deborah's desk, past the plethora of packages waiting to be scanned. There were big metal containers, wire cages, and huge brown boxes filled with packages that were to be scanned in one by one via clerk then passed to the routes for the carriers to deliver. On average, Clarkston Post Office processed around 3,000 or so parcels per day, all sorted by hand. Clerks had to have them scanned and ready to go by 9:30 a.m. The later the mail was up, the worse it became on the carriers. Most of them had families and were eager to get home to their loved ones. Besides, beating after-school traffic was preferred, rather than dealing with loads of children crossing the roads.

Evelyn opened Deborah's top desk drawer, pulled out Jackson's badge, then handed it over to him.

"Thank you, Evelyn."

"My pleasure. I wish I could show you around, but I'm really busy. I have to get the mail out to you guys for delivery, and I have no time to waste."

Jackson nodded in agreement. "I understand."

"Do you see that guy over there casing mail at the route with the number eight above the case?" She pointed Randy's way.

"I do."

"That's who will be training you. I'll give you one word of advice: take the good and leave the bad. In time you'll come to understand what I mean. Now, come on. I'll take you to him."

"It's okay. I can handle it from here. You go ahead and finish your work."

Jackson preferred not being introduced to another man by a woman. Call it sexist. Either way it was how he felt. These views were always deep down inside of him, but because he'd been in a loving marriage where he was the breadwinner, he seldom had to enforce his alpha. Since his alpha stood challenged by a cheating wife, he held tighter to his beliefs.

"Look at you taking initiative. I like that." Evelyn darted off to tend to her duties. Letters had to be done by 0850 hours.

Jackson briefly admired the motion of her hips as she departed.

He stood there for a moment sizing up the regular carrier on the route scheduled to complete his training. Randy, like most of them, was an experienced rural carrier. He'd worked on every rural route in the building. Three months prior, when Rural Route 8 became his regular route, he was no longer required to deliver any routes besides his own. Being a "regular," regular meaning a full-time carrier, gave him the luxury of having a substitute. Subs were referred to as RCAs. Jackson would be Randy's primary RCA, rural carrier assistant. Therefore, whenever Randy was off work, Jackson would be required to fill in for him. Jackson's objective was to work as many hours as he possibly could. He had hopes that working diligently would move him up through the ranks sooner rather than later.

Randy turned up his chrome thermos, taking small sips to get himself fueled up for the start of his day. He wasn't as tall as Jackson, but standing at six feet and 240 pounds, he wasn't a small guy by any means. His curly black hair was disheveled, seemingly matted to his head in some spots but blown out in others. Quite frankly, in Jackson's opinion, Randy looked like he had just rolled out of bed, heading straight into work without an ounce of water or soap. Randy popped a piece of gum in his mouth, turned up his small radio, then began casing magazines. The techno beat seemed to get him going. "Let's get it, guys!" he yelled, riling up the rest of the office.

A few carriers joined in, shouting, "Let's get this day over with!" The rest of them remained silent, wishing they were home in bed. The scorching heat that day would no doubt take a toll on them. Although mail carriers braved the elements on a daily basis, inclement change in weather was something they just never got used to. Mail trucks had no air conditioner. Sadly, another carrier from out of state had recently passed away that year due to the heat inside of her mail truck. A truth discouraging to other carriers. Still, they had to do their duty. As the oldest establishment in the country, U.S. mail stopped for no man. The United States Postal Service was the only organization that delivered door-to-door, being that no location was cut off from delivery, unlike other carrier services.

"Nice tunes," Jackson remarked as he approached Randy at his route.

"I try to keep the mood as upbeat as possible. You must be Jackson, retired military, right?" Randy extended his hand for a proper greeting.

"I am. It's good to meet you. Randy, right?" He reciprocated the handshake.

"That's me. The man. The myth. The legend."

"Well, in that case I'm honored," Jackson replied with a smirk. In reality, he found his comment rather corny.

"You're a lucky man, Jackson. Fortunately, you have the honor of being trained by the best in the building," he boasted. "Just watch and learn."

"While I appreciate being shown the ropes by the best, I prefer to be more hands-on. Would you mind if I actually case the route with you?"

"Sure! That means we'll get done a lot faster. Grab a stack of flats, read the address, and start sliding them into the corresponding slots on the case."

"Sounds easy enough," Jackson responded before lifting a stack of about a dozen magazines to begin casing.

Chapter 4

Teamwork

Just across the room, several clerks were scanning in packages. Elise, Daniel, Marcus, and Christian. Daniel had the most seniority of them all. He also happened to be the slowest. Not because he was incapable of going faster, but because he liked to assert his authority over management. He wanted them to be aware that he could control the pace of the mail flow. The vast majority viewed him as smug, resentful, and downright miserable, most days. When his vitality was at its highest, he would crack jokes that some found humorous. Unfortunately, they were usually at the expense of one of his fellow clerks. Most times it would be Marcus swallowing his pride, as he allowed his ego to be ripped to shreds regularly. You could say Daniel fancied himself the alpha male of their group. And Marcus, well, not so much. Daniel stood at about six feet even. His broad shoulders were muscular. His wide back was strong. His calve muscles resembled turkey drumsticks pumped full of genetically modified hormones, making them twice as massive. Other than his cavity-riddled teeth and solid, round belly, the salt-and-pepper-haired gentleman was mildly attractive. The joke around their office was that he could be one of Blake Sheldon's less fortunate relatives. Maybe a distant cousin, if he was lucky. Either way, the notion brought him great joy.

Now Marcus, on the other hand, was taller than Daniel by a couple of inches. His height, however, did nothing for his confidence. He was a light-skinned fellow with a narrow skull, receding hairline, and slumped shoulders. Black specs he wore to help his nearsighted vision made his eyes look even more beady than they were. Every day, he wore the same blue T-shirt and blue shorts, leaving his pale limbs to soak in the elements. Marcus nitpicked every issue he found pressing. To Marcus, though, everything was pressing. At 55 years of age, the divorced postal clerk had yet to find another woman who was willing to deal with his odd practices, or more so his peculiar behavior. Nontraditional characteristics that kept his female prospects at bay eventually caused a festering habit of purchasing prostitutes to become an obsession. He tried, but every so often, to woo a woman he deemed fit. It just never seemed to work out. Marcus imposed his obsessive-compulsive nature on almost everyone around, which made him more of an agitation than help to his coworkers. Daniel seemed to be the only person he allowed a pass. Whether it be fear or lack of confidence, he dared not cross that line.

Daniel grabbed a small cardboard box from a larger one filled with packages waiting to be scanned in then delivered to the appropriate carrier. He held it under the light until hearing the beep. Once the PASS machine had successfully logged in the package, Daniel pulled it from the glare of the scanner, tossing it into the air a few times. An action carried out purely to showcase his handling skills, no doubt.

"Hey, Marcus?" Daniel said with a maleficent smirk plastered across his face.

Marcus turned, hesitant to reply as he sensed sarcasm in Daniel's voice. "Yes."

"I bet it's been a while since you've seen a pair of these, huh?" he asked, alluding to lace underwear depicted on the gift box.

The reference pointing out his obviously lackluster love life made Marcus's face burn red with embarrassment while Daniel snickered, brandishing his tarnished teeth. He didn't know what to say, or how it would make Daniel react, if he responded. The risk was too great, prompting him to tuck his tail. It was his safest option and had worked many times before. If he just stayed quiet, Daniel would simply leave him be. There remained the possibility he would have to endure a few hours of heckling while they finished scanning parcels, at most.

Elise didn't find humor in Daniel's antics, nor could she tolerate Marcus's constant nitpicking. But, the choice as to whose side she leaned toward was an easy one.

"Marcus, what are you just standing there for? You might as well tell him."

Daniel's eyebrows wrinkled. *What the hell is she up to?* he thought, knowing how shrewd Elise could be.

Elise continued, "He had a hot date. Your mom was over just last night, Daniel. Right, Marcus?"

Elise's comment sent him into a fit of laughter. Marcus's body trembled as he giggled silently.

A wry grin settled upon Daniel's mouth. "Yeah, whatever," he replied, tossing the package into its appropriate hamper. In a small way, Elise had saved the day, or at least Marcus, from further embarrassment for the moment.

After about an hour, the clerks were done scanning in the 3,000 or so packages that had come in that morning.

"Letters are ready!" Evelyn shouted from her letter case.

"Good mail!" Deborah shouted immediately after.

"Good mail" was not to be called until letters and packages were all scanned in, letting mail carriers know that it was time to case those items processed and begin separating packages into their hampers.

Christian walked over to Elise before she could dart off to the postal store just across the street. Clarkston was one of the locations that operated from two separate offices: one to process mail, the other to service customers who required postage.

"That was so nice of you to speak up for Marcus like that. Lord knows he can use all the help he could get," Christian remarked quietly as she pushed her long black hair behind her ear, revealing only the side of her face where Elise stood. She didn't want Daniel to see her talking about the incident, for fear she'd become a target. Not even her baby blue eyes and innocent demeanor could grant her clemency from Daniel's wrath. The soft-spoken married woman in her forties also happened to be a mother to three healthy, well-mannered children, a fact that made her most proud.

"Well, somebody has to say something, or he'll go on and on to no end."

While the women continued gossiping about their coworkers, nearby, Jackson pulled out a hamper filled with packages labeled RURAL ROUTE 8.

"Who is that?" Christian inquired, before catching the edge of her bottom lip in her teeth. "What a hunk."

Although Jackson didn't let on, he'd heard the flattering comment.

Elise laughed. "Geez, calm down. What are you, in heat?"

"Oh, hush," she responded. "I'm harmless."

"Yeah, okay." Elise raised a brow. Was Christian really kidding though? She wondered.

Christian snickered as she nudged Elise's arm with her elbow. "For now, anyway," she bashfully admitted. Christian would never in a million years be unfaithful to her husband, but just like men, women too had wandering eyes that fancied attractive things.

"He's actually the new rural carrier assistant on Rural Route 8. He probably won't get many hours unless he learns other routes. Randy never misses work."

Jackson pushed the cart back over to the case where Randy waited to further instruct him.

"I'm going to show you the best way to separate parcels. The secret is to put them in order according to the path you are going to travel, from beginning to end." Randy handed over a single sheet of paper. "Here is a map of only this route. It makes it so much easier and cuts your delivery time in half. You'll be sipping beers and sitting poolside by three p.m."

Jackson accepted the keen advice along with the sheet of paper, folding it into quarters, then shoving it inside one of the pockets of his shorts.

"As a matter of fact, some of us coworkers are getting together tonight at a bar and grill over in Waterford. You should come on out, rub some elbows, ya know?"

"Sounds good to me. What's the place called?"

"Jack Hammers, right off White Lake Road. Six o'clock. Be there or be square."

"I'll be there." Jackson was eager to meet some new people. Up until then, he had stayed pretty much to himself in Clarkston. He knew the depression from his marriage ending could only subside once he'd moved forward. So, Jackson was prepared to put his shiniest boot forward. Pun intended.

His trainer preferred to be out on the streets delivering the route by 1000 hours. And so they were. By the time 0950 hours rolled around, Randy and Jackson were signing out keys with Evelyn at the accountables cart. It was where they'd check in or out anything of significant value. Once they collected their items, the trainer and his trainee pushed through the double doors.

"Let's hit the road, Jack!" Randy laughed. "No pun intended."

He had worked alongside him for only a couple of hours and already Jackson had concluded he was some sort of goofball. Attempting to make the most out of the situation, Jackson reckoned Randy's lighthearted mood was a symptom of the beautiful weather that day. *Maybe I'm being too serious.* Conflicting thoughts plagued him. Should he lighten up a bit, or was Randy not taking his job seriously enough? Jackson began loading packages into the back of the mail truck in the order indicated by markings they'd written along their sides. Randy turned on his portable radio, blasting nineties tunes. Music he listened to on a regular basis for some reason that day agitated Jackson. He pressed the tips of his pointer and middle fingers to his temple on the right side of his head, massaging them around in circles. Just then, he remembered he had forgotten to take his medication.

"What's wrong, man? You got a headache?" Randy inquired, taking a swig from his thermos.

"No. I, uh, just neglected to drink my coffee this morning. No biggie. I'll be fine. I'm going to run to the bathroom before we head out." Jackson turned to head back inside.

Randy sipped from his thermos. "Good idea. There's not a lot of places to drain the lizard out there on the route. And God forbid you gotta pinch one off! You're really in a pickle then, buddy," he shouted.

Jackson rolled his eyes at Randy's obnoxious comment as he headed to the restroom. Once inside, he rushed into a stall securing its latch without haste. It reeked of urine, plus some unrecognizable stench escaping sewer drains in the floor. Pills rattling around in the bottle Jackson pulled from his pocket sounded few and far between. He popped off the cap. "One, two, three." There were only a few pills left. The mentally fragile ex-marine needed those pills to level out his emotions, his thoughts, and even more critical, his demeanor. This job was cloaked in customer service. That his customers liked him was of great importance to Jackson. Regardless of that fact, he couldn't afford to take one of his pills just yet. He needed to make them last as long as possible. As opposed to taking his recommended dose of one per day, Jackson opted for taking it once every couple of days, hoping it would keep him balanced out. The skin between his eyes wrinkled. Worry was visible on his face as he closed the bottle and stuffed it back into his pocket. *Eighty-nine more days until I can get insurance,* he reminded himself. "Pull it together, Jackson. You've got this."

Chapter 5

Rural Route 8

By the time he made it out to the truck, Randy had already finished loading packages. "Hop in," he said, with the back door lifted, directing Jackson with a gesture of his hand to a jump seat. "It's no recliner, but it's all we got."

"I think I can handle it. If riding in a plastic Humvee while dodging a hail of bullets didn't break me, sitting in a jump seat on the back of a mail truck surely won't do the job."

Jackson climbed on board, allowing Randy to pull the metal sliding door down, locking him inside.

Finally, Randy opened his driver's side door, hopped inside, then strapped on his safety belt. "So, inquiring minds want to know. Why'd you leave the military?"

"Who are inquiring minds? And how did you and inquiring minds find out I was military?"

"Dude, they've been talking about you since the day you interviewed. Word spreads fast around the office. Especially once the ladies get wind of it."

Randy started the ignition and drove off out of the parking lot and onto the streets of Clarkston to complete their route.

Jackson snickered a bit, amused by the fact that he'd already become the brunt of office gossip. "Tell me, what else do the ladies know about me?"

"Well, from what they've gathered, and I'm sure thoroughly investigated—if not already, then it's in the works—is that you are married with at least one child. You were in the Marines, and you are in your late twenties."

"Wow. Word does spread fast around the office. And they're right on all accounts. Including the late twenties part." Jackson was flattered that they thought he looked ten years younger than he was, so he wasn't too eager to debunk the myth.

"We've got some real potential around the office, man. Oh, I forgot. You're married, right?" A question Randy posed to test Jackson's loyalty, of course.

"I've been married for three years now. My wife is . . ." Jackson paused, forcing back words that wanted to come out all on their own, then continued with something that sounded much better. He finished it off by saying, "A lovely woman. A vessel of virtue, in fact."

"So, you're happy to be on lockdown, in other words?"

"I'm happy to be in a loving and trusting relationship. It's all I've ever wanted," Jackson responded, meaning every word.

Randy took a swig from his thermos. "Damn. Kudos to you! I wish I could be so sanctified. You a righteous man," Randy replied, the latter part of his statement uttered with a bit of church in his tone.

"If that's what you want to call it." Jackson sucked his teeth as if attempting to dislodge the piece of food a toothpick couldn't reach. He didn't like his seemingly underhanded comment.

Randy yanked the steering wheel of the LLV to the right to pull into a driveway of a large colonial-style home. "Here we go."

Jackson nearly flew out of his seat until he grabbed hold of the hanging shelf above his head for stability. It was his saving grace.

Randy proceeded to divulge successful mail-delivering tips. "Now, this old broad always gets packages, and she gives the best tips during the holiday season. You just have to sit and chat with her for a second or two. You don't even have to say much. Old Mrs. Teresa will talk enough for the both of you." He shifted the gear into park.

Randy unstrapped, then hopped out of the truck to let Jackson out. "Come on, soldier," he shouted

upon lifting the back door. "Don't forget to grab
her package. 11710. It's the small white and blue
box on the right. Probably a refill on her denture
cream." Randy chuckled at the joke Jackson didn't
find humor in.

Jackson grabbed her package before climbing
down out of the LLV. "We'll all be ordering denture cream one day. If we're lucky."

"You are one serious cat. Must have seen some
crazy shit in the military," Randy remarked, taking
note of his lackluster demeanor.

"I have indeed, Randy. You just be thankful
there are people out there like me willing to risk
their life for people like you."

Randy threw up a clenched fist as he headed up
the driveway. "'Merica! Yeah, man."

Jackson shut his eyes, shaking his head with
disappointment. *This guy is a real tool,* he thought
as he followed Randy up the driveway to Mrs.
Teresa's front door. He could see her waiting on
the front porch. She'd been tracking her package
since it left the warehouse in Pontiac early that
morning. Mrs. Teresa loved to chat with whomever
would listen. Being that the mailman came six
days out of the week, it made him or her a sure
thing. Jackson waved hello as he approached.

"Oh, shit, I almost forgot." Randy turned back
to grab her letters from a tray in front of the mail
truck.

Mrs. Teresa was old yet could see them coming from the end of the street. She saw everything that went on in her neighborhood, the comings and goings. She'd lived there her entire life and made it her business to keep a clean and orderly neighborhood. You couldn't so much as build a fence on your property without the subdivision's consent. Mrs. Teresa kept a watchful eye on her neighbors to ensure the rules weren't bent in any way.

"Good morning, ma'am. How are you this fine morning?"

What a handsome gentleman, she thought as she lifted her hand to Jackson for a handshake. "Well, hello, young man."

He accepted, only to lay a kiss upon her hand as opposed to the expected shaking. Mrs. Teresa's eyes grew wide. She lifted her other trembling hand to her chest. "Oh my, what a gentleman you are. Such chivalry hasn't been shown since my younger days."

"I assure you there are still men like us out here carrying on the tradition," Jackson replied.

"Well, that's certainly delightful to hear."

"My name is Jackson Pierce. I'm your new mailman."

"It's a pleasure to meet you, Jackson." She blushed. Her rosy, wrinkled cheeks complemented her short, curly gray hair.

"Mrs. Teresa," Randy shouted as he approached. "I have your letters. You got some more mail from the Volunteers of Clarkston, too. They must be running low on funds."

"Of course he would bring letters asking for charity drunk off his ass." She mumbled but made sure it was loud enough for Jackson to hear.

"I have your package here," Jackson said, handing the box over to her.

"It's a new blouse. It's a red one just like the silver one I have on."

"It's lovely and actually matches your eyes perfectly," Jackson remarked.

"Yeah, it really brings out the tinge of blue in your eyes," Randy added, trying to make a good impression. He couldn't allow Jackson to steal his thunder.

"That's the glaucoma, son."

"Oh, uhhh, sorry."

Mrs. Teresa had twenty-twenty vision. Still, she liked to see Randy fumble over his words. She always felt like he was some sort of con artist. Which kind, she was still trying to determine.

"This is Jackson, my substitute."

"We've already become acquainted. Thank you."

"Great. So, what's been going on lately? I see the Escobars are putting in a new pool. They must have paid some big bucks for that one."

"I guess they can afford it. They need to spring for a fence as well. If someone's pet or kid wanders over there, they could fall right in," Mrs. Teresa griped.

"Do you have an extra copy of your subdivision rules? I'd be happy to slip it into their mailbox for you." Jackson's suggestion made her feel better instantly.

"Why, thank you for offering. I certainly do have an extra copy. Let me go inside and get it for you."

The scrawny old woman turned, then headed inside of her house to fetch the booklet.

"Look at you, getting in good with the right people. Smart move, man," Randy remarked, leaning in closer to Jackson so that their conversation stayed between them.

"I've got some gum if you need it," Jackson replied in hopes he'd get the message.

Randy's breath reeked of alcohol, and moreover, the heat that day intensified the aroma of liquor escaping his pores. "I already chewed my last piece. What can I say? I had a good time last night," he chuckled. Whenever Randy felt even the slightest tinge of embarrassment, he'd laugh it off. Only this time, the defense mechanism quickly shifted to worry. "Does my breath really smell like booze?"

"Man, it's seeping out of your pores. You smell like a brewery, a liquor store, like a wino, vagrant standing on the corner begging for change to cop his next bottle, like a—"

Randy interrupted, "All right, all right, man. I get the point. I'll take the gum. Geez."

Jackson handed over a stick of gum he had stashed in the pocket of his cargo shorts.

"All jokes aside. Is it really that bad?" Randy inquired as he ripped the foil-laminated paper from the chewing gum before popping it into his mouth.

"It's pretty bad," Jackson reiterated. "You're welcome by the way."

"I was going to say thank you if you just give me a second."

"I gave you more than a few," Jackson countered.

"Damn, dude, you really are a marine at heart."

"Actually, I grasped the concept of having manners before I joined the Marines."

Randy was at a loss for words. Mrs. Teresa exited her home right on time, cutting through the uncomfortable silence.

"I've got it right here, Mr. Pierce." She waved a pamphlet above her head as she tackled the three steps below her front porch, a wooden cane assisting her descent.

"Please, call me Jackson." He graciously accepted the pamphlet.

"Thank you for your kindness, Jackson. I hope they appreciate you down there at the post office."

"So far so good, Mrs. Teresa. I'll be seeing you around. You enjoy the rest of your day." Jackson nodded farewell.

"See ya later, Mrs. Teresa," Randy chimed in.

"Enjoy your day, boys." Mrs. Teresa turned, then headed back to her porch swing so that she could continue spying on her neighbors.

Randy lifted the metal door on the LLV, allowing Jackson to climb inside. "I think I'm going to walk. We can get this street done twice as fast if you drive on one side and I walk the other."

"Is that really the reason you'd rather walk?" Randy inquired, letting his insecurities get the best of him.

"That, and the fact that it's about ninety degrees on the back of this thing."

"Oh, yeah, I forgot about that. It's been so long since I was in training. You know the other RCAs call this hell week. Sitting on the back of this thing during training gets you ready for what's to come."

Well, let's just say I've endured enough hell for one lifetime. I'll do the left. You do the right side. Sound like a plan?"

"Hell yeah. Let's get her done. I need to stop at the store before we head back. I'm feeling a little dehydrated."

"I wonder why," Jackson mumbled sarcastically.

Their decision to split the route worked out perfectly. By the time the time clock struck 1200 hours, they were pulling back into the annex parking lot.

"Today was great! If this is what I have to look forward to all week, sign me up."

"I'd never steer you wrong," Jackson chimed in while massaging his temples with his fingertips. A headache was brewing. He attributed nausea he felt to the nearly suffocating heat in the rear of that LLV.

Randy climbed down out of the mail truck, then hurried around back to free Jackson from the hot seat. "I really appreciate your help today. You're a standup guy. I'll put in a good word for you. Lots of other routes could use a good substitute. I never miss work, and I'm on the overtime list to work my days off, so this route is pretty much off the list for subs getting any real hours."

"Thanks. I would appreciate you putting in a good word for me. Once my training week is up, I'd like to continue working even if it is on another route." Words he spoke conflicted with his thoughts. *This is a good job, the benefits, the hours, the pay . . . I can't pay my rent if I don't work. Child support is going to take most of my check. I have a child to support. He doesn't even have any kids. He hasn't a care in the world. Getting drunk every day, partying every day . . . This is such bullshit.* Jackson's irritability was beginning to boil to the surface.

"Maybe I could—"

Before Randy could finish, Jackson darted off toward the double doors. "Excuse me. I really need to use the restroom."

"Nature calls! I'll gather up the outgoing mail and see you inside!" he hollered out to Jackson already inside the building.

Chapter 6

What's Hidden

Randy pulled out a white plastic mail tub half-way filled with outgoing letters they collected from the mailboxes out on the route. He pushed through the swinging doors, then emptied the tub into a wire cage filled with the compiled outgoing mail. That was when he saw the bottle of medication. *It must have fallen out of Jackson's pocket while he was riding in back,* he reckoned.

Hunched over a urine-stained commode, Jackson puked up the orange juice and bagel he'd had for breakfast. "Come on. Please don't do this to me now." He shook his head in despair. Jackson lifted his leg, using his foot to push down the chrome lever to flush the toilet, then dug into his pocket to retrieve his pills. Where the hell did the bottle go? He began to panic, checking each of the pockets on his cargo shorts thoroughly. "Oh no." Fearing the worst, Jackson rushed out of the stall to retrace his steps.

By the time he made it to the exit, Randy was standing there reading the bottle of medication he found. "Jackson Pierce. Generic for Prozac. I knew it." He huffed. "This dude is psychotic."

Although Jackson heard every word, he decided against ruffling any feathers. The last thing he wanted was for them to find out he was on medication, a fact he'd neglected to note on his application.

"I'll take those," Jackson uttered, standing closely behind him.

Randy jolted from the shock of being caught reading the medicine bottle that didn't belong to him. They were neck to nose when Randy turned. "Oh, man, you scared me a little. I think these are yours."

"Thanks." Jackson accepted the handoff.

"I found them mixed in with the outgoing mail. Must have dropped them."

"The bottle fell out of my pocket. I'm glad you found them."

"Yeah, no problem. Let's head over to the case and finish up. I'll show you how to do the extras tomorrow. You don't look so good."

"I'm fine. Please, don't baby me. I'm fully capable of doing the job," Jackson professed.

"If you say so, man. I'm just trying to look out for you."

The moment Deborah saw them heading back to the case, she rushed over to greet them. "Hey, guys! How'd it go today? You're back pretty early."

"Yeah, we split the route up. He did one side of the street while I did the other. I figured it would work better that way," Randy blurted before Jackson could say a word.

Jackson's heart began to race. *Did this lying piece of shit just take credit for my idea?*

As opposed to revealing the lie, Jackson took it a step further. "That's right. We got all the mail delivered in half the time." Jackson smiled. He had other plans that would lay the groundwork for his career there at the United States Postal Service. "Hey, while I have you here, I have a question I need to ask you. I'm Jackson Pierce by the way. I don't think we've met."

"We didn't, but I'm glad we finally have." Deborah held out her hand, waiting for him to take it, all the while ogling at his bright smile, full lips, handsome face, and chiseled physique. He was her type, yet rules of fraternization were not to be broken. Be that as it may, she enjoyed looking while imagining his hands were discovering parts of her body that desperately hungered for a strong man's touch.

"As am I," he agreed. Jackson could see lust in her eyes as he took her hand. To Deborah the words left his lips in slow motion. Her stockings felt moist between her thighs.

"I, umm . . ." She was at a loss for words.

Randy stared at Deborah as if she were alien to him. *What the hell is wrong with this chick?* It was then that Jackson saw his chance. He reached for the folder compiling his choices for health insurance, knocking over Randy's thermos full of liquid in the process. It spilled out onto the floor, splashing across the bottom of Deborah's beige dress slacks. The smell of liquor stung their nostrils.

Deborah looked up, her eyes moving back and forth between them. "Whose thermos is this?"

"I was, uh . . ." Randy paused. There was no chance he could talk his way out of this one.

"Randy, in the conference room, now," Deborah demanded.

Randy knew he was in big trouble. His job was on the line, and it was all thanks to his new RCA. His gaze lowered to the floor as he headed toward the conference room to be reprimanded.

Deborah turned her attention to Jackson. "Welcome to Rural Route 8. Until further notice, this is your route."

"I won't let you down," he said, flashing that brilliant smile.

"I'm counting on it," she replied.

Jackson's smile fleeted into a twisted grin as he watched her tear off toward the conference room to deal with Randy.

At 1800 hours, the parking lot was nearly full at Jack Hammer's Bar and Grill, more so a bar than a grill. The hole in the wall establishment pulled in its fair share of locals. It was a favorite hangout for a few rural carriers, making it the go-to place for impromptu employee gatherings. On the way there, Jackson hoped his neatly pressed dark-washed blue jeans were appropriate for the night. When he heard the nineties classic by Blackstreet "No Diggity" blasting from speakers inside upon pulling into the gravel parking lot, his insecurities faded. *I hope Evelyn is here tonight. I'd love to get to know her a little better.* Jackson was up for some flirty conversation.

Several patrons gathered out front, taking drags from their cigarettes while immersed in meaningless chatter. He got out of his Bronco, smoothing down his black fitted V-neck T-shirt. "Ain't nothing to it but to do it, right, Jackson?" he encouraged himself.

"Get the fuck out of here! Are you kidding me?" Elise shouted at Pat, one of the other rural carriers.

"I swear. I saw him leaving the office. He look so mad," Pat reiterated. She was an attractive 40-something Vietnamese woman with long, thick, healthy black hair. Her small frame didn't stop her from keeping up with the best of them. She tossed her shot of tequila back after sucking on a slice of lemon.

Evelyn locked eyes with one of the other rural carriers, Tanya, shaking her head with disappointment. The petite woman in her forties had short, curly hair that was tapered around the sides and back.

Meanwhile, Elise further investigated. "How did you find out what happened?" she inquired.

"Deborah told me," Pat answered emphatically.

Evelyn spoke up, saying, "Now she knows she is not supposed to be telling his business like that. She so damn petty and inappropriate."

"That's your girl, though," Elise countered.

"Shut up, Elise."

"Truth hurts," she mumbled in response.

Everyone always gave Evelyn a hard time about being friends with Deborah. She was their supervisor, in other words, their enemy. Evelyn didn't see it that way though. To her everyone was on the same level. She didn't treat people different because of the authority they held or lack thereof.

"She's an employee just like you. Why treat her differently?"

"Because she's a bitch. Because she treats people like garbage. Maybe because she talks to most of us like we are subhuman. Everyone except you for some reason."

"Maybe it's because I treat her like a human being."

"No. It's because you're constantly saving her ass when she does or says something wrong. How long are you going to continue to cover her ass?"

"Wow. Somebody has been holding a lot in, I see," Evelyn responded with raised brows. She knew Elise had a stick up her butt about something. She just couldn't pinpoint it.

"Right," Jackson chimed in, having walked up mid-conversation.

"Oh, hey, Jackson! You came! We're glad you came," Pat spoke up excitedly.

"Jackson, did you know Randy was forced to go on leave?" Elise asked.

"I feel like I'm in the hot seat." He pulled up a stool to join the others at the black rectangular table. "I see everyone has ordered drinks."

Evelyn responded, pointing out Pat and Elise. "Some of our coworkers have been drinking since they got off at four o'clock."

"Don't avoid the question, Jackson. Did you know about what happened? I mean, if the rumors are true, you've just secured yourself a route. Through the holiday season at the very least."

"What's your name? Elise, right? I think you need another drink, Elise."

"That's the last thing she needs," Evelyn chimed in.

"Oh, he'll be back to work in no time," Pat slurred.

Her remark didn't sit well with Jackson. "What makes you say that?"

"We have protection in cases like this. He can just admit he has a problem. All he has to do is agree to counseling, and poof, just like that Rural Route 8 is his once again." Pat's words seemed taunting. There was a stiff, drunken stare plastered on her face.

With a wave of his hand, Jackson signaled to get the attention of a bartender. "Bartender! Can we get another round over here, please?"

Elise chimed in to soften the blow. She could tell the news was unsettling to him on account of the way his fists clenched up upon hearing Pat's declaration of Randy's impending early return. "Never mind Pat, Jackson. You'll have plenty of time to settle in at Clarkston."

"Elise, I'm a new hire. The last thing I want to do is ruffle feathers by stirring up gossip. Plus, I'm a man, and men simply don't gossip about other men." Jackson shrugged off his worries for the time being.

"Says the marine. Ooh rah!" Evelyn boosted his ego.

"I understand, Jackson. Just watch your back when it comes to Deborah."

Jackson looked over at Marcus sitting nearby. He sat alone, drinking his mug of malt liquor. "Oh, I didn't notice Marcus sitting there."

"He probably didn't notice himself there. Weirdo." Elise chuckled silently.

Jackson glanced back at Elise, surmising her alcohol level. "On second thought, maybe you have had enough."

"Oh no, she's always like this," Evelyn chimed in.

He leaned in toward her, whispering, "That's unfortunate."

"Indeed." She smiled.

Pat focused her gaze on the new hire. "So, Jackson, tell us about yourself."

"I think you guys know everything it is I want you to know."

"So, you're a hard ass and a smart ass!" Elise blurted.

"If that's what you feel comfortable calling it." Jackson looked up at the waiter as he approached their table.

"Uh-ohhh, I smell trouble. I see another bird has joined the flock." He waved his hand flamboyantly. Nick was in his twenties. He'd been working the bar part-time for the last seven years. It supplemented his income, though he made a pretty penny doing a fashion blog on his web-televised series. Nick's build was equivalent to Jackson's, but he had a head full of black silky curls.

"Nick, this is Jackson. He's new at the post office."

"Very nice," Nick remarked.

"Great to make your acquaintance, Nick." Jackson shook his hand. He caught on to what Nick meant by the comment but kept his innermost thoughts to himself, well aware that ass whippings didn't only come from men of the heterosexual variety.

Nick garnered an instant respect for Jackson for not treating him differently. "So, what can I get for you?"

"Nick, I'll just have a beer, thank you. Heineken in a mug would be perfect."

"Any of you other troublemakers want anything?" He motioned, wiggling his fingers out toward the others.

"How about a menu? I'm freaking starving over here," Elise responded.

"One Heineken in a mug and menus all around. Got it." Nick glanced back at Jackson, "I'll be right back with your Heinie, sir."

"Of course." Jackson dropped his head, seeing humor in his closing remark.

An hour later, Elise was out cold with her head nestled in her arm down on the table next to a plate of devoured Buffalo wings.

Marcus had called it a night, having not really involved himself in the gathering his entire time there. Pat and Tanya were busy sampling each other's appetizer platters. There were a few other carriers scattered about in the high-traffic bar. Jackson and Evelyn were busy chatting about other employees. Jackson didn't really mind gossip just as long as he wasn't the one spilling it. As his military career came up in conversation, the former marine boasted of his accomplishments and, moreover, dangerous situations he'd braved.

"So, have you ever been shot at?" Evelyn asked.

"I've been shot at, blown up, hunted, you name it. I've pretty much experienced it all." Jackson lifted his shirt, revealing scars across his abs from severe burns he'd endured. "Check this out."

At first Evelyn was inclined to look away. Not because of the distorted look of his wounds, but because she was a married woman. Her watching him lift his shirt could be misconstrued as something more than it was. Still, she looked, unable to resist the fascination.

"Damn. How did that happen?"

"I told you it was my job to burn the shit. One time I got a little squirt crazy with the accelerant and didn't feel it splashing back up on my shirt. Needless to say, what you see is what you get." Jackson let his shirt back down, covering his scarred abdomen.

"Damn. That looks like it hurt. I'm nearly brought to tears when I burn myself taking something out of the oven. I couldn't imagine actually being on fire."

"It certainly wasn't fun. It actually took months to heal from the pain."

"Well, I'm glad you didn't die."

Jackson chuckled. "What a nice thing to say. Weird, but considerate."

"Weird. I actually get it quite often," she admitted proudly.

Jackson liked the way Evelyn's mouth moved when she talked. Her smile was as inviting as her big brown eyes. Evelyn had a talent for attracting unwanted affection. Most men took her kindness for flirting, an issue that frequently found her in odd situations. She hadn't anticipated that being the case with Jackson. After all, he was married. Knowing that brought her comfort. They conversed until around nine o'clock before Evelyn decided to call it a night.

Chapter 7

Danger Lurks in Darkness

After a few alcoholic beverages, Marcus's inhibitions were at an all-time low. He waited outside of the bar, slumped over his steering wheel, hoping to catch a glimpse of a woman he'd been spying on most of his time there. She was busty with a petite frame. The woman's silk peach blouse matched the blush about her cheeks, and her black business skirt told him that she was a woman worth approaching.

Marcus assumed she was clean and fit for his needs. He had watched the unsuspecting woman order her last drink and push it away before it was finished, signaling the bartender she'd had enough. It was only a matter of time before she'd be exiting the bar. Marcus's suspicions were correct.

Fifteen minutes later, she emerged, music echoing through the opened door out into the parking lot. Tobacco smoke escaped into fresh air as she held open the door, eyes searching the lot for her vehicle. "Where the hell did I park?" she muttered, forcing herself to recollect previous actions.

As paranoia washed over him, Marcus sat back in the driver's seat, using the shroud of darkness in his vehicle as cover. He worried she'd notice him there spying.

"There it is." She breathed a sigh of relief. For a moment she worried someone may have taken off with it, but at the sight of her pearl white Mercedes-Benz, she released her grip on the door handle to head toward her vehicle. Pushing her shoulder-length blond curls behind her ears, she kept her eyes to the ground, her footing wobbling across the gravel.

Marcus wanted more than anything to approach her right then and there, but he was unable to muster up the courage before she'd already gotten into her sedan. He saw no other option than to follow his prospect. Marcus's Volkswagen pulled out of the parking lot just after her Mercedes. He hoped she lived alone and that no one was waiting for her arrival at the next destination.

As she stopped at a red light on Dixie Highway, the woman lowered her visor. She stared at her reflection, searching for signs of inebriation. The last thing she wanted was to go home drunk. If her husband found out she was at a bar, there would surely be hell to pay. The white around her warm hazel pupils was bloodshot. She popped open the middle console, pulling out a bottle of Visine. After squeezing out one drop into her right eye, she shifted left. The woman pinched the sides of the miniature bottle as hard as she could. But nothing. "Shit. Of course," she huffed, figuring it was just her luck she'd be out.

As Marcus waited, eyes transfixed on her, the person driving a vehicle behind Marcus's laid on their horn, alerting them of the green traffic signal. Startled, she pushed up the visor, then slammed her foot down on the gas pedal. *I can't go home like this. My husband will kill me.* She was supposed to be working late, not hanging out at a bar. But she needed the release. Knowing her husband wouldn't approve, she chose to keep nights like those secret. A gas station on the corner she saw as her only refuge. They had to sell Visine there, she assumed.

Marcus followed closely as the woman pulled into the gas station, parking alongside her Benz. He pushed a button to lower his passenger-side window. That was when she noticed him. Marcus pointed his finger downward in a silent plea for her to lower hers as well. She complied, wondering what he could possibly want.

"Excuse me. I was wondering, if you're not attached—"

"I am," she quickly interrupted, holding up her hand to flash a two-carat diamond wedding ring. "Now please, leave me be. I really don't have time for this." She ended the rejection, pushing a button to raise her window back up, before hopping out of her vehicle to go inside the gas station. She paid Marcus no mind, having been approached by men quite often. Turning them down had become a regular occurrence, especially when she'd be hanging out as opposed to working.

Marcus felt slighted, and more so upset by the woman's rejection. *Who does she think she is dismissing me like that?* Irritability festered in a pocket of his mind. *I'll show her who's boss.*

The woman headed straight for the register where a gas station attendant sat nodding off in his cushy chair behind a Plexiglas-encased area. "Hey. Hey," she yelled over the sound of a small box television playing behind the counter. Once she smacked her hand against the countertop a few times, the young man finally awoke. He had to be in his early twenties, she surmised. One thing she did notice was the fact that he was as high as a kite. It was his squinted eyes, coupled with the beanie atop his dreaded head, that clued her in. If nothing else, his tie-dyed shirt was a dead giveaway. "Do you sell eyedrops?"

"Sorry, lady. We're all out. Do you need any gas?" He yawned, stretching his restless limbs.

"No. I need eyedrops," she explained emphatically.

"Looks like it's not your lucky night." He closed his eyes, drifting back off to sleep.

"Of course. I'm sure you've used them all," she complained as she headed back to the restroom. She figured she could wash her face and maybe rinse her eyes out. She'd done so before. At the very least she would smell refreshed. The redness of her eyes could be explained away as a side effect of working all night.

As she pushed open the door to the single restroom, a dim, flickering light above the sink illuminated. The room smelled of urine, and even worse, the toilet was packed with tissue along with the remainder of the last person's waste. She tiptoed in, trying to avoid pieces of toilet paper stuck to dingy linoleum flooring. Catching her off guard, Marcus shoved her inside the rest of the way.

"What the fuck are you doing?"

"Shut up or I'll snap your neck," he demanded, shutting and locking the door behind him.

"Don't you dare touch me," she hollered out, hoping to wake the napping cashier.

Visibility hindered by a flickering light, she was barely able to get a good look at his face. Marcus snatched the frightened woman up by the arm, pulling her toward him, before he spun her around, masking her screams. His hands felt like blocks of ice, yet when he pulled her close, she could feel how his profuse sweating had dampened his T-shirt.

She thought for sure someone would hear her scream if she could just get closer to the heavy metal door. But first she had to free herself from his clutches. She bit down hard on Marcus's finger, prompting him to immediately snatch his hand away from her mouth, wrapping it around her throat.

His grip was tight, too tight for her to scream. "I said I'll snap your neck," he threatened, holding his lips alongside her face. She smelled like cherries. Marcus liked breathing in deep her essence. She, on the other hand, was on the verge of vomiting from the smell of garlic and alcohol escaping his breath.

Her body trembled, knees nearly buckling when she felt his lips brush against her cheek. The terrified woman didn't have much of a choice yet refused to give up without a fight. She stomped down on the tip of his shoe, digging her heel into his toe.

"Ow. You stupid tramp." Marcus shoved the woman away with as much force as he could muster. Her body slammed against a concrete wall, knocking the wind from her, almost causing her to lose consciousness. He dropped to his knees beside her, erect penis protruding through the open zipper of his shorts. Marcus slid his hands up her skirt, pulling her lace panties to the side. Her crotch wasn't shaved, but still it felt nice enough for him to explode when the time would come.

She whimpered upon feeling his manhood brush against her vagina, bracing herself for the penetration that was to ensue, yet never did. He spit on his hand, moistening her lips. His member stroked against hers, sliding back and forth until it finally happened. Marcus pulled away, stood to his feet, then released his fluids into the toilet. He used his foot, kicking the metal lever to flush it down the drain along with the rest of the waste.

"Maybe next time you'll be a little nicer. Let this be a lesson to you." He exited the restroom in a hurry, leaving the woman scared, disgusted, angry, and moreover, confused. Unable to grasp what had really happened to her, she contemplated reporting it as tears flowed down her flushed cheeks. She wept, snot sliding from her nostrils. If she said something about what happened, she would have to tell her husband the truth—an act she was hesitant to carry out. Mrs. Trionfi decided in that moment that she would keep her attack a secret. Besides, she hadn't been penetrated. How her husband would react frightened her more than the devastating experience. The only solace she found was in the fact that Mr. Trionfi would never know.

Chapter 8

Neighbors

By the time the clock struck midnight, Jackson was back at it, sitting on his sofa watching old home videos of his and his estranged wife's broken bond. Those were happier times when they loved hard, he and Sue. Jackson gazed at their images on the tube, the couple in the throes of a whimsical embrace. The entire family was there for the reception celebrating their union. When Jackson and his new bride locked eyes, passion exploded from his loins, as did Sue's desire for him burn from the very core of her. A kiss was imminent and how she preferred to express her passions. Sue craved the physicality of it. Jackson should have known it would end as it had. When he met her, she was upside down, legs spread until they made a horizontal line across from one foot to the other, while holding tight to a metal pole in one of the sleaziest topless bars in Jacksonville,

North Carolina. One wink while she held the
seductive pose was all it took. Lance Corporal
Jackson Pierce didn't know what hit him. They
were married within six months' time. A quick
start. Little did he know his wanton wife was rushing to the finish line from the moment she said the
words "I do."

A single tear fell from his left eye before he
wiped his face over from forehead to chin with one
hand. His other clicked the button on the remote
to turn off the television. "Fucking bitch ruined
everything," he mumbled. His anxiety neared
its peak. Opting not to take one of his pills until Monday morning when he would need it most,
he decided to go for a walk. Jackson needed to
blow off some steam. The air outside should be
perfect. During summer nights the temperature
was ideal for taking a stroll. He got up from the
couch, leaving the remote there on a cushion beside him. Before walking out, he snatched up his
dark gray hoodie from the standing wooden coat
rack near the door. Stretching his arms through
the sleeves, he stepped out of his studio apartment
into a dimly lit hallway. The pewter-colored car-
peting was worn, loose strings of wool unraveling
from its backing. Peeling at its corners, gray wallpaper with vertical maroon stripes lined the length
of the walls. The heavy wooden door with the 8
nailed onto the front closed behind him. Jackson
zipped his hoodie, then tossed its hood over his

head with both of his hands. A faint smell of mold compounded his worries as he made his way down two sets of creaking wooden stairs before pushing his way out into fresh air.

Although a vast number of Clarkston's residents were wealthy, every city had a ghetto or an area where residential housing required meager dividends. With the looming hammer of child support waiting to crash down upon him, Jackson thought it best he be as frugal as possible. Living in a more expensive apartment simply wasn't feasible. It wasn't a lack of space that bothered him. It was his decline on a societal level. He resented his soon-to-be ex-wife for his misfortune, of course. *Why can't people just be honest?* he asked himself. *She could have just told me she didn't want to be with me anymore. That would have been better than finding her riding another man's cock when she should have been taking care of our 3-year-old daughter.* His thoughts sickened him. Hate he harbored for Sue festered down deep. *I can do better,* he convinced himself, *for the meantime anyway. Just wait until I get myself together. I'll show her,* Jackson vowed. But then there was the dreaded loss of hours looming over his head. He thought about what Pat said about how easy it would be for Randy to get his route back. Jackson couldn't let that happen. He couldn't lose his job. It would crush him as a father and, even worse, as a man.

Something had to be done to stop him. Whatever that may be, in Jackson's eyes it would be justified.

He walked nearly a mile by the time he shifted focus to the road ahead of him. Jackson made a left. The only gas station operating that late was a quarter of a mile or so ahead. Although most of the businesses along Dixie Highway were closed by 10:00 p.m., the light beaming from the streetlamps overhead illuminated the way. When he finally made it there, a vagrant approached before Jackson could near the entrance.

"Excuse me, sir. I'm sorry to bother you, but I'm homeless, and if you could spare anything, I'd greatly appreciate it." Even bums in the area had manners, or at least they minded them once they crossed the border into Clarkston.

"Sure, man. I have a couple of dollars," Jackson replied, digging into the pocket of his cargo shorts to hand it over to the unfortunate stranger. "Here you go."

"Oh, God bless you. Thank you so much." He stared down at the three dollars as if he were staring at the face of Benjamin Franklin.

"No problem," Jackson assured him just as he spotted Marcus exiting through the gas station doors, while glancing over the vagrant's hunched shoulders.

Mrs. Trionfi hadn't quenched his thirst. Wanting more, Marcus went back to what he had become accustomed to: prostitutes.

That's the clerk from the post office, Jackson concluded by his dopey posture, pale skin, and oval-shaped head. If not, his resemblance was uncanny, that was with the added fact that coils of hair along the man's forehead receded on both sides.

Marcus rushed back to his 2001 Volkswagen GTI, Jackson assumed, to enjoy the company of the seemingly lethargic brunette leaned back in his front passenger seat. He tossed a black plastic bag containing items he purchased into her lap as he climbed inside. Marcus started his car, taking off without hesitation.

Someone is in for a wild night, Jackson thought. In a way he envied the fact that Marcus had a companion. He wondered if that was his wife or just a passing fling. Maybe it was a married woman, cheating on her husband, and Marcus was her lustful boy toy. He shuddered at the thought, dismissing it altogether as he headed inside the gas station.

After a few minutes, Marcus pulled into the alley behind his apartment building, that same apartment building where Jackson resided. He parked behind a big metal green dumpster, then hopped out, rushing to the passenger side of his vehicle. Marcus opened her door and grabbed the grocery bag from her lap, hanging it on his wrist. He would need both hands to help his date from the vehicle. Whatever he'd given her rendered her defenseless against what he had planned. Marcus lifted her from the car, hanging one of her limp arms over his shoulder to walk alongside her for assistance. He pushed the car door shut yet was only able to take a few steps before her arm slid from over his shoulders, sending her body toward the pavement. His hands gripped her sides, halting her descent. It behooved him to lift her, tossing the upper half of her body over his right shoulder, so Marcus did just that. Her long brown hair extended past his buttocks, and on the other hand, her crimson-colored minidress neglected to cover hers. A matching G-string made it seem as if she weren't wearing any underwear at all.

The back door to his building had been propped open with a small boulder, it being wedged in the door at its base. Once inside, Marcus kicked the rock out into the alley, allowing the door to close behind him. He climbed three flights of stairs with the malnourished woman hanging limp over his shoulder. The hallway on the third floor led him to the apartment door with the brass number 9 nailed onto its front side. That apartment was directly across from the apartment with the 8 on the door, Jackson's studio.

He pulled the keys out of his pocket, then proceeded to fumble with them until he found the appropriate one. Marcus had already started to sweat, stains visible at the pits of his blue T-shirt. He moved to insert the key but clumsily dropped them onto the carpet before he could unlock his door. "Damn it," he groaned. Marcus needed desperately to gain access to his apartment before someone discovered him in the awkward position. He knocked gently, just loud enough for whomever was inside to hear. The door opened almost immediately. Marcus kicked his keys inside as he pushed the rest of the way through.

"Close the door," he demanded of the 17-year-old boy waiting silently on the other side. "It's time for her to lie down."

The boy's eyes lit up as if an early Christmas gift had arrived. He pushed the door shut, then peeked through the small hole that gave a view to the hallway. No one was there. *The coast is clear,* he thought, twisting the deadbolt into the locked position. When he turned, he pressed his back to the door for a moment, reminding himself to keep composed. Ready, he pushed forward, running his fingers through the side of his greasy black hair as he attempted to tame lustful urges rising inside of him. Andre pushed a button on the radio that sat in the living room just outside his father's

bedroom door. Alice in Chains's "Down in a Hole"
was his song choice for these kinds of events.

It had taken Marcus more time than he preferred to render his companion defenseless. Now,
he could finally do as he pleased with her. He
dumped the woman off his shoulder, down onto
his queen-size bed. The sheets were black. No
blanket covered them.

He rushed over to the windows, peeking out
into the alley before twisting the stick to close
the white venetian mini blinds. At the same
time, the boy flipped the light switch, illuminating
a black light in the ceiling. Sporadic spots on the
bed linen lit up like neon lights. He walked over,
then sat on the edge of the bed, pushing her hair
back behind her ear.

The woman's widened pupils focused on Andre's
face for a moment, her eyes a dull shade of gray.
She spoke softly, so he lowered his ear near her
narrow lips to hear. "He didn't have to drug me,"
she whispered before both eyeballs rolled back
into their lids.

"I beg to differ, sweetheart. This is gonna be
a wild ride," the teenager replied in a whisper,
anticipating exactly what would happen. When
he moved to touch the top of her exposed breast,
Marcus wasted no time halting his advances.

"Not yet. It's not your turn yet. I want this one
all to myself first. Go out and take a seat." He
motioned his hand for the boy to exit.

"Can we keep her?"

"For a little while."

The teenager didn't put up a fuss, knowing his time would soon come. He left the room, then turned the volume up on the radio before taking his place on an old, checkered beige and brown recliner in their living room. The door was left wide open so that he could watch his father and their date for that evening while they performed.

Marcus stood at the end of the bed, dropping his trousers there on the spot, but he left his black boxer briefs on to cover his erect penis. He lifted her torso from the mattress, pulling both arms toward him. Even sitting up, her back hunched, shoulders slumped, and head hung low. Marcus dropped to his knees in front of her. The woman's shoulders were bare, all except for the spaghetti straps that held up her minidress. With a delicate touch, he took down her straps, letting the dress drop down around her waist. Her breasts were firm and perkier than most other working girls he'd previously purchased services from. Their large areolas heightened his thirst for her. Marcus's tongue tasted his lips. Then, out of nowhere, he delivered her a hard slap to the right side of her face. You'd have thought the slap would have stung her cheek. His large hand left a massive red welt on the side of her face. Still, she didn't react to the blow. She wouldn't remember a thing.

Marcus was sure of it. He smacked her again. That time it was with the palm of his hand before the backside immediately followed. He stood, lifting her into the air with a strong hold on her scrawny biceps. The woman's silk dress slid off onto the floor, resting on top of his trousers. He threw her back onto the bed, her small frame bouncing on the mattress. Marcus spread her legs before he crawled down onto the bed, then wrapped her narrow limbs around his waist. He rested on his knees and shins, letting her buttocks lie on his pale, hairy thighs. With a tug of one of her limp arms, he pulled her in closer. The skin of her shoulders, back, rump, and thighs felt like cashmere on his fingertips as he navigated the length of her body with a tender touch.

"So smooth," he whispered. Marcus touched his forefinger and middle finger to her mouth, running them down her lips. "What soft lips you have," he remarked. Her G-string snapped like a rubber band when he pulled them apart with both hands. "Are these soft as well?" he asked, looking down at the flesh of her naked crotch. The spit Marcus forced from his mouth onto his fingers he used to moisten her lips down below. She was completely shaved, which was his favorite. He loved to feel the skin of it. The anticipation had built to an urge insurmountable. His erection was rock hard, ready to be worked over. With one hand he grabbed hold to the side of her waist, the other he wrapped around her narrow neck, squeezing her throat as he yanked her pelvis back and forth. It felt good to him, her vagina moving back and forth across his penis. Marcus made it a point not to penetrate them as they were, in his eyes, unclean women. And so, his long-standing obsession with dry humping would go on until a woman was worthy enough to feel the skin of his erect member.

"You nasty trick. You like that, don't you? I know you like it. You want me to put it in, don't you? Tell me you want me to put it in."

He yanked her faster and harder, back and forth across his bulge, over and over, until he exploded, releasing juices into his boxers. A stain slowly came into view under the black light.

"Ahhh," he exhaled, the look on his face twisting from pleasure to disgust instantaneously. "Look what you made me do," he threatened with a tight squeeze on her throat. Marcus sat up on his knees, forcing her body down to the mattress in a choke hold. He began strangling the already-unconscious woman, releasing his grip only to deliver repeated swift open-handed blows to her face.

Jackson could hear music as he came up the stairs.

Down in a hole
Feeling so small
Down in a hole
Losing my soul

The chorus blared from that apartment opposite his. The old man in the adjacent apartment rushed out wearing a plaid robe and slippers just as Jackson was unlocking his door.

He banged his wrinkled fist upon Marcus's door. "Turn that damned music down! Four days out of the week I have to listen to this shit blaring all night long! I'm sick of it!" he demanded, pounding at the door with the number 9 on the front. Seemed the old man had recognized his pattern of frequency in Marcus's affairs.

Jackson paid him no mind as he stepped into his apartment, closing the door behind him. He had more important things to worry about than loud music.

Chapter 9

Adjusting to Life

Jackson slept most of the day away that Sunday, getting up only to relieve himself. For some reason he couldn't shake exhaustion his body was plagued with that day. He had awoken to a prickly feeling festering at the nape of his neck. Jackson tossed and turned, flipping then folding his pillow in half under his head until his dreams took him back to that hellish place from which he had been barred.

Lance Corporal Jackson Pierce stood over the box of crap, ready to get it over with. It was his duty to dispose of the human waste he and the other marines at Camp Joe Foss released daily. Jackson pulled a metal pan full of feces out from the bottom of the wooden box, poured an accelerant across the length of the pan, then struck a match.

"I hate this job," he remarked before tossing the lit match into the waste. He held a white hand-

kerchief over his nose and mouth to block out the foul smell. Jackson's job required him to watch it burn, until there was nothing left. But just then the soaring sounds from the SCUD missiles being fired from Iraq could be heard overhead. Bombs were coming, and there was nothing they could do to stop them.

"Take cover!" multiple soldiers hollered out in unison. It was best they took cover. Green natural biological and chemical warfare suits they wore made them stick out like a sore thumb.

Jackson scooped his gas mask and M16-AR2 service rifle up off the sand nearby. "Let's go! Move! Move! Move!"

Marines scrambled, grabbing their gas masks as they rushed to file into the bunkers for cover. Some of them prayed. Others cursed the Iraqis for their attacks. Jackson climbed down into the bunker, put in his earplugs, then slid on his gas mask as he waited there in silence. He wasn't too worried about the bombs. Their smaller base was rarely targeted. It was the main base the Iraqis were attempting to destroy. When bombs landed near Al Jaber, the ground shook at Camp Joe Foss. With no inclination as to when the bombs would cease, the marines would have to sleep there in the bunker for the remainder of the night, as they had many nights before. The platoons were in for another night of no sleep. But it was what they'd signed up for: no showers for months at a time, meals ready to eat that tasted like shit warmed up twice, and the constant threat of death. Jackson wondered if it was all worth it and, moreover, if he would even live to see his wife and child after the war was done.

Jackson's mind shifted, still captive of his night terrors.

He was there again peering through the window of that musty motel room. His eyes protruded as he watched Sue slowly riding that younger marine's stiffened penis. He slammed his fists against the glass. But this time it was different. The glass didn't shatter. "Get the fuck off him! What are you doing? Why are you doing this?" he screamed at the top of his lungs as he pounded harder on the glass. His efforts were futile. Sue couldn't hear him, and neither could her lover.

He turned her over, taking her from behind. The young marine tugged at her long black hair as he slammed his pelvis against her bottom. "Oh, yes. Just like that, soldier," she cried out in ecstasy, locking eyes with her distressed husband. Sue licked her lips slowly from the top right corner all the way to the left. Taunting him even in his dreams.

"I'm going to kill you!" Sprinklings of saliva shot out of his mouth, landing on the window he'd tried so desperately to shatter. Tears streamed *from his bloodshot eyes. "I hate you, you bitch! I hate you! Do you hear me? I hate you!"*

Suddenly, the alarm clock went off, ripping Jackson from his night terror. He sprung up from his pillow, bald head drenched with sweat. It took a few seconds for him to gain control of his panicked breaths. He then realized it was just a dream, that he was no longer trapped in that devastating nightmare.

The old man next door pounded at the wall adjoining their apartments. "Hey, buddy! How about you shut off that damned alarm!" he screamed.

Jackson breathed a sigh of relief as he reached over to shut off the alarm clock on the nightstand. It was 0700 hours, almost time for him to head to work. He had one hour to make his bed, shower, shave, and have his breakfast before it was time to serve the citizens of Clarkston. Monday would be his first day alone on the route. Jackson was a quick learner, so he remained optimistic that he could complete his route without incident. The moment he climbed out of bed he fixed his linens as he had been taught in the military, tight enough to bounce a quarter off them. Afterward, he made his way to the bathroom, sliding off his white boxer shorts on the way, only to toss them into the hamper stationed in a corner of the room. Jackson knew he had to make a good impression. The only thing that could possibly stand in the way

of him doing a good job was him. Increasing nightmares, irritability, nausea, even headaches, were
all symptoms of withdrawal. He opened the medicine cabinet, grabbing his nearly empty bottle of
Prozac.

Jackson popped open the cap. "One, two, three."
He peered into the bottle, counting them out.
"Only three left," he mumbled.

He was almost out. Regardless, he had to take
one. It was the only way he could get through the
day without snapping at someone. Jackson placed
one of the pills on his tongue, then set the bottle
on the sink. He reached for a small glass on the
countertop to fill it with water so that he could
wash the capsule down. It was then that he had
made a grave error in judgment. When the glass
tapped against the opened bottle it toppled over
into the sink, spilling the other two pills down into
the drain.

"No no no." Jackson scrambled to retrieve them.
But to no avail. It was too late. They were gone, as
soon would be his sanity. "Oh, my God, what am
I gonna do?" He thought about going back down
to Veterans Affairs, but his case was still under review. It wouldn't matter what he said to the review
board. They rushed for no man. You'd think the
soldiers who fought for our country wouldn't have
to struggle for a thing. Unfortunately, their needs,
most times, went unfulfilled. Many veterans ended

up living below the poverty level with minimal health care or, even worse, homeless. Jackson, like many other veterans, felt abandoned by those to which he remained loyal. After fighting for the lives of his nation, he received nothing but a big middle finger.

Jackson looked up to the ceiling. "Why is this happening? I just don't understand what I did to deserve this."

Of course, he received no answer to the questions that plagued him. So, the strong-willed marine gathered his emotions once more, pressing forward through his day. He would make this one day medicated his best. Jackson turned on the nozzle in the shower, then stepped inside.

At 0750 hours, Jackson headed out the door on his way to work. Although he was feeling a bit uneasy, Jackson was excited to be working the route alone. He wasn't scheduled to come in until 0800 hours, but he figured he'd show up early to peruse the office while getting acquainted with more of his coworkers. On his way down the hall, he ran into his dopey-looking coworker with the awkward posture rushing back toward his apartment. If anyone could ever look uncomfortable in their own skin, Marcus could.

"Hey! I know you. You're one of the clerks at the post office down the street. I'm a new hire, Jackson Pierce." He extended his hand. "I saw you at that bar on Saturday night, but you seemed a bit preoccupied with your thoughts."

"Oh. You live in this building? Which apartment?" he asked, avoiding the handshake altogether due to his sweaty palms.

"I moved in about a month ago. Apartment eight," Jackson answered, lifting that same hand to point his thumb over his shoulder at the apartment door.

"Great."

Jackson noticed dullness in his response yet paid it no mind. "I guess I should be off to work."

"I'm surprised you're not exhausted," Marcus remarked as he continued heading to his door.

"Why would I be exhausted?" Jackson turned, donning a confused expression.

"Those late-night walks to the gas station can be exhausting." Marcus unlocked his door, hesitating to go inside.

Jackson was unaware Marcus had even noticed him standing there with the vagrant when he spotted him leaving the fueling station. "When I can't sleep, I walk it off. I adapted the habit in the military. But I'm feeling pretty refreshed this morning. Can't keep a good man down."

"I guess I'll see you at work then."

"Yeah, I guess so," Jackson replied as Marcus headed inside, shutting his door behind him.

He thought Marcus was kind of weird, but aren't we all in our own little way? Jackson shrugged his shoulders, pressing onward.

Chapter 10

Putting His Best Foot Forward

As the time clock flashed 0759 hours, Jackson pushed through those green double doors at Clarkston Post Office. Most carriers had yet to arrive, so the sound of rolling carts on the soil-stained linoleum flooring was at a minimum. All the ruckus was coming from the chatter of clerks, some scanning parcels while others pulled parcel containers across the room for unloading. It was like a conveyor belt of activity, only the operation was manual. They worked diligently to process Clarkston's mail. Carriers present rushed to get their morning fix of caffeine before a day's hard work would ensue. Jackson's attention shifted to loud banging sounds coming from straight ahead near the back corner of the warehouse. He peeked around a letter case, wondering what it could be.

Evelyn. There she is. Damn, she looks great. Her skin looks so smooth. I bet it's soft. His eyes studied her frame. She must have played volleyball in school. Jackson surmised as much because of her long socks, short shorts, and clinging shirt, all fitting her firm body perfectly.

"Good morning, Jackson," Evelyn said with a smile, continuing to rapidly cast letters into the metal case, culprit of that banging sound.

Jackson hadn't paid attention to a word she said for being trapped in his thoughts. *She has got nice teeth. I love nice teeth. I wonder if that Marilyn Monroe mole by her mouth is real,* he pondered. Jackson licked his lips as he pondered the flavor of hers.

What the fuck is he doing? Why the hell is he just standing there not saying anything? Evelyn questioned silently, stealing glances from the corner of her eye. What she thought often differed from words she spoke.

"I see you've got your medicine this morning." Evelyn turned, looking him directly in the eyes.

"Medicine?" He snapped from the brief trance-like state. "What do you mean?" he questioned, wondering how she found out about his medication. *It was that drunk, Randy. I bet he went off flapping his gums,* Jackson assumed.

"I'm assuming that's coffee in your thermos." Her eyes moved to a chrome thermos in his hand.

"Oh, yeah. Breakfast of champions," he replied, having gotten over the anxiety of suspecting he'd been found out.

Evelyn moved to place a handful of letters in one of the plastic letter trays on a metal rack behind her.

"Do you drink coffee?" he inquired, staring at the thick structure of her long legs and how they met the bottom of her buttocks perfectly. *I would f—*

Before Jackson could finish the thought, Elise called out from the other side of the case, interrupting Evelyn's response as well. "Did your son get his license yet?"

Her question had nothing to do with work. Quite frankly it was a question Elise could have waited to pose. She had stopped throwing parcels just to come announce her irrelevant query.

Evelyn grinned. *Here she goes with her little nosy ass. She knows damn well I told her he got his license on Saturday. She just wants to come over here eavesdropping. With her eavesdropping ass,* Evelyn thought before speaking up. "Yeah, babe. He got it Saturday. He's pretty excited."

"Oh, good. I bet your husband is proud he got that job lined up for the summer, too." Elise continued piling on facts, figuring she was doing Evelyn the favor of not having to let Jackson down easily. She could see thirst in his eyes.

Husband. She's married? The glimmer in Jackson's eyes faded.

Evelyn knew exactly what Elise was up to, but she rather enjoyed the stir. She would much rather uphold her optimistic persona while watching Elise do the latter. The gossiping clerk often found herself in some sort of debate on a weekly basis due to her misguided inferiority complex. If there was any avenue available for her to butt into a conversation, she was definitely traveling it. Elise wanted to know everything there was to know. It was her strategy to climbing to the top.

"I didn't know you were married," Jackson blurted.

Evelyn snapped back, "You didn't ask."

"You aren't wearing a ring, so I didn't assume there was someone." His words came out aggressively. In fact, he seemed downright angry.

This motherfucker is crazy, she told herself.

"I feel like we've been having some sort of affair for the last couple of days and just broke up," Evelyn joked, considering how absurd it was that she would have to announce her marriage upon meeting a coworker.

Jackson stared at her for a moment, his outlook of her completely changed. He glanced down at her dirty hands. *Yuck,* he thought. *Why isn't she wearing gloves? Doesn't she know that will ruin her skin? She must not be very smart. Look at her. She's dirty all over, her shoes, shirt, and shorts. If she can't keep clean at work, I wonder how her house looks.*

Evelyn started to wonder what Jackson was thinking. *Why in the hell is he just standing here staring? I'm trying to be nice, but I see I might have to trip out on him,* she prepared herself. *I knew it was too good to be true. I can't have a simple conversation with a man without him assuming it's something more,* she complained in thought.

"What's going on here? Is there a party going on that I wasn't invited to?" Deborah announced as she darted from behind the letter racks. She too had seen him hovering at Evelyn's letter case from across the office.

Jackson was shocked to see thier supervisor standing there. The contortion of his face smoothed.

"We were just getting acquainted with the new employee," Elise answered, always happy to have someone new in the office to toy with. "You've met Jackson, right?"

Evelyn and Elise grinned, both with a deceptive glare in their eyes. They were aware of how attractive Jackson was and even more interested to watch Deborah's interactions with him.

"I have." Deborah turned to him. "Are you ready for your first day on the route alone? Do you think you can handle it?"

"If I can handle war, I can definitely handle delivering mail." Jackson lifted his thermos. "Besides, I've got my medicine. What more do I need?"

"Well, let's watch you work, shall we? Follow me. I'll show you to your case. We can let the clerks get back to business." Deborah turned, pressing on as Jackson followed. "You know you should really think about working at some other offices. Hours here won't always be a sure thing. But the Postal Service is a huge organization. There are plenty of places for you to go."

Deborah's offer to loan him out to other offices didn't comfort Jackson, nor did it sound like a win. It wasn't a sure thing, either. He needed stable hours, which he had working Route 8. Jackson's only objective was to ensure nothing stood in the way of that.

The moment they were out of earshot, Elise and Evelyn locked eyes, both entertaining the same idea. "You know she's ready," Evelyn blurted.

"Hot and ready, like the pizza," Elise agreed, amused by the analogy.

Jackson studied Deborah's posture from behind as he sipped coffee from his thermos. Tightness of her back told him of her rigid ways, moreover the drooping of her shoulders spoke of her insecurities. He would sit back, taking in every detail in her words, every movement in her posture. Only then could he find ways to manipulate her position for his benefit. Out of nowhere, Deborah stopped abruptly, causing Jackson to collide with her backside. The thermos of coffee poured out onto his face, neck, and shirt.

"Ahhh, shit. That's hot." He hopped back, pulling the front of his steaming, wet black V-neck shirt from his chest.

Both hands masked a wide-mouthed expression on Deborah's face, shocked at the foul she'd made. "I'm so sorry, Jackson," Deborah professed with an empathetic tone.

"It's okay. Don't panic." He set the thermos on the case, closing its top. When he took off his shirt, the sight of his nearly perfect physical frame took her breath away.

Holy shit, Batman! He's sexy as fuck. Deborah attempted to rub the liquid from his chest with her hand, copping a feel.

Jackson saw her intentions plainly, so he allowed the brief contact for a moment at least to reel her in a bit more. *She'll be in love before she knows it,* he concluded. "I'm gonna go to the men's room. Maybe I can dry my shirt under the hand dryer."

Her lustful eyes searched his for inklings of interest that remained absent. "Good idea," Deborah agreed. Jackson couldn't bring himself to go that far. Breaking eye contact to wipe the remaining liquid with his dampened shirt made the awkward moment a little less. Finally, he brandished a tight-mouthed grin as he stepped away to get cleaned up.

"Uh-oh. You got all dirty already," Evelyn remarked as she walked by on her way to speak to

Deborah. "It's hard to keep clean in this place," she added.

"I see that," Jackson responded, forging ahead.

Deborah rushed in to meet the already-approaching clerk. "He's smoking hot, huh?"

"If you like that sort of thing," Evelyn replied with an indifferent shrug of the shoulders.

"What do you mean? He's absolutely adorable."

"They're all adorable at first. Anyway, the letters are ready. Are you coming to count them so that I can pass them out before these carriers start complaining?"

Oh, screw them, Deborah thought. She too, most times, held back words that ran through her mind. Evelyn felt a sort of kinship with her when it came to such things.

"Yeah, let me get a ruler. I'll come do it now. I wouldn't want to upset the carriers," she responded, sarcasm oozing from her words.

It took Jackson about ten minutes to wash, rinse, and dry the coffee stain from his shirt. Only then did he emerge from the men's room as if the incident had never even happened. By that time most, if not all, of the carriers were there, rural and city. The office was bustling with activity. Carriers were chatting up a storm as clerks busied themselves, tossing parcels after scanning them under the PASS machine in the center of the floor.

Evelyn spoke words of encouragement, flattering the mail carriers as she pulled around a metal rack of letters. She doled out a trayful to each carriers' case, and kind words attached went a long way. The bubbly clerk was well liked for obvious reasons. One, due to her positivity being unmatched.

Deborah sat at her desk staring at clerks, hoping to intimidate them into moving faster. Daniel could see her from his peripheral sight, leering at them, which only encouraged him to move even slower than he already had been. It killed her just standing there, knowing there was nothing she could do about it. Not without being called out for harassment. In which case the union would be there in an instant if need be. It was as if union stewards wore capes on their backs with emblems plastered on their chests. Certainly, it was a headache supervisors didn't want.

Ugghh, I wish he would just drop dead, she thought. They hated one another with a passion.

Elise moved from carrier to carrier, running her mouth about Jackson, while making it look as if she were discussing postal business.

Her lazy ass is always walking around, trying to look busy. All those cigarettes she keeps chain-smoking are probably killing her stamina. She needs to just become a supervisor and sit down somewhere, Daniel complained, but only to himself.

Evelyn caught sight of Elise talking to Tanya as she passed by with letters. Tanya often kept quiet. Yet, when she did speak, she kept it candid.

Jackson approached his case as Pat debated back and forth with Marcus about unpaid postage on one of her customer's packages. Jackson had a fetish for Asian women, but something about her was more abrasive than his tastes allowed.

"She try to cheat us! She pay for media mail, but she send food in the box! Cheap customers don't want to pay! I'm going to take it back to her porch! Make her pay. Cheap customer," she ranted on, calming near the finish. Her accent was thick, and though some had no idea what she was babbling about, Tanya, the rural carrier at the case next to hers, heard and understood Pat's words plainly. Often, she would repeat whatever it was Pat meant to convey, only in fewer words.

Tanya shouted from her case loud enough for the others within earshot to hear.

"Pat said that she taking that package right back to get that money! They gon' learn today not to cheat Pat on her route!"

This place definitely has its share of characters, Jackson surmised as he stepped into his case to begin casing mail. There were at least twelve sets of eyes on him as he moved around the office. Coverage that the sides of his case furnished granted him a feeling of relief he craved. All those prying eyes made Jackson somewhat uneasy. He wondered what everyone was thinking and what rumors were being spread at that very moment.

"Jackson, the rest of your letters are on the APCs stationed near the supervisor's desk. They should be in order. The ones I'm dropping are not." Evelyn dropped a tray onto the floor next to a tub of magazines before moving along.

"Okay," Jackson replied, still allowing his anger to fester regarding their misunderstanding. That was when it hit him. That was Randy's case. He had to have some personal mail, a card, something with his address on it lying around. He searched the drawer, pushing aside markers, rubber bands, scissors, aside from a host of other things to find something. A bag underneath the counter contained some of Randy's personal belongings. Among those items was a magazine. Jackson pulled it out, checking the address. "Randy Lush, 7849 Edge Water Road, Waterford, Michigan." He took it as a sign. If he hadn't been meant to find it, it wouldn't have been sticking out there like a sore thumb. I mean, sure, he had to search for it, but no obstacles stood in his way. Therefore, it was his destiny, Jackson presumed. "Time to pay my new buddy a visit," he quietly vowed.

Chapter 11

Cementing His Place

By the time he was prepared to hit the streets it was nearly 1050 hours. The optimistic new hire was determined to get his route done within eight hours. The last outgoing mail truck to deliver to the plant in Pontiac was at 1750 hours, which gave him plenty of time.

Jackson strapped on his waist belt, pulled his sunglasses down off his head to cover his eyes from rays of sun, then took off out of the parking lot. He promised himself it would be a good day, allowing that minor misunderstanding he had with Evelyn to fade from thought. Traffic was light by that time. Most were at work or school, and moreover, the lunch rush had yet to begin. A few citizens traveled the streets of downtown Clarkston, walking their dogs or taking in brunch at one of the few alfresco bistros on Main Street. *This place is perfect,* Jackson thought, taking in the scenery. A smile emerged upon his face once he bent the corner at the sight of the numbers on the mailbox belonging to the house on that corner, 11710. It was Mrs. Teresa's house. He was eager to talk to the old woman so that he could inform her he'd be her regular carrier for a while. Good thing she'd ordered a package too large to fit into her box for delivery. Jackson had to deliver it to her porch.

The eager carrier pulled into her driveway, parking in front of the garage. He grabbed a shoe-box-sized package along with her letters from a plastic tray to the left of him, stepped out, then headed up the driveway.

"Oh, look, she's already outside," Jackson remarked, spotting the elderly woman seated on the porch swing.

"Good morning, soldier! How are you?"

"Good morning, sunshine! I'm doing pretty good. How about yourself?" he responded, placing her mail into a wicker basket that sat on the porch. Mrs. Teresa had it there for that very purpose.

"Fair to middling. I awoke this morning, so that's a good thing. It's just that my asthma has been acting up. Probably that damned cat from next door. It climbs through the doggie door in my kitchen. I've been meaning to get the thing covered up. Fefe's been dead for three years now. Fefe was my beautiful, darling bichon frise. She had heart disease. The condition eventually took her life.

Fefe was my very last companion. I just couldn't find the heart to replace her." Mrs. Teresa's eyes began to water as a dazed expression emerged across her face.

"I'm sorry to hear that, Mrs. Teresa. But I'm happy to see that, no matter the trials you've been through, you still get up every day and make an effort to live life."

"What a thoughtful thing to say. I'm so glad to see you here today instead of that drunk who usually runs the route."

"What makes you think he's a drunk, Mrs. Teresa?"

"I'm seventy-seven years old, soldier, not seven. Besides, you can smell him coming from a mile away. His skin smells like a brewery. My late husband suffered the same condition. That is, until the liver disease killed him. It's been over eight years now. I just couldn't find the heart to replace him." Her face donned that same dazed expression as she'd begun to recall memories of her late husband.

"You're a good woman, Mrs. Teresa," Jackson remarked.

"Unlike others," she whispered as she spotted the married couple next door bidding one another farewell, a kiss finalizing their goodbyes. Mrs. Escobar was cloaked in a magenta chiffon thigh-length robe with fluffy white slippers on her feet.

Her long auburn hair ran down her back beyond her butt. She lifted to her tiptoes to reach her husband's lips. He was a tall, dark-haired Hispanic American fellow. Mr. Escobar's beard and mustache were perfectly manicured, complementing his handsome face. The freelance architect adored his stay-at-home wife. She was spoiled rotten, to say the least. To him her lips tasted like strawberries when he kissed them.

Jackson and Mrs. Teresa eavesdropped on their conversation.

"How long will you be gone?" she asked in a sultry voice, hands placed flat on his toned pectorals.

"I won't be gone long, honey. Three days or so, maybe."

"I'm going to miss you. Are you going to miss me?" Mrs. Escobar stared deep into her husband's big brown eyes.

"What's not to miss?" He pulled her in closer, squeezing tight with one arm wrapped around her tiny waist. "I'll tell you what. I'll bring you something special back," he promised. He knew how much she liked gifts. It had become a normal practice, him bringing her presents whenever he returned home.

"I can't wait to see what you come up with, Mr. Escobar."

The couple locked lips once more. Jackson and Mrs. Teresa didn't hide that fact that they were gawking at the entire scene.

Mr. Escobar caught sight of them from the corner of his eye. "Shall we give them a show?" he proposed.

"I'm always up for it," his wife answered before shoving her tongue down her husband's throat.

"Maybe we should stop staring," Jackson suggested, turning his gaze away from them.

"Oh, she's nothing but a high-class hooker."

Jackson popped his neck left, relieving the tension her outburst brought about. "What makes you say that?" he inquired ominously, wondering if Mrs. Escobar suffered those same flaws in morality as his estranged wife.

"Our neighbors are very supportive. You see Mr. Trionfi over there? He's watering his grass with the hose. Meanwhile, he has an automatic sprinkler system that did the job earlier this morning," Mrs. Teresa tilted her head in the direction of a short, olive-toned Italian American musclebound gentleman across the street. Sun rays beamed off his woolly, coconut-oil-saturated, chiseled chest.

"Yeah, what about him?" he uttered quietly.

"Seems when Mr. Escobar is out of town, Mr. Trionfi mows her lawn. I've never really seen them in the throes of the despicable act, but you'd have to be blind not to see what's going on."

Jackson huffed in disgust, shooting a wild-eyed glare directly at Mr. Trionfi. *What a low-down, dirty motherfucker,* he thought.

"When the mister is away, little Mrs. Escobar comes out to play, if you know what I mean," she continued, figuratively twisting that adultery blade deeper into Jackson's gut, having no idea what consequences her words had invoked. A prickly feeling on his skin etched up along the back of his neck, prompting a scratching fit.

Another hardworking man being taken advantage of by his whore of a wife. Jackson's heart pounded so hard that thumping seemed to penetrate his eardrums. It slowly became all he could hear: the beating of his broken heart. "I do," he mumbled under forced breath. Jackson wished Mrs. Teresa hadn't clued him in on the betrayal. Yet, she had. He took it as a sign. Someone had to do something about it, at least find out if her accusation was true. From there Jackson would make his conclusion. Besides, the little old lady was only speculating. He forced back his rage, allowing sanity to have its way. "It's a shame the way the sanctity of marriage is mocked."

"Times sure are changing," Mrs. Teresa remarked.

"Speaking of changes, I'll be your regular mail carrier on this route for a while." Jackson turned his attention to the old woman, changing the subject altogether. He couldn't tolerate reflections of his tortured past ruining his day.

"Well, that's the best news I've heard all day. I'm looking forward to chatting with you again. And thank you for putting the mail in the basket. The other one just throws it up onto the porch. I watched him from the window that day, right after my husband broke it, mistakenly of course." Mrs. Teresa turned. "That one right there," she said, pointing up at the cracked window on the third floor. "I don't go up there anymore."

"That window is still broken, Mrs. Teresa," Jackson remarked, staring up at a long crack in the glass.

"I'd just as soon leave it like that. I've never had the heart to fix it." Her mind shifted to that very day.

Jackson noticed her disconnect. "Well, I'd better get going. I really want to make a good impression. It's my first day doing the route alone."

"Don't let me keep you prisoner, soldier."

"Have a good day, Mrs. Teresa." He turned to head back to the mail truck but quickly turned back to address her once more. "Mrs. Teresa, can I ask you a question?"

"I welcome it. I only hope I have an answer for ya."

"How did you know that I was a soldier?"

"I could tell from a mile away. It's all in the way you carry yourself. You know, I had a brother in the military. He died about seven years back. I—"

Before she could finish, Jackson interrupted, "Mrs. Teresa, I'd love to stay and chat more, but I see that Mr. Escobar is leaving, and I wanted to introduce myself. I'll see you tomorrow." He rushed off toward the LLV.

"Same time tomorrow, then." She waved goodbye as he hopped back into the mail truck.

Just as Mr. Escobar was about to shift his gunmetal gray 2001 BMW Z3 into reverse, Jackson pulled up, blocking their driveway's exit.

"Now why on earth would he stop there?" Mr. Escobar inquired, staring at the reflection of the LLV in his rearview mirror.

Jackson hopped out of his mail truck, waving a small package in the air. "Mr. Escobar! One moment, Mr. Escobar." Once he made it to Mr. Escobar's vehicle, he continued, "I wanted to introduce myself while I have you both here. My name is Jackson. I'm your new carrier. For now, at least."

Mr. Escobar let his rag top down to look up at Jackson comfortably, with his hand extended. "It's a pleasure to make your acquaintance, Jackson." The gentlemen shook hands. "This is my wife, Mrs. Escobar."

"You can call me Pamela," Mrs. Escobar chimed in, stepping forward with her hand extended but back side up, letting him know that she required a more delicate touch. "And I believe that package belongs to me," she added.

Jackson acted as if he were clueless, shaking her hand rough and eager like she was a used car salesman who had just presented him an awesome deal. "Great to meet you, ma'am."

Not only was she a bit put off by Jackson's gesture, but the fact that he'd referred to her as "ma'am" was an assault on her ego. In her eyes, at least. Pamela snatched the package from his hand. Jackson pretended not to notice that either. Mr. Escobar was pleased with the fact that Jackson seemed immune to his wife's flirtatious ways. It bothered him sometimes, how she would bat her mascara-saturated lashes at every man she made conversation with. Still, he never questioned her fidelity.

"Well, you nice folks enjoy your day. I just wanted to introduce myself." Jackson turned his attention back to Mr. Escobar. "If you need anything, don't hesitate to let me know."

"I appreciate that, Jackson. Enjoy your day," Mr. Escobar responded.

Jackson headed back to his mail truck with his suspicions about Pamela Escobar nearly confirmed. He could see lust in her eyes. She was one of those "for everyone" types of women. He pulled off to continue his deliveries, eager to make it to the other side of the street. By the time he'd made it, Mr. Trionfi had already finished watering his grass for the second time that day. Jackson headed up the driveway with his package in hand. The one Mr. Trionfi was to receive required a signature.

As he approached the garage door, Jackson noticed something that may later prove useful. Brick along the front sides of their garage had black streaks up and down its stones' surface. It was ash. Jackson imagined Mr. Trionfi pacing his driveway at night, peering over at the Escobars' home as he pulled slow drags from a cigarette. Presumably as he watched the couple eating dinner at their dining room table. Jackson made note of the discovery as he continued to Trionfi's front door.

As their doorbell chimed, Jackson peeked through the stained-glass windows along the sides of the solid oak front door. "Somebody's loaded," he whispered, watching Mrs. Trionfi come into view.

She rushed toward the door with her pink plush housecoat on, closed tight up to the neckline, not an inch of her chest exposed. Her shoulder-length blond curls bounced when she moved. The woman with warm hazel eyes opened her door to the sight of Jackson holding out a peach-colored slip that required her signature.

"Good morning, ma'am. I'm your new mail carrier, Jackson. I didn't mean to interrupt you while you were getting ready, but I have a package here for you that requires a signature."

"Oh, it's no bother. My husband is the one that ordered the darn thing. I'm Mrs. Trionfi. Pleased to make your acquaintance." She reached to accept the slip from his grasp.

"What are you doing at the door with your robe on, woman?" Mr. Trionfi shouted aggressively as he approached from her rear.

His wife was at a loss for words, considering his house robe was open at the top, allowing view of his hairy torso. The irascible man snatched the slip from his wife's hand. "I'll take care of this. You go and make yourself decent," he said with warning notes in his tone.

Mrs. Trionfi didn't put up a fuss, obviously conditioned to her husband's neanderthal ways. Instead, she rushed off without another word.

"Women," her narcissistic husband uttered once she was out of earshot. "You gotta keep a tight rein on them or else they'll feel as if they can step out of line when you're not around. I'm sure you know what I mean, brotha."

Out of nowhere Jackson delivered a swift jab to Mr. Trionfi's nose, causing blood to leak from his nostrils, painting his mouth and chin. At least, Jackson wished reality was as satisfying as the one he'd just imagined. *I would really enjoy punching him right in his big mouth.* He relished the thought yet remained civilized. "I just need a signature, sir."

Mr. Trionfi noticed a slight look of disgust Jackson was unable to hide. "I just need something to sign with. I don't exactly walk around with a pen in the pocket of my robe. Do you?"

"Certainly not. Here you go, sir." Jackson handed one over to him. He wasn't going to allow the man's condescending nature to upset him. He figured it best to obtain Mr. Trionfi's signature then go on his way peacefully.

"The ladies can't resist diamonds," Mr. Trionfi remarked, holding the slip up against the wall near the door to scribble his John Hancock. "Here you go." He handed the slip over, accepting the small box simultaneously. "Have a good day, Jack." Mr. Trionfi slammed the door without hesitation.

"It's Jackson," he responded, staring at the closed door just at the tip of his nose. "I hate him already." Jackson turned, then headed down the porch stairs.

Chapter 12

Frenemies

The building was nearly empty except for a few clerks, Deborah, and the postmaster. Evelyn stood at the center of the workroom floor scanning in the last of the afternoon parcels. "I'm so freaking hungry!"

"That's why you need to start eating bacon," Elise chimed in as she kept herself busy, passing out large parcels to each route.

"Cut it out. You know I don't eat meat."

"What are you gonna eat for lunch then?"

"Some Thai food. The restaurant around the corner has a pineapple-curry fried rice that's absolute deliciousness. And you get to pick how spicy you want it. You wanna come with me? Maybe you'll see something you like. God knows you need to eat something healthy."

"Sure, I'll go with you. I'm open to trying new things."

"Let's go now before Deborah decides to leave and we're stuck eating lunch here."

"That's your girl," Elise remarked, staying on Evelyn's heels as she rushed to the time clock.

"Girl, shut up before I change my mind."

"Don't get your panties in a bunch." Elise chuckled.

"Are you riding with me or am I riding with you?" Evelyn punched out to lunch.

"I'll drive. You park too far away," Elise answered, doing the same.

"That's because I don't like you guys keeping tabs on me." She revealed her true motives as they exited through swinging double doors.

The smell that penetrated Evelyn's nostrils once they climbed into Elise's Volkswagen gave her an instant headache. She complained, unable to hold back her words as she normally would. "You need some damn air freshener in here. Didn't you just get this car?"

Elise started the engine, then headed off toward their destination. "Sorry. I had tuna fish yesterday and left the open Tupperware bowl inside my car."

"I'm talking about those funky-ass cigarettes. You let your kids ride in this secondhand-smoke-ass car? You know you're wrong for that."

While she saw the truth in Evelyn's comment, Elise snapped back without hesitation, "Hey, you can always find another ride."

"Truth hurts," Evelyn mumbled.

"I knew you'd find a way to get me back."

"Just hurry up and get me to the restaurant before I have an asthma attack in this muthafucka."

"Oh, my gosh, Evelyn. I've never heard you talk like this. What's gotten into you?"

"Apparently secondhand smoke, bitch!"

"You're an asshole," Elise blurted.

"Takes one to know one."

The coworkers chuckled over their brief banter.

"You see, I wish we could all get along like this as opposed to taking everything so personally. Marcus is a fucking psycho. I'm getting so tired of him whining about how much overtime I get."

"Marcus is harmless, but that new guy, Jackson, he's the psycho. I think he hates me because I'm married. I've never seen someone get so mad over me being taken."

"I did notice the look on his face when he found out about your family. He was hurt."

"His ass is crazy, for real. He said he was married. He must want his cake and to eat it, too."

"He wants to eat his wife and you, too, is more like it," Elise replied.

Evelyn stuck out her tongue as if the comment disgusted her. "Ugghhh. Never. I'm steering clear of him whenever possible." The traffic light garnered her attention. "Damn. How long is this light?"

"Have some patience. If you ate meat, you wouldn't be so hungry all the time," Elise countered, watching the traffic light finally switch from red to green.

"If you stopped smoking cigarettes, you wouldn't need to keep eighty packs of chewing gum in your back seat."

"If you were honest with people from the jump, you wouldn't have men getting angry at you for misleading them," Elise snapped back.

Evelyn didn't miss a beat. "If you stopped scamming on everyone's overtime, maybe Marcus wouldn't want to kill you."

"If you stopped batting your eyelashes at every good-looking man you see, maybe they wouldn't assume you were single."

"If you stopped eavesdropping on everybody's conversation, maybe you'd get along with your coworkers."

"Girl, fuck those coworkers," Elise blurted before they busted out in a fit of laughter.

"I could do this all day, you know?" Evelyn admitted.

"As can I, my friend. As can I."

Later that day, around 1420 hours, Jackson pulled into the parking lot of Clarkston Post Office annex building with plenty of time to spare. His day had been a successful one. Jackson gathered up outgoing parcels he collected from blue mailboxes along his route, before he headed inside, lugging a tray of letters and small parcels.

Sounds of bickering between two clerks caught him by surprise. It was Marcus and Elise. Their argument was intense enough for them both to be flushed. Marcus, who happened to be senior clerk, argued that he was owed the overtime available that Sunday, not Elise. He needed the money to fund his habit of purchasing prostitutes, even though most times he'd easily remedy that problem. "I'm the senior clerk! I don't know why you insist on breaking the rules!"

Reading their aggressive body language wasn't necessary due to the escalating volume of their voices.

"My overtime is none of your business, first of all. And I didn't break any rules. I applied for overtime and was awarded it. Fair and square!"

"Books, ever heard of them, Elise? Maybe you should try one. You can start with the dictionary. And when you do, look up the word 'fair'!"

"Is it always your intention to be as condescending as you possibly can? Why can't you just be nice for a change? Instead of being a dick!"

"Fulfilling your needs is not a priority on my list of things to do, Elise. Quite frankly, you're irrelevant to me. Besides, who knows what un-

derhanded stunts you pulled to make it happen?
It's okay. I'm just going to call the union. I have
nothing more to say to you," he said, yet rambled
on. "Frankly, you sound like a hypocrite. Just
last week you were complaining about the PSE's
overtime hours. You're so stupid, Elise. And you
smell like a walking ashtray. It's disgusting, really!"

"Screw you, Marcus! You damn coward!" Elise
hollered as she stormed off in the opposite direction. She was furious. *This motherfucker is going
down one way or another,* Elise vowed in silence.
It annoyed her even further that Marcus had not
an ounce of respect for the women around him,
no matter how often they defended him against
Daniel.

"Don't hold your breath. Wait! On second
thought, maybe you should!" Marcus snapped
back calmly. He'd gotten the best of her. The
satisfaction of it was enough to comfort him, even
if he wouldn't be awarded the work hours.

Jackson kept his head down as Elise tore by him
in a fit of anger. "Motherfucker," she uttered under
winded breaths.

"This place is getting more interesting by the
day," Jackson mumbled, heading back toward
the case for Rural Route 8. *I sure could use a
stiff drink,* he thought, staring at a magazine with
Randy's address printed on it as he approached
his workstation. *I bet I can think of someone*

who could use one too. A way in had dawned on him. Jackson would use Randy's greatest vice as a weapon against him.

Jackson pulled onto the road to Randy's house expecting to see a host of nice homes. To his surprise, there was nothing but grass, trees, and several trailers scattered about. He let his driver's side window down, then stuck his head out to see the address of an upcoming single-wide trailer.

"All the money he makes being a carrier and he lives in a trailer," Jackson blurted upon stopping in front of the mobile home with 7849 above its door. *He probably drinks all of his money away,* Jackson concluded.

Regardless of what he thought, Randy's mobile home sat on ten acres of land, mostly wooded with lush maple trees except for two acres in the front yard. Land wasn't cheap in Clarkston, by any means. The grass was nicely maintained. There'd even been pine trees planted along the borders of the property to assess where his property line began and ended. Jackson shifted the gear into park, grabbed the 750-milliliter bottle of Jack Daniel's off his passenger seat, then hopped out, heading straight for Randy's front door. He knocked at the rickety screen door, then waited a moment for someone to answer. No one came. Jackson glanced all around him, surveying what of the property he could from the front porch steps. Randy's pickup truck was there. *Maybe he's inside passed out drunk. I should knock harder,* Jackson presumed. He thrust a clenched fist against the aluminum door. That was when he heard a loud boom sound off!

Jackson had heard that sound many times before. It had to be a gun, he guessed, more specifically, a shotgun. *Oh, this is perfect.* "Drinks and guns. What a perfect combination," he quietly remarked, stepping down from the porch to follow the sound of shotgun blasts. Randy's trailer sat at the front of his property, so the back was mainly wooded area that had yet to be cleared. Jackson stepped over toppled logs, forging his own way through the densely wooded area, snapping branches and twigs along his way. Just then, another blast sounded off. That time Jackson darted his head right in the direction he needed to go. A silver glow reflecting off in the distance told him so. It was Randy's jacket. He was busy doing his part to balance the deer population on his property. Jackson continued his trek until he was close enough to garner Randy's attention without calling out too loudly.

"How about some company?"

Randy turned, the gun swinging wildly in Jackson's direction.

"Whoa! Whoa! Don't shoot. I come bearing gifts." He held up the liquor bottle as an offering.

"Hey, soldier," Randy slurred, already having polished off a pint of Captain. "I wouldn't shoot you. You're my sub." He paused, thinking over his statement. "How's the route going so far anyway?"

"It's going good, Randy. You taught me well."

"Well, that's good. You'll need the practice for when you work at other offices. Trainers may not be as good as me."

"You coming back soon?" Jackson fished for answers, secretly hoping Randy would say he wasn't coming back for at least six months.

"I sure am. They can't take my job away from me. I'm in the union. Goody-two-shoes motherfuckers. It was just a little drink," he griped.

"Well, at least you're getting your job back, right? Hey. Maybe we should have a celebratory drink."

"Yeah, I could use a drink." Randy placed the butt of the shotgun on the ground, letting it lean against a tree. "I've got a cup around here some-where." He began searching a small clearing where he had set up shop just under a tree stand. "Here's my cup." Randy picked up a red plastic Solo cup from the ground, dusting off its sides before blow-ing into it to clean out any leaves or dirt that may have gotten inside.

"Do you use it?" Jackson inquired, his plan beginning to take shape.

"Use what?"

"The tree stand."

"I use it all the time. As a matter of fact, I've got another cup up there," he replied before letting out a loud belch. "Come on up. There's room for two." Randy placed the edge of the cup into his mouth between clenched teeth so that he could climb up first. "Grab the shotgun," he mumbled.

It all seemed perfect. A murder made easy. Jackson pulled a pair of palm-coated work gloves from his back pocket, covering both his hands before touching the shotgun. Once he picked it up, holding the steel in his grasp, he'd begun to have doubts. *I can't kill this man in cold blood.* The saint in him emerged for but a moment before the devil on his shoulder had his say. *He's killing himself anyway with the way he's drinking. Just look at the way his belly protrudes like a hot-air balloon. His liver is probably trash.* Jackson had mulled over the thought long enough. Randy had to go. *It'll be quick and painless,* he thought as he stood shotgun in hand at the base of the tree, finger lightly grazing the trigger. *You can do it. Do it,* his fractured mind coaxed him onward.

"Hey, you coming?" Randy leaned over to peer down at Jackson.

"Here it comes," he whispered. Jackson squeezed the trigger without a moment's notice. Buckshot crashed into Randy's face, shredding it beyond recognition. His body dropped to the floor of the tree stand. Blood spatter along with pieces of bone and loose flesh painted the wooden walls surrounding him. Jackson's eyes darted in every direction, casing the scene for possible witnesses. No one was around. Not for acres.

Chapter 13

A Helping Hand

About an hour later, Jackson was headed straight into the farming and tractor supply store. Waterford had nearly twice the residents, so he wouldn't easily be remembered. When he pushed through the glass door, a bell chimed above his head upon entering. Jackson didn't like that, but what could he do? It had already alerted the man at the register of his presence.

"Let me know if I can help you with anything."

"My pleasure to take you up on the offer. I just may need some assistance." Jackson played it off well. No need to be nervous. Besides, he hadn't even done anything wrong. Not in there, anyway.

"Words noting each department are pasted along the shelving of each aisle," the overweight sales-clerk responded, not really wanting to climb down off the obviously sturdy metal stool upon which he was seated.

"Please, don't get up. That's all the information I need." Jackson headed to where he needed to go without the clerk lifting a finger.

"You just holler if you need me!"

The store had a few other gentlemen roaming about. Only they were dressed in army-print camouflage pants or shorts. Manly men. At least Jackson was sure they thought as much.

By the time he headed to the counter, he'd managed to find some zip ties, a hunting blade, a pair of binoculars, a portable power drill, a box of screws, and a six-by-nine-inch piece of plywood, along with several other items he'd picked up along the way.

"Uhhh," the muffin-top, camouflage-cloaked, balding middle-aged cashier uttered in a forced breath as he lifted himself from the stool behind the glass-encased counter. "I take it you've found everything you needed?"

"I did. Thank you."

The cashier began scanning in the items as Jackson unloaded the small metal cart. "I've never seen you around here. You new in town?"

"I'm just passing through," Jackson answered, attempting to make their interaction as brief as possible.

He didn't think anything of it. There were several neighboring towns in close proximity of one another, so the salesman continued scanning in his items for purchase.

"You work around here?"

"Are you writing a book?" Jackson replied.

"What makes you ask that?"

"Because you seem to be gathering information."

"Oh," he chuckled, a bit put off by the comment. The man was a little embarrassed that Jackson had pointed out his intrusiveness, making him feel the need to explain.

"It's not what you think. Sitting at this desk all day you come in contact with lots of different people. I just like to know a piece of their story. It's our commonalities that link us and differences that interest one another. I was attempting to make a connection, that's all. No harm. No foul."

Jackson was surprised at his reply, having taken him for an idiot trophy hunter. "I work at Clarkston Post Office," he admitted.

"The post office. Nice job. I tried to get a job there once, but I guess I didn't score high enough on the memorization section of the exam. Good for you, man," he added while ringing up the last of the items.

"I apologize if I came off a little harsh. It's been a rough few months. Unfortunately, I let it get the best of me sometimes."

"We all have our bad days. The key is not to let the dark overshadow the light."

Jackson appreciated the cashier's wise words. Judging a book by its cover had surely done him a disservice that time around.

Moments later Jackson exited the farming and tractor supply store with the basket full of items. After loading them into his Ford Bronco, he pushed the basket back into the cart corral, then headed back to his vehicle, nodding at the other customers as a form of hello as he passed them by.

Jackson had carefully thought out how he wanted to go about exacting his plans. He cruised down the street, combing over each detail in his mind. What he had planned must be done no matter how unappreciated the deed may go. Jackson bent the corner in a rush, hitting the curb on his way around it. The eager soldier acted as if the faux pas hadn't taken place at all, continuing on his way. Soon, he made a right turn into the driveway, pulling all the way up to the garage door. Jackson grabbed the power drill before he exited his truck, then headed up the porch. He knocked at the door, waiting for an answer that eventually came after a few minutes.

"Well, hello there, Jackson! What are you doing back here? Shouldn't you be off by now?"

"I came to fix your window and cover that doggie door for you," Jackson replied with a bright smile plastered upon his face.

"Aren't you a blessing! What did I do to deserve such kindness?" Mrs. Teresa's face lit up with a smile.

"I'm sure your husband would do it if he were still around. Since he's not, you'll have to settle for me."

"Gladly, soldier. Come on inside." The old woman opened the door wider as she stepped out of the way, allowing him into the foyer.

Keeping up appearances on the exterior was imperative to Mrs. Teresa. She paid professionals to maintain her landscaping weekly. However, the inside of her home wasn't awarded the same consideration. As Jackson entered, the strong stench of Bengay permeated his nostrils. The wood floors were dull. Dust coated the walls, and outdated furniture decorated the home.

"Let me show you to the kitchen. The doggie door is in back."

Jackson followed, taking in the scenery along the way. A yellow hue emitted from the bulbs in the ceiling as they traveled the length of the hallway from the foyer to the kitchen. It was neat, no clutter scattered about. Things just needed a good wiping down. It became all the more apparent to Jackson, the old woman's propensity for holding on to the past. Upon glancing to the left he noticed the thick plastic covering the wild-flower-patterned sofa in the living room, her late husband's walker still stationed beside it. Picture frames containing photos of loved ones past and current cluttered the dusty ledge above the fireplace as they did the wooden end tables beside the couch. The white ruffled lampshades were dingy, obstructing what little light shined from the bulbs.

The kitchen counters were laminate as opposed to the latest stone or granite design. Mrs. Teresa pulled at the large metal lever on the refrigerator door, pulling an ice tray from the icebox on top.

"Would you like something to drink? I just made a fresh batch of lemon tea this morning. I used to drink the chamomile, but it makes me too drowsy."

"Yes, please. I am a little parched." Jackson walked over to the side door. "I take it this is the infamous doggie door here." He pointed in its direction.

"That's the one."

Jackson pulled back the white ruffled half curtain at the top of the door that covered the window, allowing a view to the backyard. Lo and behold, there was Minkzy, Mrs. Escobar's beloved cat. The feline roamed her backyard, no doubt waiting for the opportunity to come inside. "Will you look at that? I think I came right on time. Your little visitor is out here waiting to make an entrance."

"That damn cat is hell bent on torturing me. I think it knows I'm allergic and means to kill me. I've never liked cats. I'm more of a dog person."

"Well, you won't have to worry about that menacing cat any more after today."

Mrs. Teresa placed the glass of tea she'd poured for him on the countertop near the side door. "Here you go. I hope you like it. It's not too sweet. Do you like your tea sweet?"

"I prefer it less sweetened. All that sugar is not good for the body. I try to stay away from starches, as well. I've come to realize the body is a temple and we should treat it as such, on all accounts."

"I sure wish my Henry would have cared as much about his health. Maybe he would still be alive today."

"Alcoholism is a terrible demon to be plagued with," Jackson said, turning to face her.

"Indeed it is," she agreed with her head bowed sorrowfully.

"I'm gonna need to go back out to my truck to grab the wood and screws. Can I use this door to come in and out?"

"Oh, be my guest. I'll just be in the living room reading my book."

"I love to read. It's how I used to pass the time when I was enlisted."

"The book I'm reading now is the sequel to the first. It's called *Compelled To Murder II: Steven's Lineage.* I like suspense thrillers. Never took to all the fluff. I need some excitement in my life. At my age, it seems reading is the safest way to get it."

"You know what they say: a reader lives a thousand lives," Jackson remarked. "Can I pick it up around here?"

"I checked it out at the local library. Or you can purchase it at the bookstore."

"The library sounds good. I've been meaning to stop by. I just haven't had a pressing reason to go until now. I appreciate the suggestion."

"Oh, it's my pleasure, soldier."

"Well, you enjoy your book, and I'm going to get started on the doggie door."

"If you need anything, I'll be in the living room," Mrs. Teresa replied as she turned, walking in that direction.

"I think I should be okay. I'll just get the rest of the materials." Jackson placed his drill on the countertop, then headed out of the back door.

Hearing the running mower next door, he wondered if it was in fact Mr. Trionfi filling in for Mr. Escobar. Lo and behold, his eyes settled on the miniature muscular man seated atop the riding mower in the Escobars' backyard.

Mrs. Escobar exited the rear door of her home with a glass of liquid in hand. *How nice of her to bring him a drink*, Jackson thought, trying his best not to be presumptuous.

Noticing her as she approached, Mr. Trionfi shut down the riding mower.

"Service with a smile. I like it," Mr. Trionfi remarked as he tugged at the fingers of his gloves, pulling them off one after the other.

Her auburn eyes burned with the passion she longed to show him. The very same passion she hid from her doting husband. "I'm just showing my appreciation."

Mr. Trionfi searched the scene for prying eyes, the glare from the sun causing him to squint, completely overlooking Jackson peering at them from under the cover of Mrs. Teresa's awning over the back porch. It was risky, the two of them standing so close out in the open. "I could think of some other ways you can show your appreciation. As a matter of fact, I have something in mind."

An eyebrow lifted. "Would you like to come inside and show me exactly what it is you've got in mind, Mr. Trionfi? We can get out of this sun for a moment," she suggested as if an excuse were really necessary.

He never uttered a verbal affirmation, yet an edge of his mouth creased back into its corner telling her as much. She turned to walk back toward the back door with Mr. Trionfi slowly in pursuit. Her tight pink yoga pants clung to her narrow buttocks as she swung her hips from left to right. She was a petite woman who he handled with ease, making it an affair perfect for his massive ego.

Jackson emerged from the cover of the awning just as the two went inside the house. The breeze flowing in through the open windows permitted sight of them through the swaying sheer curtains that dressed them. Mrs. Escobar turned to him as if to say the coast was clear. Mr. Trionfi rushed in, the two of them colliding at the torso, her breasts against his chest. But in Jackson's eyes it wasn't really Mrs. Escobar. It was his estranged wife, Sue. Mr. Trionfi had turned into her younger soldier. Jackson's unfortunate reality had twisted into his reoccurring nightmare. His heart raced, beads of sweat glistened upon his forehead accentuating the pulsating vein down its center. His vision came closer. Jackson's eyes began to well up with tears as the neighbors' lips locked and tongues twisted around one another. Mr. Trionfi pressed forward to push her backward toward her and Mr. Escobar's bedroom. The jilted husband watched them move from the kitchen to the living room in the lustful embrace until the door to the bedroom they entered closed behind them.

It was like a switch went off in his head. The movie was over, leaving him standing outside of the Escobars' living room window. Jackson hadn't realized he'd walked over to the house. His breath filtered through the screen as he peered into the window like some sort of stalker. Jackson's perception of it all had become so skewed he neglected to see any fault in his actions. In his eyes Mr. Trionfi and Mrs. Escobar were committing the ultimate brand of treachery, and the foul just wouldn't be allowed. Not on his route. Jackson slowly backed away from the window, wiping his face over with the palm of his hand to clean whatever stray tears had rolled down his cheeks. He needed time to think, time to come up with a plan as to how he'd make them pay. They would pay for the pain they'd ultimately cause Mr. Escobar, as well as the pain they'd caused him to relive.

With glazed-over eyes, he headed back to his truck to retrieve the materials to fix the issue plaguing Mrs. Teresa. Jackson grabbed the wood and the screws from the Bronco, unable to shake what despicable acts he'd just witnessed.

Chapter 14

Dirty Dancer

About a mile from Mrs. Teresa's house, Marcus parked his car in the alley behind their apartment building. Only this time he was alone. He hopped out, then rushed over to the propped-open back door of the complex. Once he was inside, he kicked the rock out that was used to wedge the door open, allowing it to shut behind him. The eager clerk rushed up the three flights of stairs, then into his home, nearly missing the neighbor across the hall. The old man had heard him coming up the stairs but moved too slow to catch Marcus before he ducked inside. By the time he darted his head out of the door to see who'd traveled the dimly lit hallway, Marcus's door was already closing.

"Damn it. I need to talk to you," he demanded. The elderly man rushed out to catch him. "I need to talk to you," he yelled, banging the back of his fist against the apartment door with the 9 nailed to it.

Immediately after, music began blaring from the inside of the apartment.

Super freak, super freak
That girl's a super freak

The Rick James classic went on, drowning out the constant knocking.

Marcus heard the miserable old man yet couldn't care less what he had to say, having more pressing issues to attend to. A purse sat atop the speaker near the closed bedroom door. He unzipped it, removing a small black change purse. "Twenty, forty, sixty, eighty." He counted out the money from her purse, taking what was there including what he'd paid for her services, or the lack thereof. The unscrupulous mail clerk would wait until the boy was finished with her before dropping her off on the side of the road, of course her not knowing what had happened, or how she'd gotten there for that matter.

Jacksonville, North Carolina

That very same Rick James song blasted from large black speakers bolted into each corner of the ceiling in the Dime A Dozen erotic dance club. Thick floating layers of tobacco smoke hung in the air as several male patrons lingered about, ogling at each scantily dressed waitress who traipsed by. A spotlight above the stage shined directly on the closed sheer curtains, hiding the woman behind the linen. The silhouette of her slinky frame instantly garnered the attention of every male patron in the bar, mesmerizing one in particular. Squinting dark brown eyes studied her every gesture. He fancied the way her body moved, much like a feline. You see, Sue wasn't always an erotic dancer. She'd studied contemporary dance in school, but unfortunately, after her father passed away, she was compelled to help her mother pay the bills. For Sue, it was a no-brainer. Dancing at the strip club was the fastest way to make money, using her obvious talents. The bills wouldn't pay themselves, as her mother would always say.

When the curtains opened, his beady eyes studied her slender profile. The pigtails of her newly bleached blond hair lay down over her nearly exposed breast. Two daisy-patterned pasties covered her areolas, blue jean Daisy Dukes covered her tiny hiney, and calf-length brown cowboy boots were on her feet. The cowboy hat that covered the top portion of her head fell off once she flipped upside down on the long metal pole at the center of the stage. She'd climbed it as if she had the arm strength of an ape before flipping upside down with ease. Her legs opened as wide as they could as she held on tight. It wasn't time to slide just yet. Holding her position, she locked eyes with him. Sue had picked her target long before she'd stepped out onto that stage. Now all she had to do was seduce him.

As their gazes met, drawing him in closer, he took a swig of his long-neck bottle of beer, grabbing a seat at the closest table to the stage. That was when she knew she had him. Sue flipped right side up, then slid to the floor, legs still open in a full split. With an unwavering stare, the seductress crawled across the long rectangular section of the stage straight toward him.

"Come to papa," he mouthed, the edges of his bushy brown mustache covering his top lip. He looked mature enough, Sue reckoned. Different from the beau she'd snagged while Jackson was away, this one had black hair that was slicked back to his neckline. He was no Jackson, lacking the muscle tone she normally preferred, but the $50 bill that sat atop his table was inviting enough alone to pique her curiosity. *Maybe he's on his lunch break,* she guessed because of the khakis and white collared shirt he wore. *Nah. He's probably some sleazy used car salesman,* she reconsidered, settling on her latter assumption.

"Howdy, partner," she whispered as she rolled onto her arched back.

"Wanna ride," he responded, holding the $50 bill in the air between two straightened fingers.

A seductive grin along with a lifted eyebrow told him she'd consider the lewd proposition. Sue rolled over onto her flattened tummy, kicking her legs with pointed toes one after the other as she coaxed him in with a "come hither" finger. He got up, keeping his cool, remaining as suave and smooth as he was in his seat. Sue's glance shot down at the $50 bill in his hand, then back up at his eyes, telling him exactly what it was she required of him. He knew what she wanted, so of course he obliged, reaching over to slip the fifty into the back pocket of her Daisy Dukes. He did it slow, copping a squeeze before pulling his hand back.

"That's gonna cost you extra, handsome," Sue whispered.

The man dropped his arm, patting his hand against the wallet in the front pocket of his khakis.

Beams of sunlight blared into her eyesight, impairing Sue's vision as she stepped out of the Dime A Dozen strip club. The heels of her thigh-length black boots sank through cracks of broken asphalt as she traveled the parking lot to make it to her small gray Honda. There weren't many cars left as most had already cleared out for their day jobs or families waiting at home.

He watched the balancing act through the tinted window of his tan 2001 Toyota Tacoma double-cab pickup truck. He liked the black minidress just as much as the Daisy Dukes she wore just hours earlier. The way it clung tight to the top of her torso then flowed with the breeze at its skirt made her look like a ballerina. Once Sue made it to her car, she tossed the pink backpack she'd carried on her shoulders over onto the passenger seat.

"I got what it takes, darling," he remarked, leaning slightly over the middle console to blurt out of his passenger-side window.

Sue turned, startled. She hadn't even noticed him there ogling as she'd been preoccupied with not breaking her neck while attempting to navigate the pothole riddled parking lot. "What are you still doing here?" she asked, hand pressed to her chest.

"Well, waiting for you, obviously."

"Why? The show's over, buddy," she countered, climbing into the driver's seat of her vehicle. Sue started her engine, shifted the gear into the drive position, then waved at him through her raised window before pulling off. The single mother had to pick her daughter, Mya, up from her grandmother's so that her mom could head off to work. First, she'd have to get out of the parking lot.

Having taken off after her, Sue's pursuer bumped her rear bumper with his front.

"Is this guy out of his fucking mind?" she complained, staring at the reflection of his truck through her rearview mirror. Sue hopped out of the car, then threw her arms into the air. "Drive much?" she hollered out in frustration. As she rushed in toward the back to see what damage had been done, he backed up, allowing her full view. The small dent present was enough to make Sue fly off the handle. "What the hell is wrong with you? I don't have time for this! Do you even have insurance?"

"My apologies, darlin'. I didn't mean to bump you that hard. I was simply trying to get your attention."

"Well, you sure got it." Sue shook her head with dismay.

"Here, let me give you my information."

Sue moved in closer to his vehicle. "I hope you know you're gonna pay for this."

"What's it gonna take to smooth things over and get back into your good graces?" he questioned with cunning eyes.

"Well, first of all . . ." she started in on him, but she was halted by the wad of hundreds he held out the window in place of his registration and insurance information.

"How 'bout we start here?"

"Are you giving me all of it?" Her almond shaped eyes widened as she considered what she could do with the money, removing the dent not being one of them.

"I think it should cover the damage at least."

Sue snatched the money from his grasp without hesitation.

"I wasn't going to change my mind." He chuckled lightly. "Now, can I take you out to breakfast?"

"I can't. I have to pick my three-year-old daughter up from my mother's. She has to be to work soon."

"How about I take both of you out to breakfast then?"

"You really think I'm going to trust a stranger around my child? I may be an exotic dancer, but I'm not a bad mother."

"Okay. That's fair. How about this: what would you say your mother makes in a day?"

"She makes about two hundred dollars a day," Sue responded, of course embellishing a bit.

"How about we give her three hundred and call it overtime?"

"We?" she quickly countered.

"Me," he specified.

"Sounds like you've got yourself a date, buddy. So, where are we going?"

"There's a small diner up the road that has the best food this side of town."

"Lead the way. I'll follow, and that way you won't crash into my car again," she said as she headed back to her vehicle.

"I don't have enough money on me to do that," he joked. It was the most he'd ever spent to garner a woman's attention, but he was certain it would pay off after all was said and done.

"Wait." She turned before getting into the driver's seat. "I don't even know your name," she called out to him.

"Sure you do. It's Buddy." He grinned.

"You can't be serious." She chuckled lightly as she climbed into the car. "Buddy." Sue shook her head, finding the coincidence rather ironic.

Chapter 15

Smiles Masking Deceit

Back at Mrs. Teresa's house, Jackson pulled at the plywood nailed to the outside of the doggie door, checking how securely he had attached it. It was snug. "Nothing is getting in or out of here," he boasted with confidence. Next, he needed to go inside to check out the broken window upstairs. "Mrs. Teresa," Jackson called out to her as he opened the back door, stepping inside the kitchen. "Mrs. Teresa," he called out to her once more after only a few seconds of silence. *She's probably on the front porch reading,* Jackson surmised as he made his way to the foyer. On the way, he noticed her hand hanging down over the arm of the recliner she was seated in. "Mrs. Teresa? Are you okay?" He stood there waiting for her to reply. Not a peep. As he came up from behind, he noticed her head tilted back to the side. The old woman's eyes were wide open, as was her mouth gaped.

Ironically, the opened pages of the book she'd been reading, *Compelled To Murder II,* sat on her lap, cover upright. "She's dead," he whispered, moving to check the pulse along her pale, vein-riddled neck.

"Who's dead?" she spoke out of nowhere, sitting up in the recliner.

He snatched his hand back. "Mrs. Teresa. What the heck is going on? You just scared the hell out of me. I thought you were . . . ya know." He paused, not wanting to say the words again, figuring it would be rude. "Passed on to glory," Jackson finally added.

"Oh, no. I'm here still ticking. Just taking a little nap." She chuckled. "It's a condition I suffer from, lagophthalmos, and it doesn't allow me to close my eyelids when I'm sleeping, creating the illusion that I'm either wide awake or dead." Mrs. Teresa burst into a fit of laughter. "I swear the look on your face was priceless. And the book was the real kicker. *Compelled To Murder.* Oooh." She raised her hands, wiggling her fingers as if mocking how afraid he'd gotten.

"All right, all right. You got me this time, Mrs. Teresa. I'm glad I could brighten your day. That's the third time today."

"You're on a roll, soldier. Now what were you screaming about?"

Wait a minute. If she was napping, how did she hear me calling from the back door? Jackson mulled over the thought, realizing Mrs. Teresa was really toying with him. He thought she had a crazy sense of humor, but he rather liked it. "I've finished up the door. I was gonna head on upstairs to check out the window. I'll have to finish it later because I need to measure the glass today."

"Sounds good to me. I really appreciate you taking the time out to help an old lady," she uttered wearily, assuming she needed to play on his guilt.

Jackson grinned, quite proud of the good deed he'd carried out. It was his little way of letting the good outweigh the bad. "It's my pleasure, Mrs. Teresa. Would you like to lead the way?"

"Oh, no, I like to tackle those stairs as few times a day as possible. My knees just won't allow the up-and-down business. The window you're looking for is up two sets of stairs. When you reach the top, turn to your right, and it'll be the third door on your right." Mrs. Teresa flipped her book right side up. "Watch your step. The room is cluttered. I haven't been up there since my husband died," she added.

"Sure thing, Mrs. Teresa. Enjoy your read." Jackson left her to peruse her book, then headed back out of the living room to the foyer where the staircase began. He headed up the worn wooden staircase, letting his hand run across the banister, fingers collecting dust along the way. Not one light was illuminated on the upper floors, yet the natural light that shined into the hallways thanks to various bedroom doors being ajar easily guided his way.

"Okay. Third door on the right," Jackson whispered as he climbed the top step on the third floor. He headed up the hall toward his destination. The third door on the right was closed. Once Jackson twisted the small brass knob, the door opened with ease. The light shining in from outside was enough light for him to navigate the room safely. The room was full of boxes, a single wicker rocking chair, along with a plethora of clothing racks weighed down with old clothing that smelled of mothballs.

He had to travel straight back past the stacks of boxes to gain access to the window. Before he could get there, Jackson came upon multiple boxes scattered across the floor having fallen from a previously piled stack. Being the good Samaritan he was, the helpful carrier decided to tidy up the mess. *Besides, it's only a few boxes,* he concluded. One by one he picked up the five boxes, stacking them atop one another neatly, until the very last box sat on top. "There. Much better," he remarked before noticing the word written across the flaps of the cardboard box on top of the stack. One word was all that had been written: "Henry." That one word was enough to pique Jackson's interest.

The curious mailman wondered what kind of man Mrs. Teresa's husband was. What memories they'd captured together. Their marriage had lasted more than half a century. They had to have done something right. What was their secret? Jackson was eager to find out. He pulled open the flaps of the box. The first thing he laid his eyes on was a photo album. Brown construction paper covered the outside. No words marked its front. Jackson blew the dust from its cover off into the air. He coughed a little, continuing to brush off the remainder of the dust with his hand, opting not to pollute his lungs any further. There it was written in black marker: "Memories." Jackson opened the cover.

The first pictures were of the two of them, Mrs. Teresa and her husband Henry, on their wedding day. He held her in the air across his arms as if waiting to cross a threshold. The pictures were pasted two per page, snapshots of them picnicking, partying, and parading. They looked happy in each image. That was, until the baby was born. The smile had fleeted from Henry's face. In every photo thereafter, he was holding a beer. Jackson stepped backward, sitting on the stool behind him to peruse the remainder of the album. As the memories depicted progressed, Mrs. Teresa was shown wearing sunglasses, even on those snapped inside. Her gleaming smile also seemed to have faded from the photos as the bruising on her frail arms came into view. "He was hitting her." Jackson looked up from the album, catching a shimmer of light reflecting off an object as beams of sun shined into the window. *What's back there?* he wondered. The curious carrier stood, then placed the photo album back into its box. Jackson had to kneel in order to reach the object stashed behind the clutter. Once he got a good grip on it, all he had to do was pull. The cane with the chrome circular handle on top was bloodstained at its tip. "She said he broke the window," he whispered. Jackson stood, carefully piecing together his thoughts as he walked over to the window then glared out at the front yard.

Their previous interactions replayed in his head, as did her words. *"The other one just throws it up onto the porch. I watched him from the window that day, right after my husband broke it, mistakenly of course."* Mrs. Teresa turned. *"That one right there."* He remembered her pointing up at the cracked window on the third floor. *"I don't go up there anymore."*

Just then, another memory took hold, supporting his emerging theory. She had said it out of her very own mouth. *"Watch your step. The room is cluttered. I haven't been up there since my husband died."*

"She killed him. She killed him, then watched Randy deliver the mail that day," he whispered. Jackson didn't know what to do about his suspicions. He liked Mrs. Teresa, and more importantly, he had an idea of what really pushed her to do it in the first place. If she even had . . . Jackson thought it best he just measured the window, then head home. He was confused, hungry, and even more so, irritated by the fact that Mr. Trionfi was slinking back across the street to his luxury home.

Jackson leered at the adulterous man with an unrepentant glare. "'If a man commits adultery with the wife of his neighbor, both the adulterer and the adulteress shall surely be put to death,'" he recited the Bible scripture word for word.

Back at the diner in Jacksonville, Sue and Buddy partook of their meal as they immersed themselves in conversation. His intentions to learn everything about her came to fruition the more they chatted. "So, your ex"—he paused a second after accentuating the "ex" before continuing—"husband was in the military."

"He was. He's retired now. I got a letter in the mail the other day from the State. He's working as a civilian again."

"So, what's he doing now?"

"Last I heard, he'd gotten a job at the post office."

"He's got that servitude thing down bad, huh?"

"Yeah, I guess you could say that." Sue bit down into her French fry as she stared down at the crispy chicken tenders on her plate.

Buddy changed the subject, having noticed her reluctance to talk about her ex-husband. "So, what made you want to be an exotic dancer?"

"My father passed away, and it was up to me to help pay the bills. So, I went from contemporary dance to erotic. And here I am today, back at it."

"Going from stay-at-home mother back to stripping must have been hard for you." He slurped up a tablespoon full of cheddar broccoli soup, still studying her with his eyes.

"You've gotta do what you've got to do, right?"

"That's right. The difference is you're willing to do it. That takes real guts. But sometimes you put yourself in situations and get comfortable with settling. You can always have more. Are you comfortable, Sue?"

"Don't get it twisted. I make this look easy, but in no way, shape, or form am I comfortable with taking off my clothes for strange men day in and day out. Especially when they're broke and only mean to use me for a free jack-off session."

Buddy coughed a bit, choking on his soup. "Wow! A free jack-off session, huh? Give it to me straight, why don't you?"

"Sorry. I'm not one for mincing words."

"It's fine. I want you to be honest with me. The more I get to know you, the more I like you. I have to admit it's hard to see the real individual when you're dancing up on stage, but as I put a life to the woman, I'm more interested than ever. It's nice to see the real you."

What's with this guy? He has to have some sort of angle. Surely, he knows he didn't have to spend this much money just to get me to spend time with him. He hasn't even tried sleeping with me yet. Sue was curious enough to see where things would go.

"What makes you think this is the real me?"

"You've polished off two of your chicken fingers within the first couple minutes of getting your plate. What woman does that on a first date? A real one," Buddy answered.

Sue snickered. "You were right. The food is delicious," she admitted.

"How about we find you a way out of this situation you're in?"

"You mean me taking off my clothes for strangers? I wouldn't mind that at all. Just how do you plan on accomplishing that though?"

Chapter 16

Reality Settles In

That evening, Marcus cruised beyond the borders of Clarkston into a neighboring town, Waterford Township. That was when he started to see them, the working girls traipsing up and down Dixie Highway every few blocks or so. He peered into the darkness, only the bulbs of the streetlamps illuminating his view of the ladies. The perverted clerk had yet to find his type but was prepared to travel to the edges of Pontiac, if need be. Marcus would surely have more options to choose from there. The income level in Pontiac was considerably lower than that of the folks in Clarkston. With over 30 percent of the residents living below the poverty level, the place was a hotbed for drugs and prostitution. Although he preferred to find one that was clean, per se, if he had to deal with peering down at track marks during the act, he would have no other choice but to endure it. Unfortunately, the offense came with a cost. The cleaner the woman, the less abuse she would suffer. Being attractive boded better for them. While the boy liked a pretty face free of blemishes, more specifically pimples, Marcus was more about the curves of her body. The last one was a bit too skinny. While perfect in the eyes of his son, she scored fewer points with Marcus. This time he'd get someone who felt better, someone a little more plump. He hated thrusting up against what felt like bones. His eyes peered at the side of the road as if they were an eagle's waiting for the perfect moment to swoop down on its prey.

A reflection of bright beams from the headlamps of a vehicle swiftly approaching from behind shined from his rearview mirror, impairing Marcus's vision. The speed limit on Dixie Highway was forty-five miles an hour, yet Marcus kept his speed at a steady thirty miles an hour.

The driver of the vehicle behind him slammed on his brakes as he laid on the horn.

Marcus tilted his mirror, redirecting the glare from the vehicle's headlamps. He denied every ounce of his energy from the fit of road rage, prompting the angry driver to speed around the menacing clerk. "Learn how to drive, moron!" the passing driver yelled as he sped by.

Marcus's eyes remained focused on the sidewalk to his left. His mind allowed only one thing to consume his thoughts: a new prospect. Most times he'd have to find a new girl for having cheated the others. The money he promised to pay them would somehow get lost, or Marcus simply wouldn't pay up. As the horny clerk neared the boarder of Pontiac, he saw her switching her hips as she trotted back and forth in front of the Speedway gas station. She liked that spot because the bus stop was nearby. If the authorities decided to question her, she would simply use the excuse that she was waiting on the bus to arrive.

Her long platinum hair reached the center of her exposed back. The short, tight olive-toned thigh-length dress she was wearing slid up her thick lower limbs as she walked. It seemed every few seconds she was tugging at the hem of it to pull it back down to a more appropriate level. She spotted Marcus gawking her way as he pulled into the gas station's entrance, his hot breath fogging his driver's side window. Marcus parked at pump number eight, then shut off his car engine. A few minutes went by without him approaching or even leaving his vehicle. *There has to be a reason he pulled in,* she pondered. Seeing his lack of action as a sign, the opportunistic girl moved in closer.

"Hey, handsome. You looking for a date?" she inquired, ducking down to peer into the vehicle's driver's side window.

"What's your name?"

"Whatever you want it to be, handsome." She blew a bubble with the chewing gum she'd been gnawing on all night.

"I didn't ask you what I could call you. I asked you your name," he countered.

"It's Lydia," she admitted against her better judgment. It wasn't normal practice for her to reveal her name to her johns, though something about Marcus's dopey exterior seemed nonthreatening to the naive woman. She had to be no more than 24 years of age, he assumed. Her black mascara defined her lashes, a thick layer of foundation covered the acne attacking her cheeks, and a deep crimson lipstick coated her narrow lips. Though Lydia's frame was small up top, the bottom was what one would call voluptuous. Her curves earned her dividends much higher than the other working girls.

You see, in actuality, Lydia was a runaway. Just 18 years of age. Her parents hadn't seen her since her tenth grade year of high school, the current year being her senior. "More money and less rules on the street" was the motto Lydia lived by. As far as she was concerned, it was the only way to live.

"I like that name. Get in," Marcus instructed, pressing the button to release the automatic locks.

Meanwhile, back in Clarkston, Jackson waited in a booth in the back of a diner on Dixie Highway.

He ordered meatloaf and mashed potatoes, his favorite comfort meal. Normally he would choose a healthy alternative. That day, however, he needed to feel satisfaction. Like with most men, food was the easiest way to brighten his mood. He sat at the booth, staring at a photo of his daughter, Mya. Jackson wondered what she was doing, how much she had grown since he left, all questions he was too bitter to inquire about. All it would take was a phone call. Even so, the jilted husband couldn't bear hearing his estranged wife's voice. Her sultry tone was one of the things most mesmerizing about her. He knew she would surely lay it on thick to spite him.

"Here you go. It's hot. Be careful," the waitress, Janice, announced as she placed the plate full of food down in front of him.

"Thank you, Janice." Jackson looked up over at her growing belly. "So, how far along are you?"

Janice stretched, back and feet aching from the long shift she'd endured. "Seven months. This little guy is ready to get out. See the world."

"Why don't you take a break? Sit down. Get off your feet for a moment."

"I really don't want to be a bother," Janice said, declining the offer she really wanted to accept.

"It's no bother. I could use the company. Besides, you don't even have any other customers. Plus, I promise it'll land you a good tip. That baby could use some extra diaper cash. They get expensive, you know?"

"Yes, I've heard. Okay, you won me over. I guess I can get away with a quick fifteen minutes off my feet without the manager coming down on me." Janice scooted her oversized belly down into the booth. "So, who is that in the picture? You've been staring at it since you sat down."

"It's my daughter, Mya. She lives with her mother in North Carolina. She's a terrible woman."

"So is his father," Janice reluctantly admitted, glancing down at her belly.

"Where is he?"

"I don't know. I was sexually assaulted. His father was never brought to justice. And so here I am, a single mother on welfare."

"I'm so sorry that you had to—"

Janice interjected before Jackson could apologize for the misfortune she'd been dealt. "It's fine. I've come to terms with it and will raise my son with morals despite his father's vile ways. The sins of the father will not contaminate the son this time around." She rubbed her hand across her swollen belly.

"I can't imagine how you must feel, how you've managed to gather the strength to raise this child. Do you have your family's support?"

Janice looked up with a tinge of regret in her expression. "I don't have any family. It's just me and

Oliver now. I left my hometown shortly after the rape. All the questions. Who is the father? Where is the father? I just couldn't stay there anymore. I grew tired of the watchful eyes accompanied by whispers. This experience has taught me that people aren't as understanding as they claim to be. It's better this way, though. Now my Oliver won't have to be looked at as a monster. He can live his life never knowing of his father's wickedness."

"May I see your pen?"

Janice reached into the pocket of her white ruffled waist apron to retrieve one, then handed it over to Jackson.

"I know you don't know me from a hole in the wall, but if you ever need a helping hand, I'm around." It bothered Jackson a little that the woman had been taken advantage of the way she'd been. She didn't deserve it. Just like he didn't deserve to be cheated on. "Here, take my number," he said, jotting it down on one of the napkins beside his plate before handing it over to her.

"Thanks. I really appreciate it. Oh, my gosh, you haven't even had the opportunity to touch your dinner. I'm sorry. I tend to go on and on."

"No apologies necessary, Janice."

"Well, I'd better get back. I only have a few more minutes, and I should probably use it for the restroom. It literally feels like he's sitting on my bladder all day."

"I wish I could say that I feel your pain," Jackson replied.

"Be happy you don't have to. You enjoy your meatloaf. It's good. I had some for lunch today." Janice scooched across then out of the booth to stand. "I'll be seeing ya around."

Jackson glanced down at the picture in his lap before looking up to stare out of the window beside him. He wondered how Mya had spent her day. Thoughts of her darling smile warmed his heart, then that waned in an instant once he saw Marcus driving by the diner with another female companion in the passenger seat of his vehicle.

What's that guy's deal? Jackson allowed his mind to paint different scenarios as he stuck his fork into the slice of juicy meatloaf submerged in brown gravy atop the plate in front of him.

On the car ride home, Jackson's cellular phone buzzed. The caller identification displayed a number calling from a 910 area code: Jacksonville, North Carolina. "Daddy's baby," he remarked with the sincerest grin emerging upon his face. He answered without haste, "Mya, is that you?"

"Hi, Daddy! Yayyy! It's Daddy, Nana!" the tiny olive-toned girl with the curly dark pigtails screamed with excitement.

Her broken father teared up at the mere sound of his baby girl's voice. "Hey, Mya. Oh, my gosh, baby, Daddy misses you so much. I wish I could come and get you."

"Daddy, come home. Daddy, come home soon. Right, Daddy?"

"Daddy's gonna come and get you real soon, baby. As soon as Daddy is finished working. Okay?"

"I miss you."

"I miss you more! I love you, Mya."

"I love you too, Daddy."

"What are you doing? Are you having fun at your grandmother's?"

"Nana played games. And I have cookies, Daddy."

Her admission made him chuckle. Jackson missed his daughter terribly.

"Where are you, Daddy?"

"I'm driving down the road. I'm surprised you're still up. Does your nana know you have her phone?"

"Nana is right here. Here, Nana. Telephone," the little girl replied, handing the phone over to her grandmother. Mrs. Yang was a doting grandmother. The small, round-bellied Asian American woman kept her granddaughter whenever her mother was busy swinging around the tall metal pole.

"Hello," she answered, lifting the receiver to her mouth.

"Good evening, Mrs. Yang. Thank you for allowing Mya to call me."

"Mya needs her father in her life, too. My daughter make a big mistake losing you. Mya should not have to suffer."

"I'm glad you understand. Can I say goodbye to Mya?"

"Hold on, here she comes. What a busy bee," she remarked as Mya ran up. "Come here and sit still, Mya Lin! Say goodbye to your dad."

"Bye, Daddy. I love you," she yelled into the phone before handing it back over to her grandmother, then running off to continue playing.

"I love you more, baby girl."

Mrs. Yang put the receiver back to her ear. "She run off again."

"Kids will be kids."

"We talk to you later, Jackson."

"Talk to you later," he sighed as he disconnected the call feeling completely helpless, subject to the will of others where it concerned his future with Mya.

Chapter 17

Worrisome

Over at the Escobars', the cordless phone atop the nightstand next to the king-size bed rang, waking Mrs. Escobar from her slumber. She sat up, lifted her cheetah-print sleep mask, then switched on the lamp at her bedside. The number displayed on the caller identification was that of an out-of-state number, so Mrs. Escobar thought it best that she answer. Her husband would call from different numbers at all times of the day, being that he traveled the world three seasons out of the year.

She picked up the receiver, pressing it to her ear. "Hello."

"I love you, honey. Did I wake you?" Mr. Escobar replied.

"I'm so glad that you did." She smiled, leaning back against the gray leather headboard.

"I've been thinking about what you said about having a baby. About me stationing my business back home in Michigan. You know I love you, right?"

"I know you love me."

"I'm sorry that I never made you a priority. I'm sorry that I never bothered to consider the family you've asked to build with me. I've been very selfish with my time and energy, where it pertains to you, and I recognize that. When I come home, we're going to start over."

"Neil, why are you saying all of this?" she asked, mildly afraid she'd been found out.

"Because I don't want to lose you. It bothers me that you don't yearn for me anymore. I've noticed you're used to not having me around. Sometimes I look around the house and don't recognize anything there. When I'm leaving, you no longer lay out your usual drawn-out rebuttal. I feel like I'm losing you. They say it's better to love what you have before you're forced to mourn the fact that you had it. Whatever has happened in the past, we're going to move on from it. Everything is going to be better from now on."

Tears had begun streaming from her eyes the moment he referenced losing her. She couldn't believe what she was hearing. All she'd ever wanted and dreamt had been brought to the forefront. "I love you so much, honey," Mrs. Escobar professed.

"I love you more, darling."

***

When Sue strolled into the front door of her mother's three-bedroom bungalow, all the lights were out except the lamp atop the small oak table beside the sofa in the living room on her right. Her mother lay sleeping on the sofa with Mya on top of her, head to chest. It wasn't until Sue attempted to lift her that her mother awoke.

"What are you doing strolling in here this late? You said you would be here hours ago. I missed work because of you," she chastised as Sue lifted a sleeping Mya from her mother's bosom.

"I met someone, Mama. He's really nice, and he's going to help me."

"Help you do what, Sue Lin? Avoid your responsibilities? Neglect your child? You already ruined your marriage."

"He's going to help me get my life back," Sue snapped back quietly as her mother moved from the sofa to fold the blanket atop the matching peony-patterned love seat meant for Mya to sleep on.

"Sue Lin, I don't have time for these half-baked ideas. This is the real world, and in the real world, we must work to pay bills." She laid the folded blanket atop the couch cushion before turning to her naive daughter, brandishing a frowning face. A frown that quickly waned once she noticed the five $100 bills Sue held out toward her.

Her mother's eyes widened, snatching the money from her daughter's grasp before she had the notion to change her mind. "Where did you get this from, Sue Lin?"

"A man who knows about the real world," she responded with raised brows.

Later that evening, Jackson gazed out at the waxing moon as he stood at the edge of the beach at Lake Callis. "I can feel myself slipping, God. Give me the strength to fight this demon festering inside of me. I don't want to be bitter anymore." He let out a long sigh, worried about how he would piece his life back together. Jackson had gotten the job, yet still he felt angry, agitated, and unfulfilled. He pulled off his shoes and socks to bury his feet in the warm sand. As the clouds began to clear, so did the confusion in his mind.

Jackson walked toward the water, popping a squat on the sand. He thought about what Janice said about deciding to raise her son despite his father's crimes against her. In that moment, Sue's offenses began plaguing his thoughts. *How can I get past what she's done to me? I need to be with Mya. She needs her father,* he reasoned. *They say that time heals all wounds. Maybe it's just going to take a little time,* he hoped.

But were Jackson's hopes in vain? Time seemed to be somewhat of an issue for him. The little time the ex-marine had left with his sanity, in particular. His pills had run out. What would come of his fragile state of mind? Worry set in as Jackson thought about how he would make it through a day's work with no medication. Knowing what would come next, he lay back on the beach, overcome with despair. Jackson mushed his feet around in the warm sand, his feelings of discontent ebbing. All he could hear were waves crashing against the shore. It was peaceful there. His eyes were closed for only a moment before they opened back in Kuwait.

The dream felt as real as the sand covering his toes. Lance Corporal Jackson Pierce was in the middle of the desert, the Hummer just a few feet away from him. He got up. "Lance Corporal Flynn! Lance Corporal Flynn!" he called out to him, receiving no response. Jackson's bare feet shuffled through the hot sand as he ran toward the vehicle. When he made it to the passenger side of the Hummer, he saw Lance Corporal Flynn inside passed out with blood running from his right ear and nose. He tugged at the door handle, attempting to open it. "Flynn! Wake up, Flynn!" Jackson screamed at the unconscious marine, but there was no use. Flynn was unresponsive. "What the hell is going on here?" He held his hands to the sides of his head. It was confusing to Lance

Corporal Pierce. He was in Kuwait, but the clothes he was wearing were civilian. It was the same shirt and cargo shorts he'd worn to work that day.

There was no one else in sight. Jackson glanced all around him, turning in every direction. No one besides the unconscious marine in the front seat of the Hummer was visible. He had to find help for his brother in brown. Jackson ran in the opposite direction, back toward Camp Joe Foss. The others must be there, he assumed.

Ahead, there was a massive sand dune Jackson would have to climb to make it back to camp. He didn't remember the obstacle being there before, but it was the desert. Sand dunes would often pop up out of nowhere due to the wind's current. Jackson tackled the hill with mounting determination, his only focus being getting help for Flynn. After the descent, his journey went on for a few more miles before he had Camp Joe Foss in his sights.

Where is everyone? he thought, expecting to see a brigade of marines waiting in line for the phone. Jackson's mind quickly gave him an answer to the question he had posed. "The bunkers." The eager marine picked up speed as he headed for one of the shelters. When Jackson came around to the entrance, he could see a marine lying flat on his back. Blood leaked from his riddled abdomen, soaking into the sand beneath him.

"Oh, my God." Jackson turned to look inside, but it was too dark to see the others. He detached the flashlight from the waist belt of the wounded marine. "I'm sorry, soldier." Jackson aimed the light, illuminating what was splayed out before him. Every marine packed into that bunker was dead, blood draining, bodies tattered, and limbs missing from their corpses. The spine-chilling scene took his breath away. Jackson's eyes welled up with tears. His face trembled. A heavy, forced breath escaped Jackson's mouth before he bent over, resting his hands upon his knees. For a second, he was sure he'd lose his stomach, but he managed to resist the urge.

"What the hell happened here?" he whispered, the horror in his eyes showing the truth of it. The gruesome sight of his fellow man lying there lifeless overwhelmed Jackson. He staggered back away from the heinous scene to gain his composure. But where would he go from there? How would Jackson get help? He turned to the west as the SCUD missile soared through the sky. Headed straight for him, of course, Jackson surmised. "Take cover! We're under fire!" the others yelled from a separate bunker. Then out of nowhere the bomb crashed into the sand in front of him. Jackson's limp body was ejected into the air.

That was when his eyes opened.

"Are you okay, sir? You really shouldn't sleep out here. The cops will give you a huge ticket," the male of the elderly couple strolling by informed him.

Jackson raised his hand, rubbing beads of sweat from his forehead as he sat up off the sand. "I'm okay. I must have dozed off. It's been a long day. Thank you for waking me up. A ticket is the last thing I need right now."

"You're welcome," the gentleman responded as he and his wife walked on, her hand gripping his, unsure of Jackson's intentions.

The nightmare that shook him to his core quickly faded back into his subconscious, as many of the dreams did once Jackson was awake. It was 2300 hours, which meant he had nine hours to go before he would have to clock in at Clarkston Post Office. Jackson thought it best he got home so that he could get ample rest for his next day of work. The odds were already stacking against him due to his lack of medication.

Chapter 18

Figuring Things Out

At 0800 hours the following morning, fumes shot from tailpipes of the white trucks with the red and blue stripes, pervading Jackson nostrils. A smell that previously seemed to have no effect on him made Jackson feel lightheaded, almost nauseated. Trying his best to combat the effects, he held his breath as he traveled the remainder of the pathway leading him inside. He was right on time, which in Jackson's eyes meant he was late. Once the anxious carrier pushed through the green double doors, he breathed in a big whiff of the fume-less oxygen, hoping to ease the dizziness threatening to overtake him. It worked. Still, the prickly feeling on his skin took even more mental wherewithal to ignore, leaving him on edge.

Evelyn noticed Jackson pushing through the doors as she was on her way to open the customer entrance. Although he had tried hard to hide it, he looked confused. His wrinkled brows and wondering gaze told Evelyn so. "Good morning, Jackson. How'd your first day on Rural Route 8 go yesterday?"

Jackson took note of what she had shared, having forgotten the route number the moment he walked into the building. "It was fine. All of the packages and mail were delivered to satisfied customers," he responded, not really wanting to engage in conversation with her but feeling obligated for fear of not wanting to seem unapproachable.

"I heard."

"What do you mean? What did you hear?"

"Well, according to the gossip going around the office, a couple of customers called up here yesterday evening singing your praises. You're known as the friendly neighborhood carrier. Let's hope you can continue to live up to the pedestal they've placed you on."

The admission meant to make him feel uplifted only agitated him further. All Jackson really took in was the latter part of Evelyn's statement. *Is she counting on me to fail?* He huffed. "I'm sure it won't be a problem," Jackson countered with a combative tone.

Oh, he must still be mad because I'm married, Evelyn told herself, having picked up on the angst in his voice. *He is really, truly nuts.* She chuckled lightly at the notion, continuing her stride past him on her way to open the metal gate, securing the customer counter.

Jackson made a beeline toward the case for Rural Route 8, staring at the numbers above each of the other cases to ensure he stopped at the correct one. He set his thermos down on the case feeling as if he were in the Twilight Zone. A plethora of sounds bored a hole in Jackson's psyche. The rolling carts, slamming doors, banging metal equipment, even the loud beeping from the PASS machine irritated him. Pat and Tanya's early morning yakking as they stood outside their cases sipping coffee annoyed Jackson even further. "Nobody cares that your kid made the soccer team. Just shut the hell up," he mumbled, lifting the bucket of magazines to his counter so that he could begin casing them.

All the other carriers passed by expressing their congratulations to Pat for her son's accomplishment while Jackson, instead, tossed magazines forcefully into their appropriate slots.

"Is everything okay, Jackson?" Deborah asked as she snuck up behind him.

"Good morning," he responded, masking the fact that she'd startled him. "Everything is peachy. How about yourself?"

"Light mail today, so it's looking pretty good so far. The clerks are almost done scanning mail, so you guys should be able to get out of here early.

You received some kudos yesterday. A couple of the residents on your route called in about your outstanding manners and chivalry. Whatever you are doing, keep it up. You'll be on this route for quite some time, so you'll get to see the fruits of your labor come winter. We never ask for tips, but the residents of Clarkston can be very generous around the holidays, if you know what I mean."

"Well, then, at least I have that to look forward to," he responded hastily. Jackson didn't mean to blurt out what he had. Still, it was too late.

Deborah's wheels began turning. *Problems at home,* she thought. "How's the family?" she inquired, of course fishing for details that would help her to move in on him.

"They're doing good. I'd love to chat, but I should get back to work. It's only my second day, and I'm not adjusted to all of the addresses yet." Jackson knew precisely what she was up to, but he wasn't interested. Normally he would use someone's fondness of him to his advantage. That day was different. He simply couldn't stomach Deborah's advances. She wasn't bad looking. Just not his type in any way.

Anyhow, Deborah didn't let the brief encounter ruin her hopes of bedding Jackson in the future. "I'll leave you to it then." She strutted off with her head held high as she barked orders at one of the postal support employees stacking magazines on the floor at the carriers' cases. "That should have been done an hour ago," she blurted as she blew by the nervous PSE.

The postal support employees weren't protected by the union very well. In fact, within their first thirty days of being hired, they could be fired without reason. In other words, if management didn't like the shirt a new hire was wearing that day, they were at risk of being canned. Deborah used the rule to her full advantage, treating the postal support employees as if they were subhuman, even saying as much often. Still, they worked diligently, ignoring the abuse with hopes of one day securing a full-time position with the United States Postal Service.

At 1000 hours, the temperature had already reached a smoldering eighty-eight degrees. Sweat poured from the top of Jackson's shiny brown cranium down his face as he lifted full trays of mail from the white cloth cart to pack into his mail truck for deliveries. He kept his head down, evading the other carriers as they rushed by him to pack up their LLVs with the day's load of letters, magazines, and parcels. Feelings of agitation, fear, and moreover, anxiety, increased the probability of a clash arising. It was Jackson's intention to avoid conflict at all costs. So much so that he neglected to push his cart back into the building, instead deciding to leave it there after he emptied it. Jackson climbed into his truck, opting out of strapping the seat belt across his chest. The restriction would only make his anxiety worse. His fuel odometer read one-quarter of a tank, which wasn't enough to complete his route, making Jackson's first stop the nearest gas station.

The woman pumping gas from the fueling station opposite his looked familiar to Jackson. Her long, damp brown hair draped down, covering the sides of her face. Still, he could see her plainly, much better than he could that night from the car windshield of Marcus's 2001 Volkswagen GTI. The curious carrier stole glances at her, attempting to get a good look at her face. She saw him spying on her from the opposite side of the pump but ignored it, figuring he only wanted one thing.

"Hey, don't I know you?" Jackson finally spoke up after securing the metal slider in place on the pump's handle to automatically fill his tank with unleaded.

Jessica looked up with wide eyes, shocked at the stranger stepping over the divide to come closer. "You don't know me, and I don't know you," she said, halting his approach.

The skin atop her left cheekbone was a bruised mixture of purple and black. Her narrow, dry bottom lip was split down the middle. Although she was dressed in a casual black pantsuit, ready to take advantage of whatever success she was garnered that day, her makeup had not yet been applied.

"Sure, I do. I mean, we never spoke, but—"

Jessica interrupted before he could finish. "Look, man, I don't do . . ." She paused, lowering her tone. "I don't do that kind of stuff anymore. As you can see, it hasn't turned out well for me." Of course, she was hinting at the obvious abuse she'd suffered.

"I didn't mean to . . ." Jackson started to explain that he had never encountered her in that way, but he figured Jessica's situation out in his mind before blurting his rebuttal. She'd tried her hand at prostitution for easy money the night she hung out with Marcus. It made perfect sense to Jackson. He didn't think Marcus looked good enough for Jessica the night he'd witnessed them together. Therefore, it was Marcus who'd left his mark on her, Jackson surmised before continuing. "Never mind. I'm glad you decided not to do that thing anymore. Good luck finding something more suitable. By the way, the price tag for your suit jacket is sticking out of the pocket."

Jackson stepped back over to his side of the pump as Jessica self-consciously tucked the tag back into her jacket pocket. Ripping it off would depend on whether she got the job she was to interview for that morning.

The curious carrier stood by his truck in complete silence, watching the other patrons as they trotted in then back out of the gas station doors. *What are their stories?* he wondered. Jackson spied a man assisting his pregnant wife into their Jeep as he held the door open for her. Meanwhile, the man's beady eyes studied a single 20-something black female pumping her gas. She had a long black mane that seemed to stretch to her plump derriere. The woman eventually noticed the man staring at her, furnishing him with a wink. Their actions, though subtle, infuriated Jackson. He huffed, blood boiling, and his pulse raced. What could he do but come to terms with the world he was living in? As Jackson waited there, clarity came upon him. He was surrounded by liars, cheaters, manipulators, even sexual deviants. The list grew the longer he ruminated on it. Deep, heavy breaths escaped him, but before fury could set in, the gas nozzle lever clicked, alerting him of his full tank.

Once he got back out onto the road, all he could think about was Marcus. "What a spineless piece of crap he is for beating on that woman the way he did." Jackson searched his mind for a reason she'd deserve such brutality. Just then, Sue came to mind, further souring his mood. What his estranged wife had done to him was unforgivable. His wife had lied to him, taken his love for granted, and allowed her body to be defiled in the worst way. She may as well have been one of those street-walkers traipsing up Dixie Highway looking for a payout in exchange for sexual favors. The only reason he didn't strangle the life out of her was because of Mya. She had been Sue's saving grace.

Chapter 19

Clarity

Jackson turned the corner to pull up to Mrs. Teresa's mailbox, seeing the truth of it all. Everything wasn't bright and sunny in that innocent, fun-filled way. The heat was scorching hot, making the temperature in his mail truck suffocating. Of course, old Mrs. Teresa was sitting on her porch. The nice old lady who leered at everyone for the safety of her neighborhood. Only now the faithful carrier saw a different truth in the matter as she smiled, waving for him to come forward. The resentful old woman sat there day in and day out searching for prying eyes, paranoid that one day her secret would be found out. Someone had to have seen her that day, she feared. So, Mrs. Teresa sat on that porch every day, prisoner to her own guilty conscience as she searched for what fault she could find in others' actions.

Regardless of that fact, she would be useful to Jackson. Mrs. Teresa saw everything. From now on, she would be his eyes when he wasn't there to see. Jackson pulled into her driveway, curious as to what she had in store for him that day.

"Good morning, Mrs. Teresa. Just letters today." Jackson handed over the handful of mail to the old lady cloaked in her flower-patterned housecoat.

"Top of the morning to you, soldier. It's probably all nonprofit organizations. I gave money to one of those smaller organizations last year, and I think they sold my name to one of those lists. I've been getting requests for money every day since."

"I'm glad you know better. I've seen too many of our seniors being taken advantage of by these so-called nonprofits."

"Not me. I've still got my wits about me." Mrs. Teresa pointed out into her front yard at Minkzy, who'd been grazing on her front lawn for hours. "Check it out. This one has been scowling at me all morning. Even hissed at me a couple of times. I think she wants to check the front door for an opening."

Jackson huffed. He thought it was funny that the feline was feeling territorial. "I think you'd better stay on the porch, Mrs. Teresa."

"She doesn't intimidate me. I make a mean dragon, tiger, phoenix."

"I'm afraid to ask what that is exactly, but I'm sure you're going to tell me."

"It's a Chinese dish commonly prepared in the Guangdong province."

"I haven't had breakfast this morning." With a wink, Jackson hinted that he might find the idea appealing.

"Just a few more steps and it'll be chow time." The old woman tapped the mail against her knee as she swayed back and forth on the porch swing. The two of them chuckled at the notion. Though Jackson was kidding, Mrs. Teresa, not so much.

"So, I take it the door is serving its purpose?"

"It certainly is. I'm so thankful for you."

"You've thanked me enough, Mrs. Teresa. Really, it's no problem. Anything you need, don't hesitate to ask."

"I do have one special request."

"Well, spit it out."

"I made an apple pie for the young girl down the street. She recently lost her mother, so it's just her and her stepfather down there now. The poor thing always looks so lost. There's a sadness in her eyes that I just can't stop thinking about. I had to do something for her. Would you mind delivering it to her for me? My knees would surely be grateful."

"Of course I'd love to deliver it."

"And guess what?"

"What?"

"I made one for you too."

"Mrs. Teresa. You shouldn't have, but I'm so glad you did," Jackson admitted.

"Come on inside. They're on the kitchen counter." The old lady stood, slowly grasping the swing's chain with one hand, then the top of her cane with the other to gain stability on her feet.

"You need some help?" Jackson began to lunge in her direction.

"Don't you dare fuss over me. I'm fine. Just come on inside and get these pies. It'll be perfect for after dinner. You should warm it up and have some vanilla ice cream on the side. It tastes much better than dragon, tiger, phoenix and doesn't get stuck in your teeth."

"I bet," Jackson replied as he followed her down the hallway into the kitchen.

"There they are, boxed all nice for the both of you."

Jackson moved over to the counter to retrieve the pies. That was when he saw Mr. Trionfi from the view of the bay window above the kitchen sink. He kissed his wife goodbye, then watched her back out of the driveway. The moment that pearl white Mercedes-Benz turned the corner, Mr. Trionfi darted across the street, headed straight for the Escobars' home.

"Mrs. Teresa, you don't have anything planned later today, do you?" Jackson asked as he continued to spy.

"Just me and my book is all."

"I'll have the glass for the window upstairs. I just wanted to make sure today would be good for you."

"Today would be fine. Oh, now that I know you're coming, I'll make dinner for us."

"That won't be necessary, Mrs. Teresa." Jackson turned to face the old woman.

"Oh, please, it's the least I can do. Besides, I'd really enjoy the company." The latter part of her statement she said while exaggerating the feebleness in her tone.

"No dragon, tiger, phoenix, right?" With his own eyes, Jackson bored a hole into the old woman's eyes, searching for hints of deception. She had already fooled him into thinking she was dead. He wanted to be sure it wouldn't be another joke being pulled off at his expense.

"Cross my heart," Mrs. Teresa vowed with two strokes of her hand across her chest.

There was just something about Mrs. Teresa that Jackson favored despite his obvious suspicions of her guilt in the death of her husband. "Then I guess I'll see you around five o'clock." Jackson grabbed the pies before heading on his way.

As he climbed back inside the LLV, he saw Mr. Trionfi pushing his way into the Escobars' home through the front door.

"Let me in, toots." Mr. Trionfi looked at his mistress with a confused expression. "What's wrong? You knew I'd be coming. Why didn't you open the door when I first knocked? You got someone else here or something?" He searched the scene with prying eyes.

"No. No one is here."

"Come here then," he demanded, wrapping his arm around her waist to pull her in closer.

A raised hand separated her lips from his as he tried stealing a kiss. "What's going on? Why are you acting like a shy little girl? You're a woman, aren't you? Come show daddy how much of a woman you are," he requested, leaning in once more.

"Stop. Just stop, please."

"What? Come on!" Mr. Trionfi thought her actions were absurd. He looked into Mrs. Escobar's eyes. "Are you serious?"

"I don't want to do this anymore."

Mr. Trionfi released her, then lifted her chin so that she looked him square in the eyes. "You don't want me anymore. Is that what you mean?"

"I don't want to cheat on my husband anymore."

Mr. Trionfi processed a multitude of emotions at the point of her revelation. He felt embarrassed by the fact that she had the power to cause him to feel inept, then angry for the fact that she had the nerve to reject him. The lust he harbored for her burned even more now that she dared shun him.

He had her before and he'd have her still, as far as Mr. Trionfi was concerned. "You think I'm just going to allow you to walk out on me? You may be married, but you belong to me. You're mine and you always will be. Besides, nobody can make that pussy cat feel the way I do." He reached under her robe to touch her crotch, causing her to jump back instantly.

"Meow," Minkzy purred, hopping down off the marble side table in the foyer.

Mr. Trionfi's admission made Pamela feel guilty, the truth of it, dirty. Regardless, she stuck to her guns. "I'm not going to do this anymore," she proclaimed, more assured that time than the last.

"Let me clue you in on something. If I go, Mr. Escobar goes. You wouldn't want him to find out who you've really been waxing it for, would you?"

"You wouldn't." Her eyes bulged, considering the notion. If Mr. Escobar found out, his heart would truly be broken. She thought about the phone conversation they had about starting over. Her entire life was at stake. Mrs. Escobar refused to lose everything now. Especially for a scumbag like Mr. Trionfi. She knew he was a player. Not the kind of man with whom she would ever be able to have a serious relationship.

"Try me," he countered.

"You would force me to be with you knowing I don't want you anymore?"

"It's the ways of the human race, baby." He leaned in to kiss her, but again she backed away.

Mr. Trionfi's anger had been tested to its limit. He raised his right hand, giving her a swift smack on the cheek. "Stop being a bitch and get in that bedroom," he demanded.

She couldn't believe he'd laid his hands on her in such a violent manner. Her hands covered her gaping mouth, still in shock from the slap.

"Now that wasn't nice at all," Jackson said, stepping through the front door that had been left ajar, allowing him to hear the entirety of what had transpired there. "Calling another man's wife a bitch is a punishable offense," he threatened, closing the door behind him.

"Who the fuck do you think you are coming in here? You're a mailman. The mail goes in the bo—"

Before Mr. Trionfi could finish, Jackson lifted his boot from the floor, then launched it forward into the miniature man's abdomen. His compact frame flew back through the foyer then into the winding flight of stairs that led to the upper levels of the home.

"Oh, my gosh! What are you doing?" Mrs. Escobar finally spoke up.

"With all due respect, ma'am, I don't think you have room to be asking any questions here. From what I've gathered, you've been cheating on your husband with this spineless piece of shit, and now that you want to back out, he's attempting to blackmail you."

Mr. Trionfi coughed, attempting to catch his breath as he stood to his feet. "You're making a big mistake, buddy." He rushed toward Jackson with intentions of retaliating. The fist that soared through the air toward Jackson's face was caught midair by the arm. In one swift motion, Jackson spent him around, wrapping the arm behind Mr. Trionfi's back. He then proceeded to shove his boot into Mr. Trionfi's buttocks, forcing him back to the wood floor near the bottom of the staircase.

"Do yourself a favor. Stay down this time." Jackson's suggestion sounded more like a demand. The cowardly man was inclined to take the offer yet couldn't risk seeming weak in front of his mistress.

"I'm gonna kick your fucking ass," he spouted with a forefinger outstretched, solidifying his threat. In toward Jackson he rushed once more, receiving a chop to the throat. The maneuver knocked the wind from his sails. Mr. Trionfi bent over, hands gripping his neck at the collarbone. A chronic cough slowly inched him toward regaining his composure.

"This is what's gonna happen here. The crime of adultery is punishable by death."

"Since when?" Mr. Trionfi blurted, still short of breath.

"It's the ways of the human race, you piece of shit," Jackson countered with wild eyes. "Luckily, I heard you professing your regret for your actions. Which earned you a Get Out of Jail Free card, ma'am," he said, turning to Mrs. Escobar. "We can keep this whole thing our little secret as long as you're willing to accept your punishment. I'm sure you two can find it in your hearts to comply. After all, Mr. Trionfi," Jackson said, turning to him, "you wouldn't want to lose half of everything you've earn up 'til this point, would you? Divorce can be very expensive, and the alimony, well, it could go on for years."

"So, you think I'm actually gonna let you kill me?"

"Of course not. But I am going to beat the hell out of you. I'm gonna beat that devil right out of you." He glanced back at Mrs. Escobar. "And you're going to help. Just remember the slap on the cheek he so graciously delivered you before I interrupted, saving you from imminent danger."

"I guess you're right." She gazed at her lover. "He does deserve to be punished," Mrs. Escobar admitted.

Chapter 20

The Overlay for the Underplay

Buddy leaned back in the black swivel chair behind the desk in his minuscule four-by-six cubicle. His desk was clean, and not a photo had been pinned to the three gray walls that surrounded him. It wouldn't be long before he'd hear that dreaded beep echoing through the earbuds of his headphones. Automated calls were filtered to each station in the room filled with at least fifty other cubicles that looked identical to his. Unlike the others, Buddy didn't feel the need to dress up the area, being that it was only his for the time being. After an eight-hour shift would end, there would surely be another fundraiser stepping in to man the phone line.

Thirty seconds in, he heard the beeping sound, which was Buddy's cue to begin his pitch.

The man on the other end of the call answered, "Hello."

"Good morning, Mr. Jones," Buddy read the name of his prospect from the computer monitor in front of him. "My name is Joe Patriot," he lied, figuring that, under the circumstances, that name sounded much better. "I'm calling on behalf of the soldiers who protect our borders and the lands beyond. Assist the Soldiers is a nonprofit organization sending care packages to our soldiers overseas. The reason for my call today—" He tried forcing out his entire pitch before being interrupted.

"Whoa! Whoa! Whoa!" Mr. Jones shouted. "I'm not giving you no money for no damn troops. You know why? Because they won't get it anyway. I don't know who you people think you're fooling. I'll tell you what—if I donate ten dollars, how much of the money do they get?"

Buddy let out an exhausted sigh. He hated that part. There was no way anyone with any good sense would donate after finding out how much money the soldiers benefited from. Unfortunately, the man had asked, so it was required that he reveal the truth of it. The calls were recorded. If Buddy were to lie about that, he would surely be fired without delay.

"Sir, we use ten percent of—" Buddy attempted to weave a convincing reply before being cut off in the middle of his rebuttal.

"Get the hell outta here! Ten percent!" The man laughed hysterically for added effect before continuing with his counterargument. "You've got to be kidding me. You guys are nothing but a bunch of crooks. You ought to be ashamed of yourselves. Put me on your 'do not call' list right now! If I see your number come across my caller ID again, I'm reporting you to the attorney general," he threatened.

Buddy calmly twisted a single edge of his mustache. He was used to being turned down more often than not. "No problem, Mr. Jones. I'll put you on our 'do not call' list. Enjoy the rest of your day." Just as he pressed the button to disconnect the call, he could hear his coworker, Johnathan, in the cubicle next to him transferring over a successful donor.

"Hold the line, ma'am, and thanks again for supporting the troops." His coworker transferred the call to verification before quietly celebrating. "Ooh rah."

Buddy rubbernecked around the gray wall separating them. "How the hell do you get so many donations?" he inquired with a tinge of agitation in his voice.

Johnathan flashed a giddy grin, three of his top front teeth absent from his smile—the last remnants of a brutal beating he had previously been furnished, courtesy of Jackson. "I just use the old retired marine card."

"But you were dishonorably discharged," Buddy blurted.

"So? They don't know that," the younger gentleman replied, pulling off his headset. "I use every trick in the book. These people are starting to get wise to us. You've got to think of some fresh material, Buddy." He stood up from his seat. "Hey, you want something from the vending machine? I'm gonna go get me some water. All this yapping has got me parched."

"No. I'm good." Buddy recoiled into his cubicle, jealous of his coworker's success.

Sue's old beau had been working at the telemarketing firm since he was booted out of the military for sleeping with a fellow soldier's wife. It was through Johnathan that Buddy had heard about Sue. Just weeks earlier upon listening to Johnathan express his hatred for the woman who had lied to him, Buddy drafted a plan for the adulterous stripper. Not that he harbored any type of grudge against her. Buddy was an opportunist. He may not have been too effective on the phones, but in real life, the slender man was what one would deem a smooth criminal.

At 1100 hours that day, Marcus rushed up the stairs of his apartment building hoping to have his way with Lydia. He had a taste of her the night they met. She'd been on his mind ever since. Marcus didn't even have to drug her. Lydia liked it kind of rough, and furthermore appreciated the fact that he didn't require penetration. Other working girls had laughed at him because of it. Drugging them kept him from having to endure their judgmental stares. Lydia was different though. She didn't judge. As Marcus neared the door, he didn't hear any music, which surprised him. He thought for sure his son would be enjoying some time with her himself.

"What's going on here?" he asked as he entered, immediately locking the deadbolt behind him.

Lydia and Andre were both sitting cross-legged on the floor in front of the thirty-two- inch television.

"What's going on? Why is your television in here?"

Andre looked up at his father. "Lydia and me both wanted to play, so we thought it would be a good idea."

"You and Lydia, huh? Well, it's time for me and Lydia to have some time to ourselves. Lydia, in the room, now," Marcus demanded.

Lydia stared Andre in the eyes as she rose to her feet. "Yes, daddy," she responded to Marcus in a sultry voice before turning to enter his bedroom. She clicked the light switch along the wall, illuminating the black light before she plopped down atop the mattress.

Andre turned back to the television screen, stealing peeks from the corner of his eye at her until the door closed behind his father. Normally he would watch, but for some reason Andre didn't have the urge to watch Lydia and Marcus together, nor did Marcus want anyone witnessing the act. Andre could hear her giggling, even with the door closed. He heard every smack and "oh, daddy" she hollered. That was, until he turned up the volume on the television.

Mrs. Teresa stared at Jackson from the bay window as he stepped out of Mr. Trionfi's front door, wiping his forehead over with a handkerchief. Dragging the man's stumpy, limp body back into his home proved to be a daunting task, as Mr. Trionfi weighed much more than he looked.

Mrs. Teresa's eyes toggled between Jackson as he left the Trionfi residence, and Mrs. Escobar as she stared out of her living room window, watching Jackson leave. *Something just isn't right,* she surmised as she leered at Mrs. Escobar pacing the floor while gnawing at her perfectly manicured nails. Whatever was distressing her, their friendly neighborhood mailman was right in the thick of it.

"What have you done, soldier?" the nosy old woman whispered as Jackson headed up the road in his mail truck.

He flexed his fingers, closing then opening his fist back up again. Jackson's fists ached from the beating he'd furnished Mr. Trionfi with. Once he pulled up to the house where he was to deliver the pies, Jackson noticed an adolescent girl, 15 years of age at most, he assumed, darting from the black SUV parked in the driveway. The man behind the driver's seat hopped out, chasing after her. Eventually the girl turned after he yelled out, demanding she stop. *That must be her stepfather,* Jackson thought. The man moved closer to the girl, but when he reached out his hand to touch her, she knocked it away, rejecting his embrace. Jackson couldn't hear what she was yelling over the roar of his engine. What he had seen plainly was the guilty look on her stepfather's face once she had said it. Jackson saw how he looked around to search the scene for prying eyes. Something was hiding there beneath the surface, Jackson surmised.

He pulled up to the mailbox, then hopped out with the mail in hand. "Hello there! I'm Jackson, your new mailman. I've missed you the last few times I delivered." He handed the stack of letters over to the pleasant-looking gentleman.

"Hello there, Jackson. It's very nice to meet you. Thank you for stopping by to introduce yourself. I'm Mr. Sobieski, the principal over at the high school."

"It's very nice to meet you, Mr. Sobieski. Actually, I have something for your daughter."

"My daughter? What could you possibly have for my daughter?"

"It's special. From Mrs. Teresa."

"Oh. The nosy old woman down the street in the corner house?"

"That would be her."

"What did she make this time? A cake?"

"Close enough. A pie," Jackson answered.

"Her generosity knows no bounds."

"Can you call your daughter out here? I'm supposed to deliver it to her personally."

"Sure thing, Jackson. I'll go get her." Mr. Sobieski went inside the house, emerging not even a minute later, having notified the teenage girl with long blond pigtails in tow.

Jackson came toward them, having retrieved the pie from the LLV.

"Shelby, this is our new mailman, Jackson. He has something for you," Mr. Sobieski announced as they met on the front lawn.

"Hello, Shelby. I was instructed to deliver this to you personally."

She seemed shy. Not much of a social butterfly. "Thank you, Jackson," Shelby uttered quietly, accepting the box.

"Yes, thank you, Jackson." Mr. Sobieski rested his hand on his stepdaughter's shoulder. Jackson noticed the slight change in her demeanor, how she moved her shoulder from his grip the moment she felt his touch. The look of disgust on her face spoke volumes as to their stepfather-stepdaughter relationship. She obviously wasn't very happy with him. "Well, it was nice meeting you, Jackson. We should be going now."

Shelby turned, then ran inside without another word.

"Women. I'll never figure them out."

Jackson agreed. *Women are complicated,* he thought. Only, Shelby wasn't a woman, so why was he referring to her as such? That itching crept up along the back of Jackson's neckline, irritating him.

"See you later, Jackson." Mr. Sobieski waved as he headed back toward the house.

Jackson stood there, scratching at the irritation until they were both inside. There was just something about her stepfather that wasn't quite right.

Mr. Sobieski took note of Jackson's lingering gaze as he closed the front door.

Chapter 21

Love or Lust

Meanwhile, Andre stood at the door of his father's room, leaning against the molding as he stared at Lydia resting in bed. It was the first time he had felt confused about his feelings for a woman. He'd never liked anyone the way he liked Lydia. After talking, they realized they had gone to school together. Although they'd never spoken in passing, they both attended the same high school before she dropped out and he converted to being homeschooled. His father touching her skin bothered him. *I don't want to share her with anyone*, he thought. *Maybe she could be all mine. I've never had a girl who was all mine before.* Andre never thought it was possible.

"Whatcha thinking about, handsome?" she inquired upon opening her eyes.

"Nothing. I was just—"

Lydia interrupted, "You were just watching me sleep. Did you think you would have to kiss me to wake me?"

"No," he blurted, embarrassed by the sentimental feelings he felt.

"Of course. What was I thinking? I'm all used up anyway. Not the kind of girl who gets a Prince Charming, right? I lost that innocence a long time ago."

"What are you talking about? Any guy would be lucky to have you as a girlfriend," he admitted, walking over to sit at the bedside. "But you obviously like older men."

"It's not that I like them. I just became accustomed to them at an early age." Her voice reeked of sadness. She began to recall the day her innocence had been taken, forcing the terrible memories of her sexual assault back into her subconscious.

"So, you're not in love with my dad?"

"Of course not. I'm not in love with anyone."

Andre lowered his head in disappointment. Not that he could really expect her to love him. They'd only known one another for two days. Lydia noticed his dismay.

"I like you a lot more than anyone I've ever met. That I can say." She saw her opportunity to make a home out of their place. Staying there with them kept her from having to pay for a roach motel. There she didn't have to worry about where her next meal was coming from. If only she could get rid of one in the group, making their trio a duet. It was the perfect opportunity. In that moment Lydia decided to weave a web of deceit. Whichever suitor remained would win her affections.

"Really?" he said, eyes beaming with hope as his head raised.

"Really." She smiled at him. "Come here. Let me show you how much."

"Not in my father's room." Andre stood up from the mattress, then headed out of the room.

Lydia followed, ready to fulfill his every desire. After all, unlike his father, Andre quite liked penetration.

Mrs. Teresa waited a few hours after Jackson had cleared the block before she emerged from her home to make her way across the street with the extra pie she had made. She was right when she surmised making extras would come in handy. A few cars waited to pass through as she took her time crossing the road.

"Come on. Really?" Mr. Sobieski complained from the driver's seat of one of the waiting vehicles. The old woman's lingering had caused his aggravation to spike. The moment her slippers touched the Trionfi's driveway, the impatient principal peeled off, tire tracks painting the cement.

Mrs. Trionfi ran back and forth from the kitchen to the living room, trying to make her irascible husband as comfortable as possible. She grabbed him an ice pack, covered his wounds with bandages, even propped his feet up on the sofa, attempting to ease the aching feeling his body was plagued with. "I thought I asked for a glass of ginger ale!" he demanded.

"Honey, I made you a cherry Coke," Mrs. Trionfi reasoned.

"I don't feel good. I want a ginger ale!"

"And how is ginger ale going to help?"

"Vernors cures everything. Now get me some ginger ale!"

Of course, everyone in Michigan thought that Vernors ginger ale was the cure to many ailments that threatened their health. The concept was absurd, yet widely held.

"Fine. I'll get your ginger ale."

The doorbell chimed. "Honey, I'll be right back. I have to answer the door."

"Tell them to go away. I don't want to see anyone," Mr. Trionfi griped.

She couldn't stand her husband's demanding ways, but she was a devout Catholic, which meant divorce wasn't in the cards for her. Mrs. Trionfi would unfortunately have to endure her husband's abuse for the remainder of his life. Which she at times hoped would be cut short by way of tragedy.

"Mrs. Teresa! Well, hello. What are you doing over here?"

"I came to bring you one of the homemade apple pies I made the other day." She handed over the pie while at the same time stealing peeks inside the residence. Mrs. Teresa could see Mr. Trionfi moving around to get situated on the sofa. "Is that the mister? I'd love to say hello."

"He's not feeling up to having company right now. I'm sorry, Mrs. Teresa."

Mrs. Teresa's brows wrinkled as if she were concerned about something other than the gossip she could gather. "Is it the bug that's going around?"

"He wishes," Mrs. Trionfi blurted before realizing she'd already said too much.

"Is he going to be okay? I saw the mailman helping him earlier. He didn't look too good."

"It's nothing he won't get over with lots of rest."

"Well, that's good to hear." Mrs. Teresa stood there staring inside, completely oblivious to the fact that she'd already overstayed her welcome.

Mrs. Trionfi wondered if she would catch on but hadn't the time to continue waiting. "I should go."

Still, Mrs. Teresa leered inside trying to see what she could.

"I'm going to close the door now, Mrs. Teresa. Have a great day." She slowly narrowed the gap the old woman used to peer inside.

"Enjoy the pie," Mrs. Teresa uttered as the door closed in her face.

Chapter 22

Fatal Attraction

"Why are these parcels all over the floor?" Deborah yelled out to whichever clerks were on duty at the time. She hadn't anyone in her sights in particular but was confident someone would hear her daily tirade. "You guys can't keep throwing the parcels on the floor like this. It's a safety hazard. I'm tired of having to tell you guys the same thing over and over again. You guys suck at your job. Elise! Where is that PSE, girl?"

"What are you over here yelling about now?" Evelyn inquired, emerging from behind the cover of a line of tall rolling metal containers that were used to transport packages.

"Why are all of these packages on the floor? Who threw them?"

"Oh, you must be mad. Are you actually gonna do something to the person responsible, or are you just gonna throw a hissy fit, then do nothing to back it up?" Evelyn patronized.

"That's it. Somebody's getting written up for this. Who's throwing parcels?"

"First of all, it's not the fault of the person throwing parcels. It's the carrier's fault. They have a cart that belongs right here in the spot for the parcels. When they roll their cart away, they should be bringing the bucket to replace it. Apparently, Mr. Handsome on Route 8 can't follow simple instructions, because lo and behold, we have not a cart nor a bucket here. Looks like golden boy needs a bit more training."

Jackson heard everything. A small crack between two of the city cases allowed him to peek through at the women, neither of them having any idea he was there. *The enraged carrier darted from behind the cases, headed straight for Evelyn. Her eyeballs bulged from their sockets as his hands wrapped firmly around her neck, threatening to strangle the life out of her.*

"What are you looking at?" Marcus asked, having been standing behind him nearly the entire time he had spied on the two women.

The inquiry ripped Jackson from his retaliation-riddled fantasy. He hadn't rushed at Evelyn at all. His hands were at his side, not wrapped around her throat. It was all just wishful thinking, a premature thought that had failed to manifest action.

"Nothing." Jackson turned to Marcus, believing he could hide the fact that he'd been leering at Evelyn and Deborah.

"She's a real bitch. Isn't she?" Marcus remarked.

"What?" Jackson inquired, quite baffled by the fact that he hadn't really attacked Evelyn.

"Deborah's a bitch. She wrote me up yesterday for being two clicks over, then accused me of trying to steal time. I can't wait until she chokes on a big, fat—"

"Who is that back there?" Deborah interrupted, demanding to know their identities.

"Time to face the music," Marcus remarked with a foreboding tone.

He and Jackson stepped from behind the cases, meeting Deborah and Evelyn in the center of the workroom floor.

"Marcus. I should've known it was you creeping around back there. Your lunch break is over. Shouldn't you be working the window at the store?"

"I came over to see Hilary."

"Well, Hilary isn't here, so it looks like you're going to have to come back on your next break."

Marcus stood there for a moment as if they were involved in some sort of faceoff, not wanting to jump at a woman's command. He hated being ordered around by women.

"What are you waiting on? Mosey on across the street and get to work." Deborah waved her hand flippantly.

His twitching lip was a sign of the embarrassment he felt. Choking the life out of her remained a thought more than an option. Marcus finally relented, turning from them to head back to his post.

"And make sure you circle the number at the bottom of every receipt," Deborah added, making him feel even further subordinate than she already had.

"Jackson," Deborah said, directing her glare at him. "We need to talk."

"Well, I'm off," Evelyn blurted before scurrying off toward the time clock.

"I need to see you in the conference room, Jackson." Deborah headed that way, expecting him to follow. Her assumptions were correct. Once Jackson stepped into the room, he closed the door behind him. She seemed to have an issue maintaining an appropriate volume when talking to the employees, which Jackson took note of, addressing it accordingly. A coworker hearing him being reprimanded and belittled would only further his festering rage.

"Have a seat, Jackson," she instructed, taking a seat herself at the opposite end of the long rectangular table. It was all that dressed the room: a table with several chairs stationed around it.

"First of all, how was your day today?"

Jackson appreciated the fact that she had started the conversation by inquiring as to how he faired. "Much more fulfilling than the day before," he admitted, recalling the beating he'd awarded Mr. Trionfi.

"Well, I'm glad it was fulfilling for you. Let me ask you another question. Do you feel that you require more training?"

Jackson felt slighted by the comment. He thought he had done a great job, considering he'd only had a day of training. "I don't know. Do you feel like I require more training?"

"I'll say this. Which I'm sure you've already been taught. When you pull your cart from the floor, you need to replace it with the bucket at your case with the big black number eight on it. Once you finish emptying your cart, you come back, take the bucket, then put your cart back where you got it from. Are we clear on this?"

"Crystal," he replied, forcing back the urge to be combative.

"The other thing I wanted to talk to you about today was a call I received from one of the residents on your route. Someone witnessed you backing out of a customer's driveway then across the street into another resident's driveway. Jackson, you are not the only one on the streets. Nor are you allowed to back up like that. Now, you've only been here for a few days, and you already have a backing violation in your file. That doesn't look good for you as a carrier. Maybe if you require a bit more training, you can come over after work today and we can go over the manual."

Deborah looked at Jackson as if she'd just fallen from the "I wanna suck your dick tree" and hit every branch on the way down.

Jackson wasn't in the least bit surprised it had come to that, but he resented the fact that he had to go to such lengths to secure his position. "How about tonight, eight o'clock?"

"A late-night cram session. Takes me back to my college days," Deborah replied.

"Yeah, I bet you crammed a lot."

Her eyebrows wrinkled a little. Deborah didn't know how to take the remark, yet she pretended it was a good thing for fear of him changing his mind. "Here's my address." Deborah scribbled her home address down on a piece of paper, then slid it across the table to Jackson. "I'll see you at eight o'clock."

Chapter 23

Ill Intentions

Mrs. Teresa shuffled around the kitchen, preparing the meal she and Jackson were to partake of that evening. Because she was aware of his intentions to eat healthy, she'd prepared blackened salmon atop a bed of mixed greens with cranberries and pecans. The lemon-poppyseed dressing that would be drizzled on top was an old family recipe. She wanted to show her appreciation somehow. The fact that he was coming over to fix the window without her asking or even paying for it was a gesture far beyond any kindness she had ever experienced. And though she appreciated it, like I said before, Mrs. Teresa couldn't forget what she'd seen earlier that day. That evening she'd furnish him with a good meal, hoping in return to be privy to an enlightening conversation.

Finally, the doorbell chimed. Her guest had arrived. Jackson had the replacement glass along with the other tools needed to repair her broken window in tow. Knowing it would take her more than a minute or two to make it there, Jackson waited patiently on the front porch. The sound of her cane banging against the wood floor echoed through the hall, making it audible even from the opposite side of the front door. She thought about changing into something other than her housecoat and slippers but decided against it, figuring dinner was effort enough.

"Come on in, soldier," the old woman said, greeting him upon opening the front door.

"Hello again, Mrs. Teresa," Jackson replied, stepping into the foyer. "Something sure does smell delightful."

"That's our dinner. Of course, I'm gonna put you to work first. It'll give the salmon enough time to finish baking."

"I love salmon. I haven't had a good fillet in months."

"Well, you're in luck. I'll let you head on upstairs while I prepare our feast."

"Sounds good to me." Jackson headed up the creaking wooden stairs to complete his task.

The bathroom door slammed as did the front when Sue's new boyfriend, Buddy, tore into her two-bedroom apartment. Mya sat cross-legged on the green shag carpet in front of the television, watching a marathon of *Teletubbies* episodes. She paid no mind to the banging that was inaudible to her. Sue made sure she kept headphones over her daughter's ears, so that company wouldn't have to endure cartoons. More importantly, so that Mya couldn't hear the comings and goings, assuming she'd tell her grandmother or, worse, Jackson.

Sue rushed over to the bathroom door. At first, she knocked lightly, but after receiving no response she finally spoke. "Buddy, is everything okay?"

"It's fine, Sue," he answered with angst in his tone.

"Can I come in then?"

The door opened a little, giving her the go-ahead. When Sue pushed the rest of the way through, Buddy leaned over with his hands pressed to the porcelain bowl on the sink as he stared at his reflection in the mirror.

"Is there anything I can do?" she asked, rubbing her hands down the center of his back.

"I've already told you what we need to do. Are you ready now, or are you still too chickenshit to go for it?"

"I just don't think that's morally right. What about Mya? I still have to consider her needs. She needs her father."

"Needs him? He's not even here! He doesn't even take care of her. I've given you more money in the short time we've been together than he has since he abandoned his role as Mya's father. You need to make a decision, because I don't think I can do this anymore if you're not about making things right."

"Funny what you call right," she mumbled.

His threatening glare shot in her direction through the medicine cabinet mirror. "What did you say? Speak up. Let me hear your brilliant rebuttal for staying in the poorhouse."

"Just let me think about it, okay? I just need a little time."

"Of course. Time. A luxury we assume we have."

"I'll give you an answer in a couple of days. Let me do some digging. I'll find some things out, and then we'll go from there."

"Promise."

"Cross my heart," she replied, wrapping her arms around his waist to lay her head against his back.

It had taken him about a half hour to repair the broken window. Jackson came back down the stairs carrying a large, thick brown paper bag containing the broken glass.

Mrs. Teresa didn't hear him coming up the hallway. Nor had she noticed him watching her as she prepared their plates, doling out a few garlic and herb red-skinned potatoes to each.

Jackson eventually spoke, "You're all set, Mrs. Teresa. The window is as good as new."

"I certainly appreciate you, soldier. I hope the dinner I've prepared is to your liking."

"I'm sure it will be. I just need to toss out this broken glass and wash my hands."

"You can toss the bag inside the garbage can out back."

Jackson headed through the kitchen to exit from the side door. The bottle of bourbon sitting on the countertop caught his eye, and he figured it would be the end to their evening.

Mrs. Teresa placed their plates on the table in the dining room, his at the head, then hers in the first place on its left side. It was a much more formal setting than the kitchen. The only place she kept free of dust. The beautiful cherry-oak china cabinet against the wall housed a plethora of porcelain cups, plates, bowls, saucers, even tea kettles. There was barely any room inside for another item to be added to the collection. Its wood matched the extended dining room table, set with placemats for at least eight others.

"What would you like to drink, soldier? How about some raspberry tea? I brewed it this morning," she inquired as Jackson crossed over the threshold between the kitchen and dining room.

"Iced tea? Sounds good to me. Do you need my help with anything?"

"Oh, no, you've certainly done enough. Have a seat and relax. It's suppertime." Mrs. Teresa pushed the dinner cart out with her as she headed back toward the kitchen, then stopped suddenly at the door. "You did wash your hands?" she asked with her back still turned to him.

"Yes, ma'am. I'm ready to get them dirty again."

"Well, I do have napkins for that." She continued on her way to grab the glass pitcher of raspberry tea from the refrigerator.

Everything sat atop the plate so beautifully. "This all looks so delicious, Mrs. Teresa," he called out to her. Noticing the water stains on his glass, he switched it with hers without a second thought. Switching it with one of the other glasses on the table would have been more appropriate, but he didn't care as much.

"Here we go." She entered, the cane supporting her with one hand as the other carried the pitcher of raspberry tea.

"I'll take that." Jackson sprang up from his seat, taking the pitcher off her hands, then adding a full serving of tea to their glasses.

The old woman took her seat. "So, Jackson, tell me. How have you been enjoying your new job?" Mrs. Teresa sipped her tea, having worked up a sweat slaving over the hot stove.

"I like it. It's much different than the strict regimen I followed in the Marines. Management has a weird way of enforcing their rules. I will say that."

"Do you get many tips for helping out the neighbors?" She sipped a bit more tea as she attempted to gather more information from Jackson.

"This meal here serves as my first tip. But, of course, I don't do good deeds for the tips."

"Still, I'm sure it certainly helps. I noticed you helping Mr. Trionfi the other day. I doubt if he'll give you anything in return."

What exactly could she have seen? Jackson worried. "I wouldn't exactly say I was helping him."

"Would you say you were doing Mrs. Escobar a solid? I saw her gawking at the two of you from her front room window." As soon as Mrs. Teresa had uttered her reply, she began to wonder why she had. *What the hell is wrong with me? He's never going to tell me anything now.* She drank from her tea again.

"Must be pretty strong," Jackson remarked.

"What's that, soldier?" Mrs. Teresa replied, blinking lethargically.

"Whatever it was you lined my glass with."

"What are you . . . Why would you say . . ." She couldn't form the words to make a viable reply, so Jackson continued.

"I thought they were water spots, so I switched the glasses out. You've been sipping on that tea since you sat down, and since then you've become extremely relaxed. Your pupils are dilated. The muscles in your face are now making more of an effort to droop, excusing what effects age has already imposed."

"What an asshole move. You could have switched it with one of the other eight glasses on the table."

"No, Mrs. Teresa. The asshole move was trying to drug me. What are you trying to find out, and why? You want to know what I was doing with your neighbors, don't you? You want something on everybody. What are you trying to hide? People only point out the flaws of others when trying to mask their own. Tell me, Mrs. Teresa." He switched their plates before taking a bite of salmon off his fork. "What really happened to Mr. Teresa?"

Her eyes widened with fear. She didn't want to expose her deepest secret, yet the part of her in control apparently had a great desire to unleash. "Boy, did that man beat me. Sometimes within an inch of my life. I doted on him. Gave him everything he wanted, even kids against my better judgment. Still, it wasn't enough to tame the violent drunk inside of him. I was willing to take it for the sake of the children. And I did. That is, until I found out he had been cheating on me our entire marriage. He had some black broad." Mrs. Teresa's hand shot up to cover her lips. "Oops, I'm sorry. I didn't mean it like that."

"No offense taken," Jackson admitted. He recalled calling his wife an Asian bitch after catching her in the act. Anger could sometimes make you say terrible things.

"I'm no racist. It's just . . . I mean, the huzzy was sleeping with my husband for decades behind my back. So, one day I came home, drugged him with the same stuff I tried to give you, and made him tell me the entire dirty truth of it. He slept like a baby that night and didn't remember a thing the next morning. A few weeks later, I killed him. I couldn't stand looking at his ugly face anymore. There, I said it. The truth is out. Now what are you going to do?"

"I'm not going to do a thing, Mrs. Teresa. You did what you had to do. But no more trying to slip thiopental in my drink, agreed?"

"How about your food?" She was lethargic, yet able to ease out a subtle bit of humor.

"Don't slip it to me at all. Keep it to yourself," Jackson replied. "By the way, dinner is delicious. You should try some. You're already drugged now, so it doesn't matter."

"I guess you're right." Mrs. Teresa stared fixedly at her plate of food.

Two hours later, the doorbell chimed, springing Deborah into swifter action. She placed the cheese tray and bottle of gin on the stone coffee table in front of the sofa. The rural carrier manual to the left was just for extra effect. "I'm coming. Just a moment!" She rushed by the mirror, then came back, taking a gander at her reflection. Her hair was curly, makeup fresh, and outfit relaxed. Deborah made sure her crimson-colored bra could be seen through the white deep V-neck T-shirt she was wearing. Her shorts lacked length. They were much shorter than that of a woman her age would normally wear. The bell chimed again.

"Geez, somebody's impatient," she remarked on her way to the foyer from the living room.

"It's about time," Jackson said as he traipsed into her home upon Deborah opening the front door.

"Wow. Someone is definitely off of work," she remarked as to his rough-hewn greeting. His usual polished approach seemed nonexistent that night. Anyway, she ignored the slight in his nature, hoping it wouldn't become a big deal. "Please have a seat inside the living room. Would you like a drink?"

"I'm not sure if I should mix white with dark," he replied, taking into consideration the bottle of gin on the table.

"Just a little shouldn't hurt." Deborah hoped to get Jackson drunk enough for a good romp in the hay. "I'll pour you a shot. It should loosen us up."

He watched her pour the shot, secretly wanting another drink to further lower his inhibitions. "Let us have a shot then. How about lemon? Do you have any?"

"Yes, let me get some for you." Deborah rushed off toward the kitchen to fetch the lemon for their drinks, while Jackson made himself comfortable on the black leather sofa.

She opened the refrigerator, grabbing the bowl of sliced lemon she had with her tequila shots the past weekend. "Here they are," she said excitedly as she came back from the kitchen.

"Thank you." He accepted the bowl, taking one for himself before placing the bowl on the coffee table. Jackson passed a shot glass over to Deborah as she sat down on the sofa with her knee touching his. "Down the hatch." Jackson tossed his head back and the drink down his throat in one motion.

Deborah followed suit, eager to get the party started.

"Do you drink much, Deborah?" Jackson asked.

Deborah thought it was an awkward question. "I drink just as much as everyone else. I mean, I don't allow it to affect my job, unlike some people we know." A jab directed at Randy, of course. She sighed afterward, for some reason feeling sorry for him.

"So, we're here to teach me the rules, right?" Jackson grabbed the manual as Deborah poured herself yet another shot. "What should we go over first, Deborah?"

She downed the shot, then sat back on the sofa. "I don't know. What do you think I should teach you?"

"I don't really know if you could teach me much of anything," Jackson admitted.

Her face drooped, donning a clueless expression. "I think I can teach you a lot more than you think." Deborah was the resilient type, used to thinking on her feet. Being turned down so often in life, she wasn't accustomed to giving up easily.

Jackson popped his neck to the side, relieving emerging tension. "Your thinking is actually the problem. It's what has caused you to take more than you've had to in relationships. It's why you can't find a good man. You don't really feel that you deserve a good man, so you sleep around, further blemishing the way you view yourself. Pleasing men at the expense of your dignity isn't going to make you more attractive. It just tells the users that you're an easy target. They'll use you up until there's nothing left. You'll find yourself giving your body to a multitude of men who care nothing for you. It's made you hate yourself, hasn't it? It's like, why live if no one loves you? How many times have you thought about taking your own life, Deborah?" Jackson poured her yet another shot, which she took, swallowing it with haste.

"How did you know?" she replied, eyes filled with tears of sorrow.

"It's written all over your face. It's in your body language and the way you choose to deal with others. You're absolutely miserable. Everyone can see it. It's gotten to a point where the drinking and pills don't help. Sometimes it's better to just go to sleep and forget it all."

"I wish I could go to sleep and forget it all," she admitted.

Jackson grabbed the notepad and pen next to the cordless phone off the side table near the couch. "Tell them how you feel. Make them feel what it would be like if you were gone," Jackson coaxed as he handed the pad and pen over to her.

"Who do I write it to?"

"Everyone," Jackson responded with a wild-eyed, piercing stare.

Tears streamed from her dilated eyes as she poured her heart out on paper, having no idea that she was writing her own suicide note. He'd slipped her the very same drug Mrs. Teresa had attempted to drug him with. Jackson wouldn't be trading his affections for the upper hand at work. Deborah had made a grave mistake in thinking she could manipulate Jackson Pierce. It would be her last day as rural carrier supervisor at Clarkston Post Office. That night, she'd overdose on one of the many bottles of pills in her medicine cabinet.

Chapter 24

Justified

The crisp night air felt refreshing as it blew in through his open driver's side window. The maleficent carrier felt exhilarated having prompted Deborah's unfortunate demise. Jackson was at the top of his game, sure never to fall victim to another scheming woman. "'Ding-dong, the witch is dead!'" he proclaimed, patting his hands atop the steering wheel to the beat of the music that only played in his head. That was, until his cellular phone rang. Jackson looked down at the phone buzzing as it lay atop the center console. His foot eased up off the accelerator upon seeing the number on the caller identification. It read: lying bitch. Apparently, his estranged wife Sue had something to say, a concept that sent chills down his spine. The top corner of his mouth began to twitch as that itching crept up along the back of his neck. Jackson didn't know whether it was fear or anger that caused nervousness to begin simmering in his belly. He hadn't spoken with her since he'd left Jacksonville, North Carolina, and even then, he didn't want to hear anything she had to say. Of course, there was the possibility that it was Mya, although at that late hour she should've been in bed. Normally his daughter would call from his ex-mother-in-law's phone when she was visiting with her grandmother. Regardless, he felt forced to answer.

"This is Jackson," he said upon answering the call.

"I'm surprised you answered," Sue replied lethargically.

"What do you want from me? Haven't you done enough damage?"

"Jackson, we need money. How do you expect me to take care of our daughter alone?"

"I'm sure your mother told you I got a job at the post office. I managed to get a permanent spot, so I'll have insurance for Mya soon. When I get my first check, I'll send you some money. I'm not trying to shirk my responsibilities. So don't call me acting like I'm some sort of deadbeat dad. I'd be there if it weren't for you and your slutty ways."

"We need money now. I can't take care of Mya with promises. Promises aren't going to feed or clothe her. That's your responsibility as her father."

"And your responsibility as a wife was for you to keep your legs closed, bitch!"

"It just happened. I never meant to hurt you. I never meant to hurt Mya. Look, Jackson, I know you never meant to hurt me. You did what you felt was right at the time."

"You never meant to hurt me?" Jackson could tell by the slow, drawn-out pronunciation of her words that she was well into a bottle of her favorite toxic pleasure, tequila. "And what do you mean I never meant to hurt you? When exactly did I hurt you? I was nothing but a good husband to you. Let me guess, you must be drunk and drowning in your sorrows. Now you want to apologize, talk about it, right? Let's talk about the fact that I'm off fighting for our country while you complain about me being gone, yet you sleep with another marine! I don't want to hear your excuses. You're nothing but a trick!" The truck careened across the road, impeding oncoming traffic. Jackson jerked the wheel to the right, avoiding collision, yet he continued to spit the venom he'd held in for months. "A cheap whore who will do anything for a buck. How much did he pay you? Or did you suck his dick for free? I swear I hate you with every fiber of my being." His eyes welled up with tears. "Do you hear me? I fucking hate you!" He screamed into the phone not realizing she'd hung up at "cheap whore." He took the phone from his ear, yelling directly into the microphone, "I hope you fucking die!"

Out of nowhere, something crashed into his bumper. Whatever it was that Jackson hit, he'd rolled over it with his front and back tires. The phone flew from his grasp. "What the fuck was that? Great. Just fucking perfect. Now look what you've done. I swear this bitch is like a plague on my life!" He pulled over to the side of the road, then looked around for what it was he had rolled over. The black purse on the grass along the side of the road left a sick feeling in the pit of his stomach. His eyes bulged as he leered left, right, then all around him until he was turning in circles. That was when he finally saw her dragging her wounded body across the asphalt. It was the girl with the long brown hair. The same one who'd vowed never to prostitute herself again. Yet, there she was, walking the streets that night. Jackson ran back toward her. "I didn't see you. I'm so sorry."

Jessica coughed, spitting up blood that shot out onto the dewy grass. Her arms and legs were bruised, stockings tattered. Blood ran down from a deep wound in her forehead. "Help me, please," the woman pleaded, barely able to force out her words.

"I'll be right back," Jackson responded before tearing off back toward his car. He grabbed her purse up from the ground, jumped into the driver's seat, shifted the car into reverse, then sped backward to reach her. Jackson surveyed the scene as he hopped out of his vehicle. *Where is everyone?* he wondered. The streets were empty with the exception of the two of them. Jackson opened the back passenger door, then picked the feeble woman up from the grass still coughing and moaning from the pain she felt. The blood spatters left her mouth, landing on his face. At the point the blood contaminated his person, he wanted to drop her to the ground, but he thought it was the least he could endure having been the cause of her misfortune.

He gently laid her body on the back seat. "Just hang in there. I'm gonna get you some help." After closing the door, Jackson pulled the bottom of his black V-neck T-shirt up over his face, using it to wipe off her blood. *Where am I going to take her?* he worried. *What am I going to do? I'm going to lose my job. I can't lose my job right now,* he told himself. Beads of sweat ran down his forehead, drenching his face as Jackson hopped into the driver's seat, intent on weaving a master plan.

Having driven not too far, he let down his window, pressing the button on the driver-side door. "Don't die on me. I'm gonna get you some help," Jackson promised, knowing all too well he was feeding her lies. His intention was to keep her mind at ease as she succumbed to her injuries. Jessica's body had hit the grill of the Bronco yet left no visible damage besides the blood left splayed across the front of the vehicle, a dilemma Jackson would quickly remedy with a $5 wash.

The lights from the gas station car wash clued her in on his abysmal intention as they pulled inside. "What are you doing? I need help. Take me to the hospital, please," she feebly mumbled. Jessica attempted to beg for her life. "I'm not gonna make it. Please."

"Shhhh." Jackson adjusted the rearview mirror to see her lying there. "You're going to make it worse. Just relax and let nature take its course."

Her eyes widened as the space between her brows wrinkled. "You're just gonna let me die? What did I ever do to you?" Jessica struggled to get the words out, coughing then wincing from the pain she felt.

His stare was cold, devoid of any emotion. "You didn't do anything. I'm sorry, it's just your time. Now, I've come to terms with it. It's time for you to as well." Jackson shifted the mirror back in its previous positioning, then pulled out of the car wash, the vehicle looking as clean as the day he'd purchased it. All there was left to do at that point was to find a place to hide the dying woman in his back seat. Jackson pulled out of the gas station entrance, his eyes toggling left then right as he gnawed at the loose skin on his lips.

***

A news program on the television was muted. Jackson sat on his couch, his torso bare, staring at the subtitles that came across the screen. By the looks of it, you would think he was paying attention, yet the recent murder he had committed took precedence. Sweat drenched his face. The fingertips on his right hand tapped on the leather sofa cushion one after the other. Blood from Jessica's tattered body stained his hands. Jackson scratched at the back of his neck. He chewed at the loose skin on his lips, trying to think. What would he do? What would be his plan? He hopped up from the sofa, darting off to the bathroom. Jackson grabbed the bar of soap from the sink, using it to scrub some of the blood free from his hands. The water he splashed up onto his face, over his bald head, then down onto the back of his neck as he leaned over the bowl did nothing to wash his sins away. Staring into the mirror at his bloodshot eyes, he saw his life crashing down around him. Jackson couldn't let that happen. He pulled back the shower curtain, revealing the bloody corpse that lay in his tub. Jessica's bloody corpse.

Chapter 25

Stalking Prey

0330 hours. "Honey! I made you a cup of coffee!" Just as Erick twisted the cap down on the thermos, Evelyn crept up behind him. She ran her hand up then down his back again before wrapping her arms around his abdomen. The embrace was one they shared every morning. Evelyn loved her doting husband as did he love her in return. He turned to her, his hazel eyes boring into her soul. She pushed his long blond hair back behind his ears as he leaned in to taste her lips. Evelyn rubbed her hands down the sides of his face, tugging on his beard a little as she planted three tender kisses upon his. As her tongue moved down his neck, her right hand moved to his genitals, fondling him outside of his boxer briefs.

"Oh, you want more, huh?" His eyes lit up with excitement.

She glanced over at the time displayed on the stove. It was already 3:33 a.m. Evelyn was scheduled to clock in at 0400 hours. Opening before the first of several mail trucks would be pulling in to unload the mail was her first duty every morning.

"How about we postpone this until I get home?"

"Then I want you naked as soon as you come in the door, 'cause daddy's gonna take you to pound town."

Evelyn blushed, giggling at her husband's admission. After over a decade of marriage, he still had the ability to make her burn with intense desire to the point of bashfulness.

"You know I have to take my nap before I run errands and the kids get out of school."

"It's okay. Daddy's gonna put you to sleep and take care of dinner."

"Ohh, daddy. I like that." Evelyn smooched the side of his neck.

"You sure you don't want me to bend you over right now?" he reasoned.

"All right. All right. Let me stop before I'm late for work." Evelyn backed off.

Erick reached over, grabbing the thermos off the black granite countertop. "Here. Don't forget your coffee." He handed the container over to her.

"Thank you, baby."

"You're welcome, my love." He followed his wife through the mudroom, then out into the garage

where her SUV was parked next to his Harley.
Erick opened the driver's side door so that his wife
could climb into her black 2001 Yukon Denali.
"Lock it," he demanded after shutting her door.

Evelyn pressed the lock, then gave her husband
a thumbs-up. "I'll call you on my lunch break," she
yelled through the raised window as she pushed
the button atop her sun visor to lift the garage door.

Evelyn turned on the radio, switching it to a
compact disc she'd previously loaded. A compila-
tion of classical music would be her music choice
for the ride there, as it was on many occasions.
The ride to work was a time to clear her mind of
confusion before she would have to worry about
work, before kids, T-ball practice, gymnastics,
chores, and a multitude of other priorities would
take precedence. It was dark along the two-lane
highway she traveled for twenty miles to make it
to Clarkston Post Office. The area was rural where
she lived, abundant in corn fields, cow pastures,
and moreover, acres of land yet inhabited by
humans. Evelyn held her breath as she passed
by the pet cemetery on the left. She paused her
breathing not because of it, but because of the
town's cemetery directly across the street. She was
superstitious like that, believing that if you didn't
hold your breath when passing by a graveyard, an
evil spirit or someone who'd recently passed on
would have the opportunity to inhabit your body.

No matter how absurd the notion, no one could convince Evelyn otherwise.

She glanced over at the time displayed on the dashboard. It was 3:45 a.m., with only about seven minutes remaining to travel before she would reach her destination. Evelyn appreciated her job and took her duties seriously, so getting there on time was of great importance. The road to work was an easy one. She would only ever see a few cars traveling during those wee hours of the morning, which made it much more pleasant than the lunch hour rush she'd maneuver through on the way home. After she crossed over Interstate 75, Evelyn relaxed, the post office being only a couple of miles up the road. She turned up the volume on the radio. Beethoven's "Moonlight Sonata," one of her favorites, blared from the speakers.

The headlamps of her Yukon illuminated the chained fences as Evelyn pulled into the parking lot at Clarkston Post Office. Required to stop there, she shifted the gear into park, let her car window all the way down, then hopped out to unlatch the chains. Beyond the gate she'd have to travel the lot, mail trucks lining both sides, until making it to the employee parking in the back. The American flag strung to the pole overhead flapped in a gentle breeze pushing from the east. She pulled at the string tied to the belt loop of her shorts, which had her keys attached at the other end. Evelyn kept the building's keys strapped to a belt loop to avoid losing them. She often worried that they would one day slip from her grasp, then through the metal spaces of a sewer drain. Paranoia, much of the time unwarranted, pushed her to take extra precautions. After getting it unlocked, Evelyn leaned in to one side of the metal gate, sliding it back as far as it could go, then turned, doing the same to the other.

When she turned back to her vehicle, her eyes squinted initially, sharpening the view of the masked assailant in all black running full speed in her direction. Evelyn's eyes bulged with a mixture of shock yet, at the same time, disbelief of what was taking place. The frightened woman hurried to get into the driver's seat of her car, realizing by the time she'd be able to get in and drive off, her assailant would have already had her in their grasp. Acting fast, she opened the car door just as the assailant rushed upon her. Using it as a divide between them gave Evelyn the time she needed to dart off in between the mail trucks.

"Oh, my God. Oh, my God," she uttered repeatedly in a voice that was barely audible. The last thing she wanted to do was tip off her attacker as to her whereabouts. *I can't believe this is happening to me. What the fuck am I going to do?* Evelyn didn't notice the assailant wielding a weapon when they'd rushed toward her. Maybe they were just

trying to scare her, she hoped. Evelyn told herself
to calm down. *It's only a person who bleeds just
like me.* The beaming headlights allowed her to see
the assailant's shadow moving across the asphalt
as they approached. Evelyn climbed under one
of the LLVs, lying flat on the pavement. Her eyes
leered at their feet as they were about to pass by.
The black combat boots stopped right in front of
her. But then out of nowhere, the assailant quickly
turned, rushing back toward her vehicle. They
hopped into the driver's seat, shifted the gear into
drive, then sped back deeper into the parking lot.

Evelyn scooched across the pavement until
she was able to stand. She ducked and weaved,
crossing through the trucks, using them for cover
as she tried to pinpoint her attacker's location. The
frightened clerk thought about running out into
the open, but the possibility of them being faster
than her was probable. She looked down at her
wristwatch. It was 3:58 a.m. *All I have to do is wait
a couple more minutes. The semi carrying today's
mail will be pulling up soon.* She clung tight to
hope.

Suddenly, a gloved hand reached out of the
darkness, gaining a strong grip on the back of her
neck, while the other pinched down on the pressure joint between her neck and shoulder, bringing
her to her knees. "Ahhhh! Get the fuck off me,"
Evelyn screamed, forcing her body forward to the

ground before quickly rolling onto her back. The swift kick she delivered her assailant to the groin took his breath away, and at the same time clued her in as to the gender of her attacker. The heel of her shoe cracked against his scrotum not once, but two more times before she crawled backward, then hopped up to run out into the open while he attempted to catch his breath.

The truck driver who pulled into the lot neglected seeing her yet felt the bump when Evelyn's body slammed against the grill of the semi.

"Oh, my God," the driver blurted as he slammed hard on the brakes. By the time he jumped down out of the cab, her assailant had already crept back off into the darkness to nurse his wounds.

Within five minutes of the call, police and paramedics were on the scene. Two paramedics loaded the unconscious woman into the back of the ambulance. Colin, the more experienced of the two, rode in back with Evelyn. Blood streamed from an open wound atop her forehead, painting her face crimson. Colin soaked it up with gauze as it seeped down into the sockets of her eyes. Evelyn's lids sprang open once she'd gotten a whiff of the inhalant he'd waved under her nose, and she woke in a fit of panic as if still battling her attacker. She slapped, scratched, even clawed at Colin, attempting to fight him off.

"Whoa. Whoa. Whoa. Calm down."

Her arm badge flew off onto the floor amid the commotion.

"Please, calm down. I'm not going to hurt you. I promise," he assured her. Colin could tell she was frightened and, moreover, confused.

Unable to keep up the fight, Evelyn gave up, falling from consciousness.

Ten minutes later, the gurney carrying her body burst through the double doors of the emergency room. "Try to stay with me, ma'am. Please, stay with me," the paramedic encouraged, trying to keep Evelyn awake. She had been slipping out then back into consciousness since they waved the ammonia inhalant under her nostrils during the ambulance ride there. "You're gonna be okay."

"Don't . . . don't leave me," she whispered, staring into his big deep brown eyes.

"I'm right here. Everything is going to be okay," Colin reassured the dazed mail clerk before she fainted yet again.

"We'll take it from here," the doctor called out as he took control at the head of the gurney, allowing the rest of his team to move in along its sides. "We've got an injury to the frontal lobe. Patient has been suffering multiple bouts of syncope."

Colin watched as the gurney plowed through a second set of double doors before they disappeared from view completely.

When he got back to the ambulance, he noticed Evelyn's postal badge on the floor of the vehicle just as he moved to close the back doors. He picked it up, tapping it on the palm of his hand, contemplating his next move. *I should take this back inside to her.* He mulled over the thought. *I wouldn't mind checking on her later, though. It's not as if she'll need it for work tomorrow,* Colin reminded himself. *I'll bring it to her in a couple of days.* He made up his mind, shutting the ambulance doors, ready to end his shift for the day.

Chapter 26

Masking the Truth

At 0750 hours, Jackson trekked up the walkway behind the running LLVs. The smoke escaping their tail pipes clouded his way. He glanced over at Evelyn's blood staining the asphalt of the parking lot. The twisted grin that had slowly emerged fleeted as Jackson neared the group of rural carriers huddled by the double doors at the annex's entrance. Although taking both Evelyn and Deborah out in one night had lightened his lugubrious mood, he'd rather not engage in conversation with any of his coworkers. He avoided the crowd of onlookers near the double doors, continuing on his way inside.

Hilary was busy rushing around the office, attempting to manage the clerks and carriers single-handedly. "Where is Deborah? She never misses work," the postmaster complained to herself as she rushed over to Elise. Hilary hated asking the clerks for help, which most of the time was necessary. It was nearly impossible to do anything without their assistance. "Elise, can you answer the phone if it rings? I need to go to my office."

"Sure, I'll answer the phone, and one of the other clerks can answer the door. Which means that's two less clerks on parcels. I hope you guys take that into consideration while you're pushing us to make good mail early."

"Thank you, Elise. I'll take that into consideration." Hilary rolled her eyes as she rushed off toward her office in the corner of the building.

Once Hilary was inside, she slammed the door behind her. "This is ridiculous. Where the hell is she?" The big blue binder on her desk listed the phone number of every employee. She flipped through it to find Deborah's home number. "There it is." She pointed it out, pressed the speaker button on the phone's base, then proceeded to dial the number.

Of course, it rang repeatedly with no answer. That was when Hilary really began to worry. Evelyn had already been attacked. What if Deborah was attacked, as well? The next call she made was to the Oakland County Sheriff's Office.

Officer Edward Barnes, a middle-aged fellow resembling a young Barry White with a voice just as deep, cruised the streets of Clarkston. He was already on Deborah's side of town when the call came in. "I need a 10-42 at 1313 White Lake Road. The employers called in a welfare check for a forty-five-year-old white female by the name of Deborah Koch." Detective Barnes was familiar with the name. She had hit on him on more than a few occasions while standing in line at the coffee shop in town.

Officer Barnes answered the call. "This is Officer Barnes. I'll handle the welfare check. 10-4."

"Roger that, Officer Barnes. Let us know what you find. 10-4."

"Copy that," he replied.

It wasn't long before the officer was knocking at Deborah's door. After knocking three times with no answer, he began pacing the long, wooden porch, peeking into every window he could where the curtains permitted views to the inside. Lo and behold, there she was, sprawled out on the sofa in the living room.

"Ms. Koch! Ma'am! Wake up! It's the police!" he hollered through the double-pane window, hoping to wake Deborah. A few more knocks followed, this time on the window. Deborah didn't move a muscle. It was at that point that Officer Barnes began to examine the scene laid out before him.

Her arm was hanging off the sofa. A notepad sat on the table in front of her next to the 750-milliliter bottle of gin. The pill bottle between her legs was missing the cap. It became apparent to him that he was looking at the scene of a suicide. Officer Barnes rushed to the front door, lifted his foot, then launched it forward, cracking the heel of his boot against it. The wooden door flew open, pieces of the lock flying off onto the floor, along with the glass from the square window at its center. "Ma'am!" he called out once more as he approached, hoping she would wake. But it was to no avail. The pill bottle on her lap was empty. He touched his hand to her wrist to check her pulse, feeling nothing. Her suicide note that sat atop the table said what she'd been holding inside for years.

What a shame, he thought, gazing down at her lifeless corpse.

Sue kicked at the gravel under her Chuck Taylors as she sat at the park on the swings, taking drags from her menthol cigarette. Through the smoke, her gaze focused on Mya playing in the sandbox, but her mind was elsewhere. Plagued with making a decision, she'd neglected to realize what was actually taking place.

Mya grabbed up fistfuls of sand, tossing them into the air only for the grains to come back down into her hair. It wasn't until she'd begun to cry that her mother finally drifted into the present.

"It hurts my eye, Mommy! It hurts my eye!"

Sue hopped up from the swing, flicking her cigarette into the grass nearby. "Mya! Oh, my God. Mommy's coming, baby!" She dropped to her knees at her daughter's side. "Did you get sand in your eye?" she doted on her whining daughter.

"The sand hurts, Mommy," Mya cried.

Sue took the pink book bag off her back to search through it. She pulled a small bottle of Visine out of her bag. "Hold your head back, baby." She spread one of the little girl's eyes open with her thumb and forefinger, yet when she pinched the sides of the bottle, nothing came out. She tossed the empty bottle back inside, then reached in again, grabbing a bottled water in its place. It too was empty. What bothered Sue even more was the fact that she didn't have enough money to buy more. The frustrated mother yanked at the zipper to close her backpack after stuffing the empty plastic bottle inside, then wrapped the straps over her shoulders. "Come on, baby. Mama's got you." Sue lifted Mya's tiny frame from the ground, letting her rest on her hip as she jogged to the closest restroom. "Mommy will get it out, baby."

She rushed inside the outdoor restroom, then over to the sink. When she turned on the faucet, water shot out like a fire hydrant, splashing up on her shirt from the bowl. "Fuck!" She turned the nozzle back to lessen the flow. "Mama's so sorry.

Come on, baby. Let's wash your face and get that sand out." She leaned Mya over the bowl to rinse her eyes with handfuls of water while she stared at her reflection in the dirty mirror, thinking, *how did my life end up such a train wreck?* She felt as if the weight of the world were on her shoulders. Sue had grown tired of struggling and, moreover, going without when there was another perfectly capable parent available to assist.

Marcus was busy making copies in the office across from Hilary's when the call came through.

"Clarkston Post Office, this is Hilary," the postmaster announced upon picking up the receiver.

Although Marcus couldn't hear the person on the other end, he could hear Hilary's words plainly.

"Dead. Are you sure? Oh, my God!" She sprang up from her seat behind the desk, shutting her office door so that no one else could interrupt.

Marcus had a sneaking suspicion that the dead person she spoke of was indeed their supervisor, Deborah. Needless to say, he managed to hold back tears of sorrow. The wheels in his brain began to turn. Who had he seen speaking with them last? It was Jackson who was angry at them both. He had watched him spying on the two of them from behind the cases. Marcus stepped out of the copy room onto the workroom floor. Three of the clerks were busy casing magazines and letters, while the others passed parcels around the office with them breaking off every so often to answer the door and ringing telephone. The carriers were busy casing mail at their route stations. Now Marcus knew it was his duty to join the others so that he assisted in the efforts to get good mail, yet he couldn't force back the urge to speak to Jackson.

Jackson had made it safely to his case without having to converse with any of his coworkers. The chatter about what happened to Evelyn swirled around the office among the employees as they worked diligently.

Pat stood just outside of her case next to Tanya's, the two of them making their thoughts about the situation heard. Pat stood with her hands covering her gaped mouth. "I can't believe this happened to her. I feel so bad. She is a good person. I just hate that there's so many bad people out here in the world. Poor girl." She shook her head in despair.

"Girl, you'd better be careful out here. These folks is crazy. I told you. I told you," Tanya remarked.

"You did," Pat professed with worried eyes.

"Get you some pepper spray for these fools," she added.

"I thought the truck driver hit her," Marcus chimed in, interrupting their conversation.

"She told the truck driver that someone was chasing her before she passed out."

"She had to have been terrified," Marcus replied, not really caring at all that she had been through the ordeal.

"I would have sprayed him, then kicked him in the balls," Tanya replied before stepping into her case to sort mail.

"Marcus, you are a big, strong man. You'll protect us, right?" Pat asked.

Marcus simply went on his way without a reply, grinning, as he was undoubtedly flattered by her comment.

"Oh, Marcus, don't be so shy," Pat urged as she lifted the tub of magazines from the floor to start casing.

Marcus had other things to attend to, picking Jackson's brain being at the top of his list.

He walked up to the workstation with RURAL ROUTE 8 posted at the top, giving Jackson no room to exit if he happened to get the urge. "So, I take it you've heard about Evelyn."

"I've heard. It's terrible." Jackson continued casing letters, seemingly unbothered by the comment.

"Had you seen her since she snitched on you?"

Jackson didn't reply instantly, giving Marcus the opportunity to dig himself even further into a hole. "Funny thing is, I hear Deborah's not doing too well either." He leaned in a little closer, then whispered, "I think she's dead."

This motherfucker is going to be a problem, I see, Jackson told himself.

"Have you talked to her since you got in trouble the other day?"

Jackson kept silent, deciding not to give Marcus any more to go on.

"Pleading the Fifth, eh? I won't tell anyone. Come on, spill it. What exactly were you up to last night?"

Jackson couldn't take another moment of his ridicule or the smell of his garlic breath as it permeated the atmosphere inside his case. He stopped abruptly, awarding Marcus his full attention. "How do we know you didn't kill them, Marcus? Maybe Evelyn turned you down and you got all pissed off. What would a man like you do with a woman like her? You wouldn't know where to start. Maybe you got tired of Deborah telling you what to do, treating you like a peon. Is that why you killed her? Was she too much woman for you?"

Marcus straightened his posture, the revelations resonating with his nature. He definitely had a violent streak toward women.

"Don't come to my case accusing me of things you'd much rather keep hidden yourself. I know exactly what kind of man you are. I can smell the perversion seeping out of your skin. Now get your perverted ass out of my case before I force you to reveal what's really under that mushy exterior. Don't start no shit. Won't be no shit," Jackson threatened.

Marcus let out a weak chuckle even though he'd neglected to find the humor in Jackson's words. It was merely a cover for his insecurities. Marcus knew it would be in his best interest to back out of Jackson's case quietly. And so, the cowardly clerk backed away to tend to his duties.

Elise stood nearby, keeping busy by switching flat tubs to the opposite side of Route 9, a ploy to eavesdrop on Marcus and Jackson's interaction. Unfortunately for her, their conversation was inaudible. She needed something she could use to stick it to Marcus. He had really struck a nerve when he insulted her prior. Her beady gray eyes leered at him as he exited Jackson's case. Something just wasn't quite right, she surmised. Her intention was to find out exactly what was amiss.

Once Marcus moved out of earshot, she moseyed on over to Jackson's case. "Hey, Jackson. You ready to tackle the day? I see you've got your morning coffee."

"Yep. Gotta have my coffee." Although he would rather not chat, he entertained the small talk because he was aware of how at odds Marcus and Elise were.

"I'm sure you need it, dealing with Marcus. He's been acting aggressive and argumentative lately. Yesterday, he was going back and forth with Deborah on the workroom floor. It's probably why she called off work. She probably is taking a break from his constant questioning of her every decision. I'm surprised I saw you two chatting. Frankly, I didn't think he liked you very much."

"What makes you think he doesn't like me?"

"Well, he's always frowning up his face when he sees you stroll by in the morning."

"Maybe it's just a coincidence," he countered, believing it to be true.

"No. I'm a pretty good judge of character. He hates you. I'm sure of it."

"Great. Just what I need, someone hating me for no apparent reason."

"It's okay. He hates me too. I don't care. Just watch your back. He can be pretty shrewd."

"Thanks for the heads-up, Elise. I guess you should be going. Looks like some of the carriers are going on a cigarette break. I know you don't want to miss that."

Elise suspected his remark was a low blow but couldn't really get upset about it. She often went out with the carriers for their morning smoke. "No problem," she replied, backing away from his case to join them.

Once she'd turned from his direction, he called her back for extra effect. "Hey, Elise?"

"Yeah." She turned to face him.

"You should be careful around him. His fuse seems to be burning low if you know what I mean. I saw you two arguing the other day. It looked intense."

She shook her head in agreement. "I'll do that."

Chapter 27

Is Blood Thicker Than Water

That evening at dinner, Marcus didn't say much. The three of them—Marcus, Andre, and Lydia—sat around the small, round glass kitchen table, eating pizza off Styrofoam plates. The plastic red Solo cups next to them were filled with cola. The conflicted man stared into the murky depths of the dark liquid. Was he just a coward? Why didn't he say more to Jackson? He questioned his decision to back away. *I'm not scared,* he told himself. His mind shifted, remembering Jackson's words as they stood face-to-face: *"Don't start no shit. Won't be no shit."* Out of nowhere, Daniel's cavity riddled teeth pervaded his thoughts, taunting him. He laughed at Marcus's cowardly ways knowing he wouldn't dare lay a finger on him. Marcus snapped out of the disparaging daydream, letting the excuses have their say. *I'd just much rather keep my job. An altercation would only cause havoc in my life. Then who would take care of Andre and me?* he reasoned.

The chatter between Andre and Lydia had failed to garner his attention until Lydia reached her hand across the table, touching his. "Marcus, what's wrong? You've barely said a thing since you've been home." She seemed concerned, yet Marcus wouldn't allow her show of empathy to cloud his judgment.

Andre glared at her hand upon his father's, heat festering in his belly. He didn't like it. Not in the slightest. But, what could he do? Lydia was pay for play. Unfortunately, it was Marcus who had all the money. Andre was lucky to be able to share Lydia's talents with his father.

"Who said there was something wrong?"

"No one. I just assumed."

"Assumed what? That you could make it better somehow?"

"I don't know. I guess. Maybe," she rambled, unsure of what he meant exactly. Lydia pulled her hand back. Her insecurity roused his nature.

He liked them submissive and unsure of themselves. Only then did Marcus feel in control. "Don't pull back now. Tell me, how did you plan on making it all better?"

"I thought you said there was nothing wrong," she countered.

"I lied. There is something wrong."

"What is it?"

"Your pretty little mouth keeps moving, yet I'm not inside of it," Marcus said, planning to take his frustrations out on Lydia.

Lydia didn't reply. Marcus looked over at Andre, sensing feelings of unrest as he watched his jawbone clench. Andre lowered his head, aware of his father's suspicions.

"Go into the room, Lydia. Looks like the opportunity to make it better has presented itself," Marcus instructed, keeping his eyes on his son the entire time.

Lydia got up from the table, leaving a slice of pizza on her plate.

"She didn't finish eating." Andre lifted his head, finally speaking up.

"She'll finish once I'm done with her," his father snapped back. "You finish your pizza, boy. We'll be back."

Marcus got up, followed her into the room, then closed the door behind them. Andre shoved his plate of pizza off the table down onto the floor. His eyes began to water, jaws trembling with anger. The boy was nearly in tears at the thought of his father having his way with Lydia. It didn't matter. There was nothing he could do to stop it. Nothing he had the guts to do, anyway. He'd sit there, all night, listening to her screams of pleasure mixed with pain.

***

Jackson sat on the fire escape peeking into Marcus's window through the open blinds. Normally they would be closed, but since Lydia had no problems with the intercourse being rough, he didn't feel the need to close them.

"Let me stay here," she said with his hand firmly wrapped around her throat, his eyes staring into hers as she straddled him.

"Why should I let you stay? Why would you want to stay? Tell me and don't lie," he demanded.

"I have nowhere else to go. You seem to like me. I like you too. Plus, you wouldn't have to pay as much if I lived with you."

Marcus mulled over the thought. It was a great idea that would save him tons of cash. He and Andre were pleased with her talents. The proposition was a win-win. "Okay, you can stay. But you'll have to show me how much you appreciate it."

Jackson watched undetected with bulging eyes as Lydia did just that.

It was almost time for Sue to drop Mya off at her mother's so that she could head straight in to work. She had finally gotten tired of sliding up and down that metal pole. The look on her face said so. Buddy could tell something was on her mind even though she barely said a word to either of them the entire time she had been home.

"You should say whatever it is you have to say before you leave. Come on. Say it." He rubbed the leather sofa cushion, giving her the cue to come sit next to him.

Sue walked from the kitchen, where she was busy making Mya's lunch, into the living room to take a seat beside Buddy.

"What's wrong, darling?" He rubbed his hand down her spine, forcing her to straighten her slumped posture.

"I think I'm ready to do it."

He knew exactly what she was referring to. "Was that all I had to do to give you a backbone?"

"You think you're funny? So how are we gonna make this happen anyway?"

"Leave everything to me, darling. Buddy will handle the details. I just need you to handle something for me before you head off to work." He rubbed his hand across her bare thigh, moving up under her shorts, hinting that it would be sexual in nature.

Mr. Sobieski stood in the doorway between the kitchen and the living room, watching his stepdaughter prepare their meal for the evening. "I thought we'd have dinner here on the sofa. There's a show on tonight that I don't want to miss," he called out to her.

"Do I really have to watch it? I'd much rather eat in my room."

"You can't keep hiding out in your room. You need to be among the living."

His remark rubbed her the wrong way, considering her mother had recently passed on. *How can he be so crass?* she wondered. Mr. Sobieski and her mother met when she was working as an administrative assistant for the school board. They weren't sleeping together for an entire month before he'd moved into their home and asked for her mother's hand in marriage. Shelby always had suspicions that Mr. Sobieski was just hunting for a woman with a house since his last wife left him, winning theirs in the divorce. But after seven years of marriage her suspicions waned. He had a good job and kept her mother happy, so she'd tolerated his lewd remarks accompanied by odd behavior, dismissing it as "a guy thing."

"Fine. We'll have dinner in front of your boring show," Shelby said as she rinsed the strainer of steaming bow-tie noodles under the kitchen faucet. She cooked them perfectly al dente for the pasta primavera she was preparing.

Just then the oven beeped. "The garlic sticks are ready!" her stepfather yelled upon hearing the oven alarm chime.

"You do realize I'm in here," she said, turning in his direction. Shelby counted the four empty beer bottles on the table. *No wonder he's being an idiot. He's almost drunk.* Instantly, she regretted her decision to eat dinner with her stepfather.

After a few more minutes, Shelby approached him with two plates in hand. She placed hers on the side table near the opposite end of the sofa, and his on the tray table in front of him.

"It looks delicious, Shelby. You always cook a great meal. You know you're gonna make some man a good wife one day."

"Well, I'm only fifteen, so that won't be for a long time, will it?"

Mr. Sobieski took a bite of pasta off his fork, then immediately chomped down on his garlic bread. "One day, baby. One day." Chewing and moaning, he bobbed his head obnoxiously, expressing its deliciousness.

"I'm glad you like it. You should chew it a bit longer. I wouldn't want you to choke," Shelby sarcastically remarked as she rolled her eyes, secretly wishing just that.

"Sit down. Enjoy the show. It's about to start." He turned up the volume.

When the *Saved by the Bell* rerun started, Shelby couldn't believe her eyes. "Are you seriously watching the rerun of an episode from a nineties television show?"

"Hey, what do you mean? This was a great show!"

"Yeah, for a thirteen-year-old girl in the 1990s. What, don't tell me, you fancy yourself being Mr. Belding?"

He didn't like the snarky comment. The truth of it bugged him. There were many days he'd fantasized about working in a high school with girls as beautiful as the ones on the sitcom. The concept was his heaven on earth.

"What's so wrong with that? I am a principal," he replied.

"Well, you have fun watching your rerun. I'm going to my room." Shelby got up from the sofa, then exited the living room, taking her plate of pasta along with her. She couldn't wait for the day she could leave that house. Just two more years and she'd be college bound.

He paid her no mind. *She's just jealous,* he thought, continuing to enjoy his dinner and show.

The room was depressing with four walls the darkest shade of brown you could imagine with black borders. There was a computer that sat atop the desk in the corner of the room. His thirty-two-inch television sat on top of the tall dresser beside the door. No family photos lined the dresser, nor were there posters plastered on the walls like most teens his age. Lydia wondered what he liked besides sex and video games. She wanted to know

what Andre was really about and why. The best
way to find out was to ask, she thought. Snooping
around wasn't really an option being that she was
never left there alone.

"Hey, where's your mom?" Lydia asked, head
still perched on Andre's frail chest. The fingers
on her right hand twirled one of the few hairs
sprouted among his pale pectorals. The muscle
tone he lacked didn't seem to impede upon her
passions for him.

Andre remained silent, not really wanting to
answer her probing question. "Why do you want
to know? What does it matter anyway?"

"Don't be like that." Lydia lifted from his chest,
pulling the black sheet up to her bosom to hide
her exposed breast. "You can tell me. I won't tell
anyone. Whatever you say to me stays between you
and me. And I expect the same in return."

His eyes finally met hers. "If I tell you, you have
to tell me something about you. Agreed?"

"Okay. Sounds fair enough."

"Promise."

"Cross my blackened heart." She gestured, drawing an imaginary cross over her heart.

Andre huffed before his mouth twisted into a
smirk. "That really makes me believe you."

"Was that a laugh? Did I make you chuckle?" she
inquired excitedly.

"Not a chance," he answered, quickly relaxing his face.

"Okay, fine. I swear on my life," Lydia relented.

"That's better. Come on. Let's get out of here before my father comes back."

"When is he coming back?" Lydia asked.

"I'm not really sure, so let's try to go before he walks in." Andre got up, grabbed his jeans from the floor, then slid them on over his plaid boxers.

"Where are we going?"

"Do you like carnivals?"

"You want to go to a carnival with me?" Her eyes widened as if hopeful for love.

"Why wouldn't I?"

"I don't know." She shrugged her shoulders before lowering her head. "Because we might see someone I had sex with before."

"So?" He shrugged.

Lydia looked up in disbelief. "Don't. You don't have to do that."

"Do what?"

"Act as if I'm not damaged goods."

"Damaged goods? What are you, food?" Andre sat back down on the bed. "Look, everyone's got a few skeletons in their closet. You've just got a little more than a few."

She lightly punched at his bicep. "Heyyyyy."

"Calm down. I'm right there with you. I'm not judging. Now, get your butt off that mattress and into a pair of jeans so we can get going." Andre stood up. "I'll wait for you in the living room."

"It's not like you've never seen me naked before," she remarked as he exited his bedroom.

"Then why'd you cover your chest when you sat up?"

She thought about the question for a moment, unable to furnish him with a viable answer.

"See, everyone has a comfort level. I'm just respecting your space," he called out from his father's room as he pulled a shoebox from the closet. The same size, color, and brand of blue shorts filled his closet along with plain blue double-XXL T-shirts to match. Andre opened the shoebox full of cash, pulling out what he felt he would need to treat himself and Lydia to a fun night out on the town.

Chapter 28

A Taste of Normalcy

A nervous Jackson bit at the skin of his lips as he peered through the peephole on his front door. From the looks of the hallway, all was quiet on the residential front. That was, until Andre and Lydia exited the apartment across the hall. It was the first time he'd ever laid eyes on either of them, concluding they were just kids. He watched the pair until they drifted from view. After they'd disappeared, Jackson rushed over to the window that gave him a view to the street, waiting for them to surface. Soon, the teens exited the building, hopping into the back of a taxi.

Lake Callis was bustling with activity that wouldn't clear out until well after 2:00 a.m. There were easily over a few hundred people there. Rides lined the grass not too far from the beach. Lydia stared up at the lights of the Ferris wheel from the passenger window of the taxi as they came upon the carnival. "It's beautiful, Andre. Look at the Ferris wheel." She smiled, taking it all in.

Andre, though, had allowed his gaze to be mesmerized by Lydia's beauty. "You sure are," he whispered.

The moment the cab driver pulled over, Lydia hopped out, leaving Andre to pay the man.

"I can't believe we're here. I haven't been to a carnival since I was a little girl," she admitted, hands perched at her chest in awe of the many colorful lights.

Andre stepped out of the cab. "What do you want to ride first?"

"The Ferris wheel, of course."

"I took you for more of an excitement junkie."

"What did you think I'd choose?"

"Honestly? The Salt and Pepper Shaker."

"How about we start slow? The Ferris wheel will get me warmed up."

"Whatever you want is fine with me."

His admission brought a smile to Lydia's face and, moreover, a spring in her step. She latched tight to his arm as they began their stroll.

"Is this okay for you?" she asked, brows raised.

"You don't see me complaining."

They trekked across the gravel parking lot, approaching the booth to pay for their tickets. "Have you thought about what you wanted to ask me?"

"I have. I think I'll wait until we're on the Ferris wheel. That way you can't get away from me."

"That's one thing you definitely don't have to worry about." Andre turned his attention to the man selling tickets in the booth.

The corners of his mouth looked as if they'd been sliced with a razor then healed over, leaving a mound of scar tissue at the edges of his mouth. "How many do you want?" the rugged, graying old man groaned.

"We'll take the unlimited pass. Two please." Andre passed him the money under the Plexiglas window, switching it with the tickets that sat there on the counter.

"These are for the games. I need to stamp your and the miss's hands for unlimited ride access."

"Stamp away," Andre replied, holding a fist in place. After receiving his mark, he stepped aside to allow Lydia to be inked.

When she stuck her arm under the glass, the carny worker grabbed hold of her hand, admiring the softness of her skin. "You got soft hands," he remarked, flashing a mirthless grin.

Andre interjected, halting the free feel. "Hey, Chester, you done?"

"Have a nice time, sweet thang." He stamped her hand, smooching his lips at her.

Lydia snatched her hand from under the glass. "Not a chance, grandpa."

The moment they crossed the threshold, beyond the gate Lydia took in a big whiff of the melody of aromas lingering in the air. Cotton candy, popcorn, caramel, even elephant ears were among the many. "I feel like I'm a kid again." She smiled softly. "Thank you for bringing me, Andre. I knew you were special."

"You don't have to butter me up. We're here now. I already bought the tickets," he joked.

"You're kind of a comedian, huh?"

"Well, that certainly isn't funny." Andre pointed at the long line of people waiting to ride the Ferris wheel.

"See? It's not just me. The Ferris wheel is the most popular ride."

"What have I let you drag me into?"

"Come on." She latched on to his arm, excitedly dragging him along with her.

Marcus hurled the dense, spongy balls at the target as Andre and Lydia rushed by. The teens were completely oblivious of his presence, as was Marcus theirs. He'd attended the fair alone. Mostly to gawk at the women, while filling his belly with tasty treats. It wasn't until he heard one teenage carnival goer heckling another that he turned to see what was going on.

"I didn't know streetwalkers liked carnivals," the light-skinned boy with the miniature high-top fade blurted. Two of his teammates stood nearby, chuckling at the rude comment. Both wore similar letterman jackets and sported matching high-top fades but with skin tones a different shade of brown.

Lydia turned to see who it was flapping their gums. She'd already suspected someone there would give her a hard time. Clarkston was a small town, so most of the teens at the high school had been acquainted with each other at some point in time or another. To her disappointment it was Richard, a guy she'd slept with very briefly before she'd dropped out. Lydia turned, attempting to ignore the ignorant comment. The trio closed in on them. "How much for tonight?" he taunted her further.

Andre glanced back, then over at Lydia, his eyes brandishing a look of concern more for her feelings than anything. "Is he talking to you?"

Lydia dropped her head. "Just ignore them."

"What?" His look of concern twisted into a demented stare as his gaze moved from Lydia over to Richard. "Who the fuck are you talking to, bro?" Andre snapped back.

Richard chuckled. "I'm not your bro. And I'm talking to the streetwalker you've got on your arm, so why don't you mind your business and let the slut speak?"

"Why don't you and the Doublemint twins fuck off?"

Richard laughed, cuing the other two to follow suit. "You know that's gonna cost you, Count Dracula. Then, once I'm done kicking the shit out of you, I'm gonna give it to your girl again, all . . . night . . . long," he replied sarcastically, alluding to Andre's milky complexion and dark persona.

"Bring it on, Shaft." Andre didn't back down.

Lydia quickly stepped between them. She leaned in toward Richard, whispering in his ear, "You're right. You did give it to me all night long, but how'd you like for everyone to find out you're serving endless shrimp? You're all balls, no bat, bro. Quit while you're ahead."

Richard considered the consequences, deciding he would rather spare himself the embarrassment. "I'll be seeing you around," he responded before backing away with his compadres in close pursuit.

All the while, Marcus had stood silently watching the scene unfold. He was proud of his son for standing up to his peers so courageously. Andre's act of bravery was more than Marcus had ever shown in his entire life. Regardless, he was furious that Andre and Lydia were out together. It wasn't as if it was against the rules, by any means. Marcus would simply rather Lydia preferred him over his son, even though he was there to look at the other women. At carnivals, many females wore skirts, which made it easier for him to peek, especially when riding the Ferris wheel. Marcus knew that spending time with a woman would win her affections much sooner than the occasional romp. Andre was treating her like a girlfriend, not a live-in prostitute. Although Marcus didn't want her as a girlfriend, he saw her as his possession. After all, he was the one paying for her services. His anger threatened to overtake his calm exterior, yet Marcus knew better than to cause a scene. He would wait until later to handle Lydia and the boy.

Chapter 29

The Fallout

The light was out in Marcus's room, making it nearly pitch-black inside. Even so, it was a risk Jackson was willing to take. Wearing black leather gloves, he pushed up on the wood panel to open the window from the fire escape. Jackson was in luck. It was unlatched. He carefully crept inside, standing slowly as he attempted to survey the scene. Considering his nerves were shot, his steps were rather steady, almost methodical. Jackson refrained from clicking on the small flashlight he'd pulled from the pocket of his jeans until reaching the nightstand beside the bed. Jackson pulled open the top drawer, pushing around Marcus's undergarments. There was nothing there that interested him. In the drawer beneath it though, the maleficent marine found exactly what he needed. "Bingo," Jackson whispered, pulling a strand of hair from Marcus's brush. He put the end of the small flashlight in his mouth to hold it where he could see, then used his free hands to place a few coils of hair into the sandwich bag he'd brought along. Moving the flashlight around the room, he noticed the closet door was ajar. That was when another vital piece of his plan presented itself. Jackson grabbed one of the folded black sheets at the top of Marcus's closet. He was in their apartment no longer than five minutes before he was climbing back out onto the fire escape.

Jackson had to hurry while the alley was empty. It was the most opportune time to exact his plan. He closed the window, then trotted down the fire escape until he reached the point where he had to jump. The plummet being barely a story off the ground, Jackson was sure he'd make it safely. He dropped the sheet on top of the dumpster, climbed over the rail, then leaped. Landing on his feet much like a cat, Jackson sprang back up. He grabbed the sheet, then took off through the dark alley.

Andre maintained his silence until they got through the line then onto the Ferris wheel. They pulled the bar down across their laps, allowing a ride operator to ensure it was locked into place.

"It's secured. Eight is good to go," he hollered out to a fellow carny at the controls. The wheel turned, taking the teens up a notch so that the next car could be filled.

"You're mad at me, aren't you?" Lydia asked sheepishly.

"No. Of course I'm not mad at you. I'm mad at that group of meatheads who decided to act like assholes for no apparent reason. Just something to do, I guess. I'm so glad I'm homeschooled. Being subject to the social hierarchy of high school was a nightmare."

"Agreed. I'm glad you didn't allow their ignorance to make you angry at me. I know it wasn't easy standing up to those guys. There were three of them, and you handled it like a boss."

"I've got nothing to lose at this point," Andre replied.

His comment made her think about the question she'd posed earlier that night. "So, are you ready?" she asked again.

"Ready for what?"

"To tell me about your mother. You said you would tell me once we were on the Ferris wheel."

"I did, didn't I?"

"Sure did. So, go ahead. Tell me. Where is she?"

"The story in a nutshell . . ." Andre paused for a moment. "I don't know why she left. She just left. Left me and my dad for a man with more money and plenty of prescription pills."

"I'm sorry, Andre. It must be hard having your mom around but not actually in your life."

"She lives in Dallas. When she left, she got as far away from my dad and me as she possibly could. I was only eight years old. She took my fifteen-year-old sister with her though. She wasn't my dad's kid, so I guess my mother had no choice but to take her."

"Have you ever thought about contacting your sister?"

"Nope," he answered emphatically.

"Why not?"

"She was fifteen when they left. I was eight. If my sister wanted to talk to me, she would have contacted me by now. Besides, I'm not one to get my hopes up for lost causes."

"Well, they sure are missing out on having a great guy in their lives."

"You mean me or my dad?" he sarcastically replied, attempting to lighten the mood.

"There's that comedian again."

"All right, I've revealed my secret. Now, are you ready for me to ask my question?"

"I guess I'm ready. It's not as if I can run anywhere. Plus, you kept up your end of the bargain, so I fully intend on keeping mine."

"Okay. Why did you really drop out of school and start being a working girl?"

Lydia hesitated, pondering how she wanted to tell Andre her truth. She wanted him to know, yet at the same time, she didn't want him to think she'd always been this careless with her body. What happened to her back in high school was the catalyst for who she'd become. Granted, after sleeping with countless men, the effect the event had on her emotions had since waned. "That sure is a story I never thought I'd have to tell," she uttered in a dull, quieted voice.

"I'm all ears," Andre replied, looking fixedly at Lydia's face as she stared out at the murky lake.

Lydia's memory took her back to the first encounter. She remembered it vividly, reciting it to Andre in great detail. "I rushed into the office right past the school secretary's desk, carrying a box of decorations for the homecoming dance. Mrs. Senkowski stopped me at the principal's door, waving her long red fake fingernails. 'You can't go in there,' she said. 'The school day is over and I'm heading home.' 'But I need to have these decorations approved by tomorrow. We're announcing the theme in the morning over the PA system,' I told her. It took a little convincing, and she never really gave up. That was, until Mr. Sobieski came out of his office. 'I can check out the decorations,' he said, assuring her she could go. I should have turned around and walked out right then. I was just a high school sophomore when I walked into that office with him. I came out a woman. At least, that's what he called it. That man took my innocence from me time after time. He never even apologized. In fact, he bribed and manipulated me. He made me out to look like a drug addict, a confused, promiscuous troublemaker who needed to be separated from the normal children and moved to the alternative school in the driver's education building. Fuck that. I finally quit. He made me give up. I gave up on my education, my family . . . I even gave up on my life a few times. It just never worked. Nothing ever did. I guess I'm meant to live out this hellish punishment. Maybe I was a horrible person in my past life, and now I'm paying for it. I don't know. But what I do know is that what happened to me in the past is in the past. I'm not going to fret over it on a daily basis. I need to get over it. The world stops for no one. Not even us, Andre. Not even us."

"I don't know what to say. I . . ." Andre was at a loss for words. He had no idea she'd reveal such dreadful memories. "I feel silly now, thinking what I've been through even compares in the slightest to the horrible things you've endured. I wish that never happened to you."

"Well, it did and I'm still here, aren't I? I'm a big girl. Trust me. I've learned to roll with the curveballs life seems to throw my way at ninety miles an hour. Besides, it's led me to meeting you. You're the nicest person I've ever met. I can't remember a single person who's treated me with as much compassion and empathy as you have. I want to thank you for that. In case I never get a chance to."

"Why would you say that? You're not going anywhere."

"You say that now."

The ride came to a halt, leaving the teens at the platform. "Come on, it's time to get off."

Andre refrained from responding until they were off of the ride.

"You wanna check out the Salt and Pepper Shaker now?" she asked, taking off in a hurry.

"Hey, slow down."

Lydia slowed her pace so that he was alongside her.

"You're not going anywhere. Do you hear me?"

She kept her words to herself, maintaining the belief that it would eventually all come crashing down around her.

"Stop and listen to me, Lydia."

Marcus watched from beyond a passing crowd as Andre lifted her chin with his hand. Whatever it was he'd said to Lydia made her smile. She leaned in, furnishing Andre with a peck on the lips before the couple strolled off together hand in hand with fingers intertwined.

Marcus knew then he had underestimated Lydia. He had anticipated the first time Andre would stand up to him, and as he leered at them then, he surmised that day would be soon.

***

At 0200 hours, Marcus sat on the love seat in his living room with every light out in the apartment. Fifteen more minutes of silence coupled with darkness dragged by before Andre and Lydia strolled in the door.

"Oh, my gosh. It's so dark in here." She giggled a bit. The dim lighting in the hallway was their only illumination.

"Are you scared? Do you need me to protect you?" he teased, poking his forefinger gently at her side.

"Shhh." She pressed her finger to her lips. "I think I see something," Lydia whispered, squinting deeper into where there was a complete absence of light.

Marcus yanked at the string, illuminating the lamp on the side table nearby. "Close the door," he instructed with the calmest of demeanors yet coldest of stares.

Andre closed the door in haste.

"I'm gonna go take a shower." Lydia attempted to escape the ambush.

"You're not going anywhere. Not in here anyway," Marcus countered.

Andre huffed, finally speaking up. "What's the deal, Dad?"

"Don't, Andre," Lydia cut him off, fearing he'd anger his father. "We know exactly what's going on here. It's time for me to go." Her plans to get

rid of one or the other had changed after the conversation she had shared with Andre on their date.
Genuine feelings of love began to bloom at the carnival that night. She would much rather go than
pit them against one another. "It's fine. I'll leave.
There's no need for argument."

"No, Dad. Why?" he protested.

"Which one of you took the money out of my
closet?"

Andre spoke up immediately. "I did. It wasn't
Lydia's fault."

"Lydia's the reason you took the money in the
first place."

"What are you even talking about, Dad?"

"I saw you two living it up on my money at the
carnival. Did you think you could just steal from
me and nothing would come of it?"

"I see now," Andre replied. "You're jealous.
Jealous that Lydia chose to go somewhere with
me. Do you think you can keep me locked away in
this sex dungeon of an apartment and never let me
out to live in the real world? You got to go to the
carnival, obviously. Why is it that you never asked
me to go?"

"Don't try to turn this around on me. I go to work
every day. I earned that money."

"Oh, please, Dad. You don't think I've seen you
stealing from the women you bring here? Every
dime in that box came out of a woman's purse, and

you have the audacity to get all holy with me. What can I say, Dad? I guess the apple doesn't fall far from the tree."

Marcus sprang to his feet. "You're not gonna steal from me, boy. I don't care how you justify it," he argued with hints of warning in his tone. He could feel the anger boiling up inside him. Everything he had held back from Jackson boiled to the surface. The shit he'd taken from Daniel wasn't far behind. Now his son was deliberately defying him. What made matters worse was Lydia standing there by Andre's side, taking in the entire scene.

"And you're not gonna keep me locked up in here anymore. I'll pack my shit and go."

Marcus rushed at his son, grabbing hold of his throat. The jolt disheveled the hair atop his head. What was once slicked back hung loose at the sides of his face. The large vein in his forehead pulsated, seemingly threatening to explode. His mouth hung open, trying to gasp for air that hadn't a chance of making it to his lungs.

"Stop it! What are you doing? You're gonna kill him! Let him go, Marcus! He's your son!" Lydia pleaded.

"Hey, what's going on in there? Cut that noise out. Damn you!" The old man from across the hall pounded on the door from the hall.

Lydia's pleas went unanswered. It wasn't until Andre delivered a swift knee to his father's scrotum that he released the death grip. Marcus doubled over in pain. That was when Andre's knee slammed into his nose. His father fell to the ground, still unable to force out anything other than a wincing cry.

"Let's go, Lydia. Grab your bag."

While Lydia rushed to his bedroom, Andre tore toward the opposite direction. He made it to his father's closet, nabbing the remainder of the cash inside, which happened to be the rent for next month. By the time Lydia tossed her purple book bag over her shoulder, Andre burst into the room. "Come on. We've gotta get out of here," he said, grabbing his black bag from the closet.

"You already have a bag packed?"

"I figured one day it would come to this. Let's go."

The teens rushed out of the room, past Marcus, then out the door.

The old man from across the hall watched from his doorway, wrapped in his robe. "Hey, keep that noise down!" he demanded. But Lydia and Andre were in the wind. They kept running, not stopping until they were a block up the street.

"We have to find somewhere to sleep tonight. I have the money Marcus paid me."

"And I have the money he should have paid all those other women. We'll be fine. I promise."

"I know we will. Let's get to a phone to call a cab. The hotels in Waterford are way less expensive." Lydia knew every hotel, motel, diner, and dive in the area. Her time as a runaway had caused her to be extremely street smart.

Chapter 30

A Change of Heart

Back in North Carolina, Buddy lay in bed while in the opposite room Sue tucked her 3-year-old daughter Mya in for the night. "Grandma told me you talked about what you wanted to be when you grow up," Sue remarked, perched along the bedside of her twin-sized canopy bed.

"I'm gonna be a ballerina like you, Mommy," sweet Mya admitted proudly.

"That's so awesome, baby. You can be anything you want to be."

"I want pizza, Mommy."

"It's late, baby girl. You have to get some sleep. You can have pizza tomorrow."

"Promise, Mommy?"

"I promise, Mya. Now get some sleep," Sue said, pulling the Cinderella-patterned sheet and blanket up to her daughter's chest, reaching her braided pigtails. "Good night, Mya. Mommy loves you." She kissed her atop her head.

"I love you, Mommy. Night-night."

Sue exited but left the door cracked after flipping off the light switch. Mya didn't like complete darkness, plus she wanted to be able to hear her if something were to go wrong.

"Come on over here to daddy," Buddy instructed upon her entering the bedroom.

Sue locked eyes with him and pulled the string of her silk pink robe, allowing it to slide off her shoulders then onto the floor. Her matching pink nightgown stopped at the halfway point of her thighs. Lace covered her breasts.

"I have to admit, that's the sexiest thing I've ever laid my eyes on, darling."

Sue climbed into bed, crawling from the bottom up toward the headboard. "Tell me what you want," she said.

"You know what I want. Did you get it for me?"

"Of course I did, daddy." Sue sprang back up from the mattress, grabbing a folded piece of paper from a jean jacket hanging off a hook on the back side of her bedroom door. "Here it is," she revealed, rushing it back over to him. "What are you gonna do with it?" Sue cuddled up by his side.

"I'm gonna make sure you get everything you want and more." He wrapped his hand around the back of her neck, pulling her into a passionate lip-lock.

***

Having arrived at their destination, Andre and Lydia stepped into the cheap, musty motel room off Dixie Highway. Andre was able to pay for a month's stay with the rent money he nabbed from his father. "I can't believe you paid for an entire month," Lydia remarked as they crossed the threshold.

"I told you we're gonna be okay. That'll give me time to find a job so I can get us out of this place."

They dropped their bags on the full-size mattress with the thin brown comforter. Andre looked up, noticing a wobbling ceiling fan above the bed.

"Hopefully it doesn't fall on us in the middle of the night," Lydia remarked, noticing the look of concern he brandished.

"If it does, they're giving us our money back."

Lydia smirked, gazing at Andre with genuine affection. "You know, you don't always have to be funny around me. I know it couldn't have been easy to endure what you did with your dad. I can't even believe he did that to you. Do you think he would have let go on his own?"

"Judging by the look in his eyes, no. It was like he was looking at a stranger. Like he didn't know me at all. I'm starting to feel like my mother left for good reason." Andre sat down on the mattress, resting his back against the wooden headboard attached to the wall. "I'm glad it's over. I just need to go back and get the rest of my stuff."

***

Livid, Marcus paced the floor of his apartment back and forth in front of the television. "Ungrateful little punk. I'll kill him. Just wait until he comes home. When I get my hands on him . . ." he spouted. Marcus bolted into Andre's room in a rampage. He ripped the sheets from the bed before flipping the mattress onto the floor. "Trying to hide your games, huh?" he yelled once he saw the PlayStation discs, having been tucked there securely. Marcus opened every game case, snapping the discs in two one after the other. His wild-eyed stare combed the room for his next target. *Where the fuck is that PlayStation?* "It has to be here somewhere." Marcus began to search the drawers of his dresser, but not before pushing the television onto the floor, busting it beyond repair. The top drawer he pulled open yielded not one result the entire time he pushed the garments around searching. Even so, Marcus snatched them out onto the floor. The second drawer he yanked completely off the track, tossing it and the clothing inside out onto the floor. He pushed the entire dresser onto the floor in frustration of it all.

"Where is it?" Marcus dropped to the floor on his hands and knees. There was Andre's most prized possession. Marcus's beady eyes lit up.

"We'll go back by the apartment tomorrow while he's at work to get the rest of my things," said Andre.

Lydia climbed across the bed, cuddling up close to him. "I hope he doesn't catch us there. If he was angry before, he's gonna be livid once he finds out that money is all gone."

The two of them quietly mulled over the thought. Each scenario they pondered caused them further anxiety.

Back in Clarkston, Marcus lay in bed staring up at the ceiling, the same crazed look in his eyes. He had plans for Andre and Lydia. Whether he intended for them to live or die, he hadn't decided. One thing he knew for sure was that he wanted them to feel pain and embarrassment just as he had that night. He was fed up with the constant testing of his manhood. It was time to start showing the others how dangerous underestimating him could really be.

Across the hall, Jackson lay awake in bed tormented by images of Jessica's bloody corpse dragging across the cement. He remembered screaming into the phone. That was when the accident began to replay in his head.

He recalled the bump before poor Jessica's body spun under the truck tires like roadkill. Jackson shook the unnerving images from his thoughts. Or at least he tried.

His life had changed forever in that moment. In his eyes he had killed an innocent woman. There was no going back at that point. But how far would Jackson go to cover up his crime?

Chapter 31

The Plot Thickens

Mrs. Escobar stood at the granite kitchen countertop, repeatedly dunking a teabag into a mug of hot water. She stared fixedly at the liquid until it was as dark as the night sky from the view of her kitchen bay window. The two cubes of sugar she had picked from the small ceramic bowl on the counter would make it sweet enough for her taste. Mrs. Escobar picked up the mug, liquid steaming inside. As she put it to her lips to blow, she heard something that startled her. The cup dropped from her hands, crashing onto the counter and causing it to shatter into pieces that spilled down onto the wood floor. She turned, raising her hands to her chest.

"Did I scare you, gorgeous?" Mr. Escobar said as he approached with a bouquet of roses in his left hand. And just as he promised, her gift was wrapped in his right.

"Honey, oh, *papi!* I've missed you so much. I'm so glad you're home," she said, rushing in to close the gap between them, her house shoes pushing aside shattered pieces of the mug. "Why didn't you call me?" Mrs. Escobar wrapped her arms firmly around her husband's waist, holding him as if worried he'd disappear.

"Aw, *mami,* I missed you more." He kissed her atop her head as she rested her face against his chest.

"Don't ever leave me again," she remarked.

"That's the plan, sweetheart. That's the plan." Mr. Escobar reciprocated the passionate embrace.

Just across the street, Mr. Trionfi tossed and turned in his king-size bed, attempting to gain at least a moment's comfort from his injuries. Jackson had really done a number on him. It seemed the more time went by, the achier his body became. He stared up at the mirrors in his ceiling. His wife lay next to him sound asleep, exhausted from having waited on him hand and foot the entire day. The beating he had taken haunted his dreams. Each time he'd fall asleep, thoughts of the heavy blows to his face and body would frighten him from his slumber. Bound to a chair with his wrists tied behind his back was how Jackson delivered the majority of his punishment. *How could this have happened to me?* the adulterous neighbor thought. *That motherfucker has no idea who he's messing with.* That night, staring up at his battered reflection, Mr. Trionfi silently vowed his revenge against the maleficent mailman.

Several houses down, Mr. Sobieski was winding down for bed. He approached Shelby's closed bedroom door, knocking to see if she was still awake. "Shelby, are you sleeping? Can I come in?" he asked with his mouth near the crack of the door.

"I'm changing. What do you want?"

"I'm going to sleep. I just wanted to say good night," he replied.

"Well . . ." She rolled her eyes. "Good night."

Mr. Sobieski walked into his bedroom beside hers, shutting his door behind him. He too craved a little privacy. The plaque on the wall to his left commanded his attention. At least, that was the story his eyes told. In actuality, it was what was underneath that he had in mind. Shelby's stepfather took down his award of achievement, revealing an eyeball-sized hole that allowed him to peek through into his stepdaughter's room. Like many nights before, he peered through to her room ready to watch her undress. The moment Shelby took off her shirt, allowing a view of her hot pink bra, Mr. Sobieski's slacks dropped to the floor around his ankles, his boxer briefs following immediately after. The lotion on the dresser next to him was the closest thing available to soften his touch. It allowed him to glide his hand up and down the shaft of his extremity as he watched her pants come off. Her panties matched, making the show even more to his liking. Mr. Sobieski imagined what it would be like to bend her over. Would she sound like his late wife? Her body was certainly more toned. He wanted to feel her warmth on his penis, but knowing it would be to his detriment, he settled for allowing his daydreams to fulfill his urges for her. The palm of his right hand slid up then down his eight inches of manhood over and over until he ejaculated onto the floor. "Oh, yeah," he moaned quietly, satisfied with the results of his peepshow.

It was nearly the crack of dawn when Andre and Lydia trekked up Main Street on their way to the apartment. "Come on, we'll make it just after he leaves. It'll give us enough time to get everything and go without running into my dad," he remarked before quickly tugging her wrist to pull her back into the shadows between the buildings. He'd taken cover at the sight of his father's car bending the corner.

"What's wrong?" Lydia inquired, having no idea why he had stopped them.

"Stay back. I think it's my dad," he said, holding her at bay as he stole peeks around the corner of the building.

Marcus zoomed by, oblivious of the teens' presence.

Andre waited until he was sure they would be out of his father's rearview sights before ushering Lydia from the cover of the building's shadow. "Come on. He's gone."

The teens started back up the road, traveling to the end of the block to make it to his father's residence. Fearing they hadn't a moment to waste, they tore up the stairs to the apartment. Andre used his key to get inside. The bedroom door was closed. He thought nothing of it.

"We should go quickly," she remarked, stepping inside after him.

"I'll pack my things." Andre rushed to gather his property. Not a thing had changed since Marcus trashed the room. The mattress lay on the floor among a sea of clothing. "What the hell?" he complained, applying force to the jammed door to push his way inside. The dresser scraped across the floor, scratching at the surface wood, worsening the more Andre pushed his way through. He and Lydia slipped inside, brandishing the same gap-mouthed expressions once they laid eyes on the destruction splayed out in front of them. "He's ruined everything I have," Andre admitted, shaking his head in dismay as he surveyed the scene.

A big green garbage truck bent the corner on Main Street to pull into the alley behind the apartment building. A sanitation worker stood on its backside, holding on tight. "Whoa, there!" He banged at the sides of the truck, alerting the driver to stop. "Whoa!" he blurted once more, waving his free hand in the air.

The 50,000-pound truck came to a screeching halt in the center of the alleyway. The driver lowered the passenger window. "What's the problem, Charlie?"

"Hold on. I see something." Charlie hopped down off the truck. His eyes focused on the black purse with the broken strap lying on the cement near one of the large brown dumpsters lining the alley. "What the hell?" he mumbled, looking up at the fire escapes above to see if maybe it had fallen from there. Nothing was visible to suggest that was the case. Charlie knelt to closer examine the bag as he swatted at the fly buzzing around his head. A mixture of sweat and dirt coated his chocolate profile. "Is that blood?" His beady brown eyes squinted to confirm what he was seeing. He quickly sprang upright, turning his attention back to the driver. "Ay, man, there's blood on this purse," he yelled, brandishing a look of concern. Charlie wondered what could have happened there.

"Come on, detective, we've got work to do!" his partner yelled sarcastically, not budging from the driver's seat of the truck.

Lydia stared out of the bedroom window into the alleyway, watching the scene unfold as Andre attempted to salvage what he could of his belongings. "What the heck is he doing?" she whispered, keeping her eyes on the garbageman.

A mass of flies swarmed nearby. "Something's just not right," Charlie mumbled, swatting them away. The buzzing horde brought his attention to the garbage dumpster on his right, it too having visible blood smears. "I knew something wasn't right." Charlie swallowed hard, his thick Adam's apple jumping in his throat. "And I think I found out what it is," he said, opening the lid of the dumpster to reveal Jessica's decomposing body. Her dull gray eyes were wide open. "Oh, my God!" He turned back to his partner. "Call the cops!"

"Oh, my God, Andre!" Lydia screamed, lifting her hands to her nearly exposed bosom. "I know her!"

Andre swiftly approached, hopping over his scattered belongings to take a gander at what she'd seen. The moment he laid his eyes on Jessica's corpse, he recognized her. He remembered the night Marcus brought her home and, more importantly, her words to him after realizing his father had brought her there. *"He didn't have to drug me,"* *Jessica whispered into his ear before both eyeballs rolled back into their lids. "I beg to differ, sweetheart. This is gonna be a wild ride,"* Andre remembered responding as he'd anticipated what acts of violence his father was capable of.

"That makes two of us, unfortunately. Three, if you count my father. And I'll give you one guess which one of us did this," Andre remarked, having snapped back from his brief trip down memory lane.

"You think Marcus did this?"

"I know he did. He was angry at me and took his anger out on her. I didn't think he'd ever get that bad again."

"What do you mean, again?" Lydia turned her attention to Andre as he continued peering out of the window at the battered woman.

"I was no more than about five years old. I saw him grab my mother by the throat. He forced her up against the wall in the kitchen. It didn't take much effort at all for him to lift her from her feet. He used his free hand to punch her in the stomach again and again, the blows becoming more aggressive each time he hit her. My dad was so angry. She'd worn something out in public he didn't approve of. He warned her she wasn't to dress like a slut. She had to be punished. Once he let her body drop to the floor, she vomited, crouched on her hands and knees. I remember my mom had the most beautiful head of long brown hair. My dad grabbed a fistful of it, dragging her across the kitchen floor to clean up the mess. She screamed so loud I covered my ears. When he released his grip, his boot came crashing down against her belly. She curled up into a ball, sobbing. I was too scared to come to her rescue. I just stood there in the corner of the room, frozen in fear. Afraid I'd be next. But I never was, not until last night."

"Andre, that's awful. I had no idea he was that bad. What are we going to do? Should we call the cops?"

"No. I've got other plans for my dear old dad," Andre proclaimed, brandishing an ominous stare.

Within minutes, the alley was bustling with activity. The Oakland County Sheriff's Office had quickly dispatched a team of detectives to survey the scene. Some traveled the alley on foot, peering behind dumpsters then inside others. The forensics team snapped pictures of the corpse.

Detective Barnes pulled up, almost immediately being briefed on the situation at hand by a fellow female officer. "Detective Barnes, this is the second female fatality within just a couple of days of each other. And both incidents are tied to this central area. This can't be just a random thing," Officer Jen Fackender rattled off the moment he stepped foot out of his cruiser. Although her masculine demeanor intimidated some of the men on the force, Barnes saw her as a real go-getter. To be completely honest, he'd rather she be by his side more than any of the other officers on the force. Her five-feet five-inch frame seemed to be more of a benefit than a hindrance in most situations. Jen had learned early in life to use her size to her benefit. What most larger officers could do she could do, and more.

"What's the victim's name?" Detective Barnes jumped right in, ready to get the case solved.

"Her name is Jessica Walkin. The garbageman found her purse on the ground." She pointed at the 20-something waste management employee being question by another officer.

"But the body was found in the dumpster." Barnes inquired for clarity, moving his gaze about the area.

"I'm thinking a vagrant found the body first, pulled the purse out of the dumpster, took the wallet, dropped the bag, and kept going. Her body was somewhat wrapped in a black linen sheet. It still had fold lines in it."

"We'll have to wait for forensics to see if they find any DNA other than the victim's on the body. Make sure they order a rape kit. Until then, let's make ourselves useful. I'll check out these two apartment buildings. Talk to the manager and get the names of each resident. We'll run the names through the database to see if we can find any violent offenders. I'd like you to find out what she's all about. Get her fingerprints and run them ASAP."

"You got it. We'll debrief back at the station."

"Keep your eyes peeled, Officer Fackender."

"Will do, sir," she replied, taking off to do her duty.

By the time Lydia and Andre came rushing down the staircase, Detective Barnes was about to enter the lobby of the apartment building. He pressed the buzzer next to the door to gain access to the office where the leasing staff would be. The teens backtracked, hiding on the landing at the top of the stairs, waiting for the officer to be let inside before they continued their exit.

"So, what's the plan?" Lydia inquired as they headed back toward their motel.

"Let's get something to eat. I'm starving," Andre suggested.

Chapter 32

The Hunt

Jackson awoke to the sound of an ambulance racing up the street to retrieve Jessica's corpse. He lay there for a moment, staring up at the dust-coated ceiling fan, before sitting up and allowing his eyes to scan the apartment. His jeans and shirt were tossed across the dresser. Beer bottles—some upright, others toppled over—were scattered across the coffee table in front of the television in the living room area. A streak of blood smeared across the white wall near the bathroom roused Jackson's panic. He hopped out of the bed, tossing the sheet off of himself, then rushed into the bathroom, searching through the cabinet for something to remove the stain. *A sponge and spray bottle of Clorox should do the trick,* he surmised. Jackson could have sworn he remembered cleaning that very same stain the night before. Still, he sprayed it down, wiping it with concentrated force to clean it entirely. Sirens caught his attention again, pulling his gaze to the window that gave a view to Main Street. Jackson hopped to his feet, then tore off toward the window. He stood there for a moment wearing only his white boxer briefs, his focus aimed at the ambulance going by. Once the sirens faded, the unnerved marine turned back to his previous task. The stain looked as if he hadn't cleaned it at all. "Are you fucking with me?" he spoke as if someone else were there with him.

The alarm clock buzzed. It was time for Jackson to get ready for work. He rushed over to the clock, shutting off the ringing alarm. When he turned back to the wall, the stain was no more. "Hold it together, Lance Corporal Pierce," he coached himself.

The woman in the lab coat seated on a metal stool at the counter in the laboratory peered through a microscope, her face covered by her lengthy dreads. Her bifocals were pressed to the lens as Jen entered the room, rattling off her request. "BranDi, I need a favor. I know you can get it done, so don't try giving me the runaround. I'm calling in the favor you owe me."

"Of course you are," she replied sarcastically, moving her attention from the task at hand.

"How fast can you rush these fingerprints for me?" Jen held up a Ziploc bag full of evidence she was sure she needed to crack the case.

"Give me a few hours. I'll see what I can do," BranDi replied, accepting the bag from the officer.

"So, how do you figure this is gonna play out?" Lydia asked, staring fixedly across the table at Andre, who sat pushing his spoon through his oatmeal in a cyclical motion. He had been fiddling with the breakfast since the waitress put the plate down in front of him. Lydia had yet to touch her bacon or hash browns. Maybe it was the dead body they had gazed upon from the window of the apartment that had spoiled their appetites.

Andre looked up, his gaze meeting Lydia's stare. "Here's how it's gonna go." He leaned in closer, then lowered his volume. "I'm gonna send him a letter. I'll tell him I've been watching him for a while and that I know he murdered the girl found behind his apartment building. I'll tell him I've seen him with her before. His options will be to pay up or I go to the cops."

"What makes you think he even has money to cough up?"

"He has the money, trust me. And if he doesn't have it on hand, he can surely get it. But that's only part of the plan. We're gonna double our payday by killing two birds with one stone."

"And how do you plan on doing that?"

"Our old pal Mr. Sobieski is gonna get a note too. He's not just gonna get away with what he did to you. He's been living the good life long enough. It's time to pay up."

Lydia brandished a sly grin. An eyebrow raised. "I'm liking the way this sounds."

The man wearing the plain black baseball cap sitting in the booth behind them sipped his coffee, quite entertained by the conniving teens' whispers.

When Jackson stepped into the office, the atmosphere felt heavy. Groups of people huddled together in different areas whispering their speculations about recent events. The when, why, and how Deborah died had clearly taken precedence. The only person who really noticed him moving about was Marcus, who was busy scanning parcels under the PASS machine. He couldn't take his eyes off of him, even after Jackson finally looked his way. Both donning looks of disgust, they locked eyes. A heated stare-down ensued, causing both of their blood pressures to climb.

"What are you all hot under the collar about? The new guy pissed you off, huh? What did he do, try to take some of your hours?" Elise teased, knowing all too well how they felt about one another.

"Eat shit, Elise. Oh, wait, it smells like you already have," Marcus uttered calmly, intent on not breaking the death stare he'd bestowed on Jackson.

Blood rushed to her head, making her complexion as red as a beet. She turned her attention to Daniel, blurting the first thing that came to mind. "Daniel, Marcus told us you'd finally be going to the dentist to fix your teeth."

"What?" Daniel frowned, embarrassed by the comment. "I told you, don't talk shit about me, man. I'll kick your ass."

"What a lying little bitch you are," he said, relenting from the death stare to shift his attention to Elise.

"Are you calling me a liar, Marcus?"

"Damn right! I'm calling you a lying little bitch in fact!" He had completely lost his cool and apparently the awareness that he was at work.

"Marcus! In my office, now!" the postmaster demanded of him.

"Explain that one away, prick," Elise mumbled as he took the dreaded walk to the postmaster's office.

Mrs. Teresa lifted her cane, using it to push back the vertical blinds as she sat comfortably in the recliner near the living room window. It was the only light that illuminated the room. She decided to spy from inside the house as opposed to the porch, intent on avoiding Jackson as he'd come by with the day's mail. That was when she saw Andre and Lydia strolling up her block. She recalled Lydia's face yet couldn't place where she knew her from. The short black body dress and combat boots she was wearing did nothing to jog her memory. She didn't associate with those kinds of people.

"It's just at the end of the block," Lydia remarked as the two marched onward to their destination.

"You've actually been to his house?"

"I used to play with his daughter. Well, his step-daughter."

As the mail truck bent the corner, Mrs. Teresa snatched her cane down out of the window. It wasn't long before she could hear the mail truck pulling into the driveway. Jackson grabbed the letters, climbed out of the LLV, then headed for the front door. After ringing the doorbell a couple of times, he waited a few minutes for a reply, knowing it could take her a moment. Three minutes passed before he pressed the button again, holding it awhile that time. "I know you're home," he whispered. "Don't be shy now." Jackson came down the porch steps and began his trek around the house. He could have sworn he'd seen the curtains moving as he approached. Maybe it was just his paranoia or hallucinations from lack of medication. It, quite possibly, could have been the vehicular homicide he'd committed.

A territorial Minkzy hissed at Jackson as he approached the back door. "Beat it, furball," he warned, moving her body with a swift but gentle shove from his boot.

"Meoooow," she cried, scurrying off toward the Escobars' home.

Jackson pulled a pocketknife from the pocket of his cargo shorts, loosening the screws that secured the wood covering the doggie door. Mrs. Teresa's eyes lit up with shock when she saw his gleaming bald head pop through the previously covered hole. "Knock knock, Mrs. Teresa. Is that you in there?" he asked, staring through the kitchen into the dark living room. She maintained her silence, sure that he couldn't see her sitting there. Regardless, the look in his eyes sent chills up her spine. It was a chill she had felt before. It was the look of pure evil. The same evil she'd seen in her late husband's eyes before he'd get to wailing on her. Mrs. Teresa could barely hear herself breathing until Jackson backed out of the small space then away from her home. The old woman let out a long sigh of relief once she heard the engine of the mail truck start up.

Marcus rode up Dixie Highway in search of Andre and Lydia. His eyes toggled left then right,

canvasing the area around each motel he passed
by. They had to be somewhere in the area, being that they took off on foot. The angry father
was sure of it. All he could think about was how
much of his life he'd put into raising his son. How
could he be so disrespectful? *I was the one who
raised him when his gold-digging slut of a mother
ran out on us,* he griped silently. *I should have
known he would run out on me just like she did.*
"Like mother, like son," he muttered. Marcus approached the motel across the street from the gas
station where he had first seen Lydia, pulling into
the parking lot the first opportunity he had.

The older woman confined to the small room
with the thick Plexiglas window scraped her thumb
across the flint wheel of the lighter, sparking up
her eighth cigarette that morning. Other butts lay
smashed into the ashtray on the counter next to
the pack of menthols.

"Hey!" Marcus called out to her as he forced a
photo of Andre against the glass. "Have you seen
this boy?" he asked.

The nearly decade-old photograph did nothing
to jog the woman's memory. The bottle of whiskey
hidden under the counter made sure of it. "I ain't
seen no kids here. This ain't no place for kids."

"He's not a kid. He's seventeen years old now,"
Marcus rebutted.

"Like I said, this ain't no place for kids. Now if you ain't renting a room, you'll have to excuse me. I've got work to do."

"Yes, I'm sure you have cigarettes to smoke," he snapped back before heading on his way.

Chapter 33

Pay to Play

A while later, the old man living in the apartment across from Marcus's waited by the string of mailboxes in the lobby dressed in his robe and slippers. Marcus rushed into the building, prompting him to take his opportunity. "Hey, you! I've been trying to talk to you."

Marcus ignored him, tearing up the stairs.

"Forget it. I'll just call the office and report you then."

The admission caused Marcus to turn back. The last thing he wanted was an inspection or, worse, for someone to come snooping around his apartment when he wasn't there. "What's the deal, old man? What do you want from me?"

"I want you to turn down that damn music and cut out all of that ruckus that goes on over there. You're not the only person who lives in this building, ya know. You should have some consideration.

Ever since you riffraff moved in it's been nothing but trouble. Dead bodies, police, fighting, arguing. You all should just go back to where you came from," the old man complained.

Dead bodies? Police? Marcus had no idea what the old man was referring to, nor did he have the time to sit there continuing to listen to him rant. He attempted to end the conversation on a friendly note. "I'll keep the noise down. Is there anything else you were thinking about going to the leasing office about?"

"Well, uhh . . ." The man paused, attempting to recollect past offenses against him. "I can't recall anything else pissing me off as much as that noise you keep up over there."

"Problem solved. Enjoy your day, old man from apartment 10." Marcus turned, then headed up the staircase.

"It's Trekul, you ill-mannered prick!" The man groaned at the fact that Marcus had given in so easily. He had bottled up the anger so long, he rather fancied a good verbal sparring. Besides, it was boring in his apartment all alone. Communication in any form would surely be a treat for him.

Marcus heard him yet refused to award the angry neighbor an ounce more of his attention. The small white envelope attached to his apartment door caused a knot to form in his throat. *That snitching old fart called the office on me,* Marcus thought. *If I get kicked out of here, I'm gonna strangle the bastard.* He vowed vengeance before he even found out who the letter was from. Marcus snatched it off the door before heading inside. Andre's bedroom door was closed. Therefore, Marcus had no suspicions of his son and Lydia having returned. It had been a terrible few days. He had been cheated, betrayed, stolen from, lied on, sent home from work to cool off, and now he had this letter in his hands. What it read was a mystery to Marcus, but for some reason he had a feeling the news wasn't good. He opened the letter, unfolding the page-long instructions in which he learned of Jessica's death. Marcus didn't see a way out. He was sure he'd be blamed for the murder. Not only had he slept with Jessica, but he'd also been physically violent with her. His brain mulled over all the ways he could possibly be linked to her death, coming up with several within seconds. They would surely throw him behind bars the moment he was offered up to the police. *What am I going to do? I don't have ten thousand dollars. I'll have to take money from my retirement, the only savings I have,* Marcus concluded.

Just then, there was a knock at the door. "Who is it?" Marcus shouted.

"It's the police," Detective Barnes called out from the other side of the door.

Panic set in, in response to Barnes's reply. Instantly, Marcus's stomach was in knots. Had Jackson set him up for the murders? Marcus worried. Had he decided to tip off the police as opposed to bribing him? Marcus started to perspire. Sweat stained his blue T-shirt at his pits.

"Sir, can you open the door? I'd like to talk to you," Barnes added, still waiting on the other side of the door.

I wonder if they're here to arrest me. I'll just tell the truth. Everything will be fine, he hoped.

The detective knocked once more, peering down at the small notepad in his hand. "Mr. Renegat, are you going to open the door? Or should I—" The door opened, halting his oncoming suggestion. "Mr. Renegat. May I come in? I'll make it brief."

"Of course. Come inside." Marcus stepped aside, allowing Detective Barnes entry. "I apologize for the delay. I had to change my shirt. I was all sweaty from work."

"No worries. Where do you work, by the way?"

"I work at the post office up the road."

"Oh, no wonder. You guys work hard. I can't imagine how you handle delivering during Michigan winters."

"I'm actually a clerk, so thankfully I don't have to work outside."

"Lucky you."

Marcus closed the door behind him. "Would you like something to drink, Officer?"

"No, thank you. I won't be long. I'm just questioning the residents to see if they may have witnessed anything strange going on around here last night. Maybe someone creeping around in the alley?"

"I can't say I have. I have to be at work pretty early in the morning, so I'm usually winding down by nine o'clock."

"Have you ever seen this woman?" Detective Barnes flashed an enlarged photocopy of Jessica's license.

Marcus stared at the photo for a moment, for the purpose of making his reply seem believable. "I'm sorry, Officer." He shook his head no. "I wish I could be more helpful, but to be honest, I have not. May I ask what this is all about? Did something happen in our building?"

"The woman in the photo was found dead in the dumpster behind your building."

"Oh, my gosh. That sort of thing never happens around here," Marcus remarked.

"Well, considering recent events, things like this are becoming more common than you know. You work at the post office. Wasn't one of your coworkers recently attacked? She's still in the intensive care unit. Did you know her?"

"Evelyn is her name. She's a clerk. I really hope she can pull through this. We're all rooting for her. She has a husband and children who need her."

"I hate to cross cases, but would you happen to have any idea who'd want to hurt her?"

It took every ounce of forethought Marcus had not to offer up Jackson's name. The fact that the suggestion would ultimately lead back to him influenced his decision to keep quiet. "She's the nicest clerk we have at the post office. I can't imagine anyone wanting to hurt her."

Detective Barnes had no reason to disbelieve him. He searched his eyes and, moreover, his body language to see if he was hiding anything. Marcus remained cool, calm, and collected. "Well, I won't continue to take up your time. I'm sure you have business to attend to. Should I have any additional questions, will you be in town to answer them?"

"Of course. I'm not going anywhere."

Detective Barnes turned to exit, then turned quickly back to Marcus for one more question. "Mr. Renegat, I've noticed you have two bedrooms in this apartment. Do you live alone?" It was his last attempt to find a foul in his demeanor.

"Actually, my son and his girlfriend recently moved out. So, it's just me now."

Further studies concluded he had been truthful. "Have a good day, Mr. Renegat. And thank you for allowing me to come inside to talk."

"Anytime, Officer."

***

At 1400 hours, Jackson strolled into the diner for lunch. He finished his route but couldn't help thinking that Mrs. Teresa would somehow cause him to lose his job. She had called to sing his praises. What was stopping her from calling to defame his character? Then there was Jessica, the woman he had killed in cold blood. Soon they would come asking questions, wanting to know if he'd seen anything. The maleficent mailman was well aware of how the process went, but he felt he had to stash the body close in order to further implicate Marcus. Jackson was feeling claustrophobic, as if the walls were closing in on him. A heavy sigh wrought by regret left his body as he slid into the booth he'd sat in previously. It being familiar to him brought him at least minimal comfort. It was actually why he picked that very same diner time after time. Well, that and Janice.

The moment Jackson sat down in her section, Janice exited the kitchen, coming from behind the counter, menu in hand. "Hey there, stranger," she called out to him, waddling over to his booth. Janice paused, allowing the man in the black ball cap to squeeze by before she continued to close the gap between herself and Jackson.

"I'll be right with you, sir. You can have a seat anywhere you'd like," she said as the man crossed her path.

He uttered no verbal response yet nodded in agreement with her remark.

"How are you today, Jackson?" Janice placed the menu down on the table in front of him.

Jackson looked up at her, hiding his frustrations. "I'm doing okay. Just got off work actually. How are you feeling? How's the baby feeling?"

"He's kickin', that's for sure," she replied. Janice rubbed her hand around in circles across her rounded belly. "What is it you feel like trying out today?" She removed her pad and pen from the pocket of her white apron.

Jackson peered down at the menu's many choices, having no idea what he had a taste for consuming that day. "What are your specials today?"

"Let's see. We've got shepherd's pie, beef stroganoff, and goulash. Take your pick, unless you want something else off of the menu."

"Which one do you recommend?"

"The goulash, of course. I love pasta, and the chef makes it just like my mother used to." Janice grinned, remembering its taste from her childhood.

"Sounds like I'm having goulash then. Does it come with cornbread?"

"What kind would you like, traditional or hot-water?"

Jackson was surprised. "You make hot-water cornbread here?"

"Our chef is from the South. He makes all the good stuff."

"I guess I'm in for a treat."

"What would you like to wash it down with?"

"Just a glass of cold water will do."

"Okay, I'll put your order in and be right back with your water if you don't need anything else."

"To be honest, I was kinda hoping for some conversation," Jackson revealed.

"I was hoping you'd say that." Janice smiled. "I'll be back with your lunch and mine too."

"I appreciate it."

"Pleasure's all mine." Janice stepped to the side to address the gentleman in the booth behind him. "Sir, someone will be right over to take your order. Can I have them bring you something to drink?"

The man in the ball cap kept his eyes on the newspaper he was reading, not bothering to look up at her. "Just water," he replied.

"Water coming right up." Janice headed to the kitchen to put in Jackson's order.

It took her no more than ten minutes to return to Jackson's table with their plates of goulash.

"That didn't take long at all."

"I had incentive," she chuckled, placing the plates down on the table before squeezing her tummy into the booth.

"It's getting close, huh?"

"Yep, my little creation will be here soon enough. Then the hard part begins. How's your little girl doing, by the way?"

"Mya. She's doing good. Last time I spoke with her she was filling up on snacks at her grandmother's house."

Buddy laid on his horn, alerting the woman exiting the front door of her residence with baby and car seat in tow. The woman's soft gray eyes lit up with excitement. She whipped her thinning blond ponytail behind her shoulder before wiggling her pastel pink–painted nails in his direction.

"Showtime." Buddy shifted his truck into the park position, then hopped out, heading in her direction. "Hey, doll face. Where you headed?"

The woman smiled softly, enamored by the fact that he'd called her doll face. Much of the time the widowed miniature, pudgy single mother was plagued by depression due to the loss of her husband and inability to lose the baby weight she gained during her pregnancy. The fact that Buddy took an interest in her she saw as a blessing. It was a naive notion adapted by a grieving, gullible woman. Regardless, the attention seemed to be healing her aching, lonely heart. Who could blame her? Buddy had swooped in so heroically, awarding her the time and attention she so desperately needed.

"Hey there, handsome. I missed you last night. I thought you were coming over," she replied.

"I've been really busy working and trying to find a place for us."

His revelation comforted her. All she wanted was to be a wife again. She struggled with being single. The day Buddy walked into her life, that all changed. He doted on her, giving her the attention she craved and, more importantly, the love she had been lacking in the bedroom. "Are we really going to be together?" she asked, ever so hopeful, forehead wrinkling as her eyes protruded from their sockets.

"Of course we are. Did you go take that money out of the bank like I asked you?"

"Yes, I did just as you asked," she replied, placing the car seat down onto the cement porch to dig into the diaper bag hanging off her shoulder. The folded manila envelope she pulled from the bag was thick with every dollar accounted for, Buddy concluded, positive he could count on her as he'd done on many occasions.

"Here it is. It's all there."

"I know it is, doll face," he responded, laying a kiss atop her forehead before accepting the envelope.

"I hope you can find us someplace nice. You know, we could always just stay here."

"I told you, I'm not going to stay in another man's house. Everything in here reminds you of the life you had with him. I want us to start fresh in our own place. It may not be as swanky as the three-bedroom cottage you live in now, but it'll be sufficient. I promise, you'll be happy." Buddy laid it on thick.

"Whatever you say. I trust you," she replied, a soft smile plastered on her face.

"I know you do." Buddy didn't feel an ounce of regret. He'd been scamming the lonely widow out of her money for months, since her husband died in the line of duty. "I should be going."

"You're leaving already?" Her smile diminished.

"I have to go to work. I'll tell you what. I'll give you a call when I'm about to get off. Maybe we can make a night of it, provided you can find a sitter for the baby."

She frequently found herself pawning off her 8-month-old baby boy on whichever relative would watch him so that she could be with her new beau. And although some protested, they'd much rather the baby be with them as opposed to being around a stranger. "I'm sure I can find a sitter. Don't you worry about that, handsome." She laid her hand softly upon his chest, closed her eyes, pursed her lips, then lifted her chin for another taste of his.

Buddy rolled his eyes, already tiring of her. Nevertheless, he granted her desires, planting a tender, passionate kiss upon her thin, glossy lips. He had no intention of actually moving in with the woman. Buddy needed the money to fund his next cash cow, which meant he'd hang around long enough to spend all of the insurance payout the poor widow had received from her husband's death. Growing up in foster homes while learning how to survive on the streets had created an intense desire in Buddy to never have to go without. He'd adopted the principle and upheld it by any means necessary.

Chapter 34

Who to Trust

Mrs. Yang could hear Buddy's truck as it pulled into the driveway. She inched the cream curtains to the side, peeking outside to get a glimpse of him without being too obvious. Although she had never laid eyes on him, Sue's mother didn't trust Buddy one bit. The old woman wondered what he'd gotten her daughter into. There had to be a catch to him giving her that much money for a babysitter. He didn't even know her that well. Something just wasn't quite right. Mrs. Yang was intent on finding out precisely what was amiss. Due to the tinted windows on his pickup truck, she couldn't get a good look at him.

Sue walked in through the front door, carrying her napping 3-year-old. "Mama, what are you doing?" she inquired upon entering the living room.

"What is going on with you and this man?" Mrs. Yang let the curtain close.

"What are you talking about, Mama?" She carefully laid Mya down on the sofa so that she'd remain in her slumber.

"I'm talking about all the money he gave you the other day. Just for babysitting. He doesn't even know you, little girl. Why he give you that money?" The more Mrs. Yang spoke, the thicker her accent became.

"He's my boyfriend, Mama. He's just helping me out like he's supposed to do."

"All help not good help, Sue Lin. You remember that."

"Please don't lecture me, Mama. I'm already going through enough. My husband left me a single parent, and I'm struggling to pay my bills. Buddy has been the only thing keeping me afloat."

"Buddy! So, he is the only one? What have I been doing all this time?"

"Mama, please calm down. I didn't mean it like that. You're going to wake Mya."

Buddy laid on the horn a couple of times, demanding Sue's return.

"I have to go, Mama. Buddy is taking me to work today. Something weird is going on with my car, and he's going to fix it for me. See, Mama? He's a good guy. You just have to give him a chance."

"I don't have to do a thing. That will be your headache, not mine." Mrs. Yang rubbed her hands together in two swift motions as if wiping them clean of the entire situation. "Just keep my grand-daughter out of it," she warned.

Jackson turned at the corner to park at his building, changing his mind at the sight of the caution tape and blockades restricting access to the alley. With his mind being so preoccupied, he completely missed the fact that the man from the diner had been tailing him since he left. You know, the stranger wearing the black ball cap? Furthermore, the plain green T-shirt and jeans he wore did nothing to make him stand out. Which was what the man in the ball cap wanted. The sedan he was driving had a big, round no-smoking sticker pasted to the outside of the glove box. He'd picked up the rental the moment he'd gotten to town, opting out of driving his personal vehicle around Clarkston.

The stranger watched patiently as Jackson parked his car on the street next to the building, not taking his eyes off him. That was, until his cellular phone buzzed.

"I'm here now," the unidentified man answered. "If you want to change your mind, you'd best do it now." The stranger paused, listening to his instructions coming from the caller before con-tinuing. "I'll call you when it's done then. I'll be expecting payment immediately," he responded, then disconnected the call.

By the time Jackson was headed up the hallway, the stranger was in hot pursuit. But just then, something caused them both to be on high alert. The cop.

"Okay, thank you for your help," Detective Barnes said, stepping out of the old man's apartment just next door to Jackson's apartment.

The stranger in the ball cap didn't want Jackson or the officer leaving the old man's apartment to pay too much attention to him, so he continued calmly down the hallway, passing them both by.

Jackson's heart pounded. He was too worried about the officer to worry about the unidentified man strolling by. Jackson took out his key, attempting to enter his apartment without incident.

"Hey, there." Barnes looked down at his notepad. "Just the man I needed to see. Jackson Pierce, I assume."

He paused, key stuck inside the lock. "What can I help you with, Officer?"

"Actually, I'm a bit thirsty. You mind if we go inside to talk?" Detective Barnes replied, attempting to gain access to the apartment.

Jackson's mind raced. *Did I clean up all the blood?* he silently questioned. *Did I leave any of her belongings inside?* He knew he had little time to mull his inquires over before the officer would become suspicious. "Of course you can. Anything for a fellow man in arms," he replied, gaining his

favor almost instantly. Jackson was smart. He
figured pulling the military card would bode well
for him as it always had.

"Fellow man in arms, huh? Which division?"
Barnes excitedly inquired.

"Actually, I'm Lance Corporal Jackson Pierce."

"All right then, a soldier. I'm happy to hear that,
brother." He held out his hand for a more appropriate greeting. Jackson quickly reciprocated,
shaking the officer's hand.

"It's a pleasure. Come on inside. I'll get you
something cold to drink and answer any questions
you have. I've heard a bit of the gossip, so I'm
curious to hear what's happened," he rambled on
as he unlocked the door, allowing them entry.

The moment Jackson's door closed, the man
who'd been tailing him got the hell out of there. He
wanted no part of the authorities.

Jackson's eyes scanned the studio apartment
in its entirety as the two crossed the threshold. Not
a thing was out of place. There were no beer bottles on the table. No clothing on the dresser, nor
blood on the wall. "Would a bottled water be okay?"
he inquired, confidence restored.

"A bottled water will do just fine. I appreciate
your hospitality," Barnes replied, taking in the
scenery. "I can tell you're a military man. There's
not a thing out of place in here."

"It sticks even after you've retired," Jackson remarked, pulling a bottled water from the refrigerator in the kitchen area. "So, what can I help you with, Detective? Please, have a seat if you'd like. I'm gonna get off my feet. I've been working all day." Jackson approached him, handing the water over to Barnes.

"Thank you. I think I will too."

They sat on the sofa in the living room. Jackson knew he'd made a good impression. He could tell by the officer's demeanor. He'd gone from suspect to comrade within just a few minutes of being in Detective Barnes's company.

"I heard through the grapevine we had an incident here. I'm assuming that's what you're here about."

"The grapevine?"

"I'm a mail carrier at the post office down the street. What can I say? Word spreads fast in Clarkston."

"The post office? You're the second person I've talked to in this building who works at the post office. I assume you're acquainted with your neighbor across the hall."

"Marcus? Yeah. He's a clerk. He works inside with the women."

The two of them chuckled at his sarcastic remark. "Yes, he told me he works inside on the early shift."

"I don't have much interaction with him, but we've spoken in passing from time to time."

"Your neighbor complained about the noise that goes on in his apartment."

"He's always blasting his music. It pisses off the old man next door. I will say in his defense, though, the man bangs on my wall if my alarm clock goes off for too long."

"So, you think he's overreacting?"

"Sometimes, yes. But there have been nights when I wanted to walk over there myself and knock on his door to tell him to keep the noise down. Luckily, I have earplugs. The good ones we used in combat. Once I put those in, I can't hear a thing."

Detective Barnes pulled a photo from the breast pocket of his shirt. "Have you seen this woman here before?"

"Oh, my God. That's the woman who walks Dixie."

"I don't follow. What do you mean, she walks Dixie?"

"She's a working girl. You know? A prostitute. I've seen her picking guys up in front of the diner, the gas station . . . she's always around. Is that the girl they say was hurt?"

"She wasn't just hurt. She was murdered."

Jackson's pupils expanded. "She was murdered here?" he inquired, of course pretending to be shocked.

"Her body was found in the dumpster outside. So, you're telling me you haven't seen or heard anything?"

"I'm sorry. I wish I could help, but my apartment doesn't even allow me to see the alley. I'm facing Main Street. The other side of the building faces the alley," Jackson answered, shrewdly casting suspicion back on to Marcus.

Detective Barnes huffed, finding the veracity in his response. The revelation prompted him to probe deeper. "The woman who was attacked at the post office a couple of days back, does Marcus know her? I mean, do they seem to get along?"

"Evelyn is a clerk, like Marcus. I'm sure they work more closely with one another than the carriers do, but I can't say I've really seen them interact. I'm sure the other clerks at the post office could help you with that information. I really wish I could be more help to you. That poor girl didn't deserve to die. I can't imagine what she'd already gone through in life to push her to become a prostitute. What a terrible way to go."

"It's a cruel world we live in, soldier. A cold, cruel world."

"No matter how bad it is though, I can't help but think at least we don't live in the Middle East. I'll pick the United States over that hellhole any day of the week."

"I'll take your word for it. I don't want the experience. Policing is tough enough. War? No thanks," Barnes replied.

"Smart man."

"Well, I should be going. Thank you for answering my questions and being so hospitable. It makes my job so much easier." Detective Barnes stood, preparing to make his exit.

"Anytime, Detective Barnes," he replied, finally reading the name stitched on his shirt.

Barnes shook his hand, even more fond of Jackson after he referred to him by name.

At the station, Officer Jen Fackender sat at her desk, perusing what information she had gathered so far regarding Jessica's identity, when a call came through. The eager officer pressed down on a speaker button to answer the phone without lifting the receiver. "Whatcha got for me?" she yelled, recognizing the call was coming from an inside line.

"Something you definitely want to see," the woman on the other end responded.

"I'm on my way down." Officer Fackender disconnected the call.

When she entered the lab, BranDi was there waiting to give her the news. "So, what's the word, my favorite forensics tech?"

"No need to blow smoke up my ass. You can buy me lunch, though."

"That all depends on what you got for me."

"Well, come on over and take a gander at what I've found so far."

Jen closed the gap between them to look over lab work she compiled.

"The fingerprints you gave me didn't match the victim, but whoever they belong to isn't in our database. We also found hair fibers on the body and a sheet that didn't belong to the victim. We've got the DNA strand, but you're gonna have to find me a suspect to match it to. The woman's body endured massive blunt-force trauma. I'd advise an autopsy to see exactly what damage was done. Have you found her next of kin yet?"

"I'm actually researching that now. I was hoping the fingerprints would yield a match. At least we've got DNA from the hair. Good job."

"Good job I'll be getting lunch sometime soon, or good job I'm eating leftovers from last night's dinner?" BranDi inquired.

"Call in the order from a restaurant of your choice. I'm paying for it."

"The Union," she suggested, it being the restaurant with the tastiest vittles in town.

"Fine. The Union gets me another favor though," Officer Fackender replied, knowing the meal would be costly.

"Deal." The ladies shook on it.

***

A buzzer rang at the front counter of the annex building. Detective Barnes waited there for a postal employee to answer. "I'll be right with you!" he heard a woman's voice shout from the back.

The officer waited patiently for her to emerge. Elise came rushing around the corner after a few minutes. "Hello, Officer. What can I do for you?"

"I wanted to ask you a few questions."

"Me in particular?" she asked, figuring it involved Evelyn or Deborah.

"Well, whatever clerks are in the building would be nice."

"I'm the only one here as far as clerks go. I'd be happy to answer any questions you have. I'll let you inside. We can go to the conference room."

"That would be great. Thank you."

"Sure. Hang on. Let me come around and unlock the door for you." Elise walked around the counter, then opened the door, allowing him access to the back.

"Follow me. The conference room is right back here," she said, leading the way. Elise entered the room, taking a seat at the end of a long rectangular table. Officer Barnes sat opposite Elise. "My name is Elise, by the way."

"I'm Officer Barnes. It's very nice to meet you, Elise. I won't take up too much of your time. I know you have work to do. I just have a few questions, and I'll be on my way."

"Okay. Shoot." Elise thought about her choice of words. "On second thought, don't," she chuckled. "I'm sorry, I had to laugh. I apologize. I know this is a serious matter. I don't mean to seem insensitive."

"It's quite all right. Elise, how would you say your relationship was with Evelyn?"

"Evelyn and I have a great relationship. We're always very candid with one another, but no real issues have ever come about."

"Did she get along with everyone around here?"

Elise thought about Evelyn's brief interactions with Jackson and how Evelyn thought he was crazy, but once Marcus came to mind, Elise decided she would weave a completely different tale. "We only have one clerk here who didn't really see eye to eye with Evelyn, and that would be a guy named Marcus. He had a little tiff with Evelyn and our supervisor Deborah just the other day. May she rest in peace."

"Had anyone else witnessed this tiff?"

"I'm not sure. I wasn't there. Deborah was the one who told me about it. News spreads fast around here."

"What about the new guy, Jackson?"

"The carrier? Oh, he's awesome so far. He's actually had a few residents call up here singing his praises. He's going to do well here at Clarkston." Elise paused. "Why? Is he a suspect?" Her eyes lit up as if intrigued by the notion.

"No. No. It's nothing like that. I'm just asking questions. We have no suspects as of yet." Detective Barnes quickly extinguished the fire, having a feeling she would be eager to spread the word. The last thing he wanted to do was ruin a good man's reputation. "I think I've asked all the questions I needed to. Thank you, Elise."

"No problem, Detective Barnes. I'm happy to help. I hope you find out who did this. Evelyn didn't deserve what happened to her."

Chapter 35

Missing the Point

Just as Barnes made it out to the police cruiser, Jen was chirping through on the radio.

"Detective Barnes? Detective Barnes, are you there?"

Barnes quickly picked up the radio. "This is Barnes. What you got for me, Fackender?"

"We've got some new developments into Jessica's case. Are you on your way back to the office yet?"

"I'm on my way now. I actually have a few developments to discuss with you as well."

"Copy that. I'll see you when you get to the office."

"Over and out." Detective Barnes hung up the receiver.

When Detective Barnes tore through the doors at the police station, Officer Fackender was there at her desk, still perusing case files. Barnes pushed past a swinging half door at the front counter on his way back to his office.

"Sir, I've got good news and I've got bad news. Which do you want first?" She stood, following closely behind as he entered his office.

Detective Barnes took a seat behind his desk. "Give me the good news first, Fackender."

"Okay. So, apparently we were able to lift fingerprints from the body that did not match the victim's. They also found hair fibers that didn't belong to Jessica."

"And the bad news?" He leaned back in his chair, rocking back and forth.

"We can't find a match in the database, fingerprint or DNA."

Detective Barnes mulled over what she revealed. "We're dealing with a first-time offender or a very clever criminal. I think I may have a suspect who's a match for the DNA. I just need to get a sample."

"Really? Well, who do you suspect did it?" Officer Fackender took a seat in a chair opposite his.

"One of the residents who live in the building with access to the alley where she was found has a view of the dumpster from his bedroom. He also happens to have ties to the woman who was attacked at the post office just days prior. He seems to be a viable suspect. The only thing that could complicate things is the fact that she was a prostitute."

"A prostitute?" Officer Fackender repeated, shocked by the information he'd presented.

"Apparently she walks Dixie Highway. She could have any number of men's DNA on her person. It'll be hard to pin it down, being that he could just claim they'd had sex before. But I've already questioned him, and he denied even knowing her. We've got to get that hair somehow. Hopefully, he doesn't lawyer up."

"What about the sheet her body was wrapped in? If we can prove it belonged to him, it'll be the nail in his coffin."

"Let's hope we can catch this guy. If I'm right, he's already attacked two women just a few days apart from one another. His next victim could be popping up soon."

"Maybe we should put a tail on him."

"I don't know. I wouldn't want to tip him off."

"Sir, with all due respect, we can't risk him taking another life."

Detective Barnes fought with the decision, ultimately agreeing with Officer Fackender. "Okay. Put a tail on him. See if we've got a couple of cadets eager for a stakeout."

"Will do, Detective. I'll get right on it. I think I've got just the pair in mind."

A waxing moon shined over the Sobieski residence that evening. Mr. Sobieski sat at the edge of his bed, clutching that letter he discovered at his doorstep. There was no way he was going to let someone take his job away from him, to ruin the good reputation he'd worked so hard to fabricate. It wasn't as if he didn't have the money they were attempting to extort from him. A small part of him felt he owed the money that was demanded of him. After all, the perverted principal had ruined a fair share of girls he'd come in contact with over the years, Lydia not being the first of them. Mr. Sobieski had a nice chunk of change left from his ex-wife's death, her insurance policy having paid out great dividends. Sitting there for over an hour, he concluded paying up would be the best option for all parties involved, though he had no idea who was doing the extorting. $22,000 was what his nefarious deeds would cost him. Either way, it was better than prison.

Authorities were closing in much faster than Jackson thought they would, so the following day he called in sick to work, for fear of not having his i's dotted and t's crossed. Too much had transpired, and he needed to ensure he'd effectively placed the nail in Marcus's coffin. Waiting for him to surface, he spied through the peephole at his front door. Jackson knew exactly what time Marcus came home for lunch. He was just waiting for him to head back to the post office. He surmised that only then would he have sufficient time to complete his task. At twenty-five minutes after eleven, he peered down at his wristwatch. That was when he heard a door close across the hall. As he hoped, patience paid off. Marcus had emerged sooner than Jackson anticipated. Edges of the demented carrier's mouth turned up, brandishing a sinister grin. He heard Marcus's footsteps become faint as he headed farther down the hall. That was when Jackson darted over to his living room window. There he peered through the blinds until his nemesis's car cruised down Main Street.

It was time. Jackson grabbed his black T-shirt off the bed, sliding it on before his jeans and Chuck Taylors. The marine in him had everything needed to break into Marcus's apartment. Jackson hadn't made a peep that entire morning, which he'd hoped would keep that old man next door out of his metaphorical hair. When he opened his door, he peeked left, then right. Everything was quiet on the residential front. He stepped out into the hall, closing his door with a gentle hand.

Once he pulled tools from a back pocket of his jeans and went to work, Jackson was inside apartment number 9 in no time. He quietly closed the door behind him with his eyes focused on Marcus's bedroom. There, Jackson would look for anything he could to further pin the blame on his coworker.

On his way to the room a loose-leaf piece of paper on the coffee table in the living room caught his eye. Jackson walked over staring down closely at the print. The more he read, the more a wry grin formed about his lips. Marcus had more than one nemesis, and the revelation was just the leg up Jackson needed. Not to mention the fact that he himself could use that money being extorted.

Over at the high school, Mr. Sobieski stood peering from a window in his office, which gave a view to the courtyard. He pondered how he'd gotten himself into such a mess. His sexually deviant ways nearly cost him a quarter of his savings. You would think his newfound dilemma would become a lesson learned. Unfortunately, he continued leering at the young girls traveling the courtyard in between classes. *I'll just smooth this all over. It'll go away,* he surmised with wavering confidence.

Just then, a voice came through the speaker on the phone atop his mahogany desk. "Mr. Sobieski," she summoned.

The perverted principal moved over to the phone past trophies and plaques lining his bookshelf to answer the call. "Mrs. Senkowski?" he answered, pressing a button to speak.

"I was able to cancel the rest of your conferences for the day, so your schedule is free and clear, sir."

"You're the best, Mrs. Senkowski. I appreciate you calling everyone. I'm gonna head out and will be gone for the remainder of the day. There's something I need to take care of, and it can't wait," he replied, staring fixedly at that dreaded letter in his opposite hand.

"You enjoy the rest of your day, sir. I can hold things down on this end."

It wasn't the day's work being completed he worried over. It was getting through the deal without his life becoming the latest Clarkston scandal.

Within fifteen minutes of their conversation, Mr. Sobieski was pulling two stacks of cash from the safety deposit box at his bank.

At the same time, Marcus strolled into the bank to complete his transaction. He kept his eyes trained on the room where the boxes were stored, knowing it was where he would be headed. That was when he noticed his son's old principal exiting. The two locked eyes. Mr. Sobieski furnished him with a nod, recognizing Marcus as well. They'd had talks about Andre's future at the high school, those that eventually led to him being homeschooled.

"Can I help you, sir?" the bank manager asked as she approached Marcus.

"I need to get into my safety deposit box."

Just outside, the deputies sat in their cruiser, waiting for Marcus to emerge. It took him nearly twenty minutes to complete the transaction before he resurfaced, rubbernecking left, then right. There were a few pedestrians traveling the street by foot, yet none were the person for whom he searched. Marcus's paranoia was at an all-time high. He was sure Jackson was somewhere watching to be sure he had withdrawn the money, ensuring everything went as planned. Marcus had no idea that the ones he should really be concerned with were two officers tailing him since the night prior. Nodding his head in despair, he continued his trek to the parking lot to get back to his vehicle.

He got inside, slamming his car door behind him. Marcus's face burned red. The angry clerk repeatedly slammed both hands against the steering wheel, attempting to release his frustrations. "Motherfucker!" he screamed, glasses lying crooked on his face as he gripped the wheel, wanting to rip it from the steering column. From his peripheral view, he caught sight of the two gentlemen leering at him from their cruiser, instantly causing his meltdown to subside. *Maybe they're just watching the bank. They could be security,* he guessed, teetering toward hope. Quickly composing himself, the nervous clerk straightened his glasses, then started his vehicle. Marcus refrained from turning their way, so the officers had no idea he noticed them there. He started his car, pulling out of the parking lot and figuring he would drive around aimlessly in order to determine whether he was being followed. Marcus cruised up the street past the bank, stealing glances at them through his rearview mirror as he made several unnecessary turns. Turns that ultimately brought him back around to the bank after just a few minutes.

"I think we've been made," one officer alerted the other.

"Maybe he forgot something and is coming back to the bank," his partner reasoned.

That was when they noticed Marcus hopping out of his vehicle and heading their way on foot.

"What should we do?" the driving deputy inquired.

"Pull off before he gets over here."

The deputy pulled off down the street, passing Marcus by without awarding him any eye contact. Marcus stared as they drove by, even more perplexed by their actions.

Chapter 36

So Close Yet So Far

A call came through as Officer Fackender stared down at photos of the late Jessica Walkin inside a case file atop her desk. "Officer Fackender here," she answered.

The deputy on the other end of the line informed Officer Fackender of recent developments.

"Goddammit, Deputy! No. Just head back to the office. He's already made you. I'll take it from here." She slammed the phone back down on its base.

Wanting to remain inconspicuous, Jackson traveled on foot down Main Street to get to the postal store across the road from the annex building. He assumed that driving his vehicle could draw too much attention his way. At the end of his ten-minute trek past shops and quaint little houses lining Main Street, he found himself in the rear post office parking lot, where employees' vehicles were parked. Marcus's Volkswagen GTI was there among the others, just as Jackson surmised. He took a stroll alongside the vehicle, ducking to attach a tracking device to the underbody of the sedan. The action was swift. Jackson was down then up again within seconds.

"Hey, Jackson. What are you doing here? Elise said you called in because you weren't feeling well today," one of the other clerks, Christian, inquired, having noticed him as she headed toward her vehicle to leave for the day.

Jackson thought quickly. "I'm heading over to the drug store to get some ginger ale and Pepto." He placed his hand on his abdomen for added effect.

Skin between her eyebrows wrinkled. "You're walking?" She thought it odd he was walking around but couldn't come into work.

Damn, this bitch is nosy, he thought, yet refrained from uttering the words. "I prefer the exercise," he replied nonchalantly, creating a bit of distance between them.

"Well, I certainly hope you feel better. I guess I'll see you tomorrow, maybe."

"Yeah, sure. I'll see you later, uh . . ." He paused his inching backward, unable to recall her name.

"Christian. My name is Christian."

"My apologies. I'm not very good with names. I'll see you tomorrow, Christian. And I promise I won't forget again."

"I sure hope not." She smiled as he turned away from her to leave.

"That was a close one," he mumbled.

Detective Barnes indeed believed Jackson's claims that Jessica was a prostitute, but he wanted to confirm rumors. Being that he was picking up his order from one of the diners on Dixie Highway, he'd decided to question his waitress. Maybe she'd seen Jessica around and could provide clarity as to who she was in her everyday life. The officer walked into the restaurant headed for the counter, where Janice was busy refilling drinks for other patrons. That evening was busier than usual. Janice wasn't in the best of moods, being that she'd been on her feet all day.

Barnes took a seat at the counter.

"How can I help you, Officer?" Janice inquired, continuing to fill the glasses with water from the plastic pitcher.

"I called in an order for Edward Barnes."

"Let me see if your order is up." Janice turned to look in the window, which gave a view to the kitchen. No boxed orders had been placed in the window. "I'm sorry. It'll be a few more minutes on your order, Detective," she remarked, turning back to address him.

"That's fine by me. It's worth the wait. I ordered goulash."

Janice shook her head in agreement with Detective Barnes.

"Do you have a moment? I know you are working, but I wanted to see if you could help me with something."

Janice forced out a long sigh. "Sure. What can I help you with, sir?"

"I promise it'll only take a second. I just wanted to ask you if you've seen this woman before." Detective Barnes pulled a photo of Jessica out from the breast pocket of his shirt, then slid it across the counter. "Have you seen this woman before?"

Janice peered down at the picture. "I have," she admitted.

"Does she eat here?" he asked to gain clarification.

"She would frequently walk the block. She came in here one day pretty beat up. When I asked her what had happened, she told me that one of her johns had gotten rough with her. The owner offered her a job. Ya know, to get her off the streets. She came in for the interview. Got the job and everything. But when it was time to come in for work, she never showed up. I guess prostituting is easier money than working for a living."

"Have you ever seen her with one of her johns?"

"I'm sorry. I can't say I have. Is she okay?"

"She was murdered. Her body was found in a dumpster in Clarkston. I'm assuming that's why she never showed up to work."

"Oh, my God. How awful." Janice held her gaped-mouth expression.

"Yes, it certainly is. Do you know where she lived?" Detective Barnes needed to find her next of kin. The address displayed on her license had led him to an abandoned house in Pontiac.

"I can get her current address off of the application for you."

"That would help. The one on her license doesn't seem to match."

"I'll be right back. Let me go to the office and get it for you." Janice headed to the back behind the swinging door that led to the kitchen.

Once Detective Barnes had eaten his dinner in the comfort of his cruiser, he decided to ride by the address on Jessica's application. Notifying her next of kin was of great importance to him. There had to be someone who cared about Jessica. At least, he hoped so. Although different than the one on her license, the alternate address led him to a run-down home in Pontiac, Michigan. When he pulled up to the house, there were multiple women sitting out on the porch, all in disheveled clothing. They couldn't have been any older than 30 years of age. Three of the women stood in a circle, each waiting to take a drag from the single cigarette they shared. The other two women sat on the wooden porch steps, one sitting between the other woman's legs as she got her long black hair braided into two cornrows. When they noticed he'd pulled up, the three standing in a circle rushed inside, but not before tossing the cigarette into the dead grass in the front yard. When they slammed the front door, the outside door with the tattered screen flew open, remaining ajar.

"Go inside," the oldest woman who happened to be braiding instructed the other.

"Can I have a word with you ladies?" Detective Barnes asked as he approached.

The younger women got up, then headed into the house without awarding Barnes an ounce of attention.

"We didn't do nothing wrong. I don't understand why y'all have to keep harassing us. We're just trying to make a living like the rest of you," she spouted.

"I assure you, I'm not here to harass you ladies. I just have a few questions I wanted to ask."

"Well, I don't know nothing," she quickly snapped back, flipping her long genie ponytail behind her back.

"Listen, sista, I'm not here to give you a hard time. I won't even ask you any questions about what you've got going on here. I just want to know if you can tell me anything about this woman." The detective pulled a photo of Jessica from the breast pocket of his shirt, then held it out for the resistant woman to see.

She studied the photo for a second, noticing exactly who it was. "I don't know who that woman is," she replied, looking out toward the street.

"Please." Detective Barnes stared into her eyes. "I just need to find her next of kin," he reasoned.

"Why you lookin' for her next of kin? Did something happen to her?" the woman inquired, finally showing an inkling of concern.

"She was found over in Clarkston. Her body was in a dumpster behind an apartment building."

"You sayin' she's dead?"

"Yes. She's no longer with us."

The woman's big brown eyes welled up with tears, but for fear of falling apart completely, she maintained her composure. "I thought she got out free and clear."

"So, you do know her?"

"She used to live here, but I kicked her out. She just couldn't manage to get along with the rest of the girls. Jessica thought she was better than the rest of us but never could manage to pay her way. Every time she came home, she had some excuse about why she didn't have any money. We can't pay no bills around here with excuses. If you gon' stay here, you gon' pay," she rambled on, tone hardening the more she spoke.

Detective Barnes shook his head with disappointment. "When was the last time you saw her?"

"Shit, I don't know. About a month ago. Jessica thought she was gon' ride off in the sunset to get a good job, a nice house, and a man who wanted her for more than what she could do in the bedroom. Last time I heard, she was sleeping in her car and staying in one of those roach motels up on Dixie."

"Do you know which motel?"

"I don't remember the name, but it's in Waterford across the street from the topless bar. That's all I know. I can't give you no mo' information."

"You don't know any of her family?"

"Same ol' story. Her daddy is dead, and her mama is a crackhead. What else you wanna know?"

"Nothing. I'll be on my way. Thank you for helping me. I appreciate it."

"Mm-hmm," she huffed as she watched Detective Barnes walk back to his cruiser.

Barnes opened his passenger side door to reach into the glove box. He grabbed a small rectangular card, then headed back her way.

"What he want now?" the woman mumbled before smacking her lips together.

"Here. Take this card." He handed it over to her.

"What I'm supposed to do with this?"

"It's a safe place. If you ever decided to get help.
You can get on your feet there for free and without
judgment. After you complete the program, they'll
even help you get a house. It's called Great Centers
of Hope. You should check it out. All of you should.
There's a much better life out there waiting for you.
Just think about it. When you're ready, they'll be
there. Tell them Detective Barnes sent you."

She looked down at the card, considering what
he had proposed. "Maybe I will."

"I sure hope so. What's your name, by the way?"

"Trixie," she replied.

The detective knew her name wasn't Trixie but
decided not to press the issue, knowing all too well
extra hoops he'd have to go through to obtain her
government name. "Trixie, you have a nice day,
and don't forget to give that number a call."

"You have a good day, Officer," she said, finally
having dropped the attitude in her tone.

Chapter 37

The Getaway

2200 hours. Night had fallen. It was almost time to exact their plan. Lydia had been unusually silent that entire evening. She sat at the edge of the bed, neatly folding her clothing into a suitcase that lay open atop the double-size mattress in their motel room. It was visible to Andre, the worry that plagued her, yet, preoccupied with his own, he refrained from addressing the melancholy expression she'd donned since waking that morning. Fear held a tight grip. Thoughts of losing the intense connection they shared ate away at her sanity. What if something tragic were to happen? She'd go back to being alone and, even worse, unloved. Lydia was sure that no one could love someone like her, someone so damaged and used. She didn't want anyone else, and neither did Andre. He'd had his fair share of women. All paled in comparison to the love he had found with Lydia.

Andre had always dreamed of the day he would be out on his own, free to do as he pleased with whom he'd chosen. Although it was Marcus who brought Lydia into his life, he felt that it was fate that connected them.

Andre's heart raced as he watched Lydia gather her belongings. Everything about her spoke to lustful urges he harbored: her full lips, the curves of her hips, even the delicate touch of Lydia's fingertips. When she touched him, malice and anger seemed to melt from his bleeding heart. It was a feeling he never wanted to lose, a feeling he was willing to do anything to keep.

Lydia's eyes lifted, catching an admiring gaze he'd bestowed on her. "What is it?" she innocently inquired.

"Everything is going to work out," he answered.

Lydia sighed. "Promise," she said with pleading eyes. The teen hoped for adequate reassurance, yet the relief Andre intended to grant her remained absent.

"I promise that everything is going to be fine. We're gonna be okay. I just hope you're ready, because after this, you're stuck with me."

"There's nothing in the world I want more, Andre," the lovesick teen admitted.

Andre narrowed the gap between them once Lydia lowered her head, overtaken by feelings of sadness. A single tear fell from a corner of her eye as she closed them. Her lover placed a finger under the girl's chin, lifting her head. "Open your eyes, Lydia," he instructed. She complied with her lover's request.

"It's you and me now," he continued, eyes gazing into hers.

The cab driver pulled up into a gravel parking lot outside of thier motel room. He pressed the horn, alerting his passengers to his arrival.

Andre darted over to a window, pulling back the curtains to peek outside. "Our cab is here. It's time to go."

"I'm ready." Lydia zipped her small suitcase, stood, then threw her purple backpack over her shoulder.

The headlamps of the cab illuminated a thick fog that had settled in the air that night. With their bags in tow, the teens walked out of the motel room, headed for their ride.

Back at his apartment, Marcus grabbed an envelope of cash, stuffing it into a back pocket of his shorts. Everything in him told him not to walk out that front door as he peered its way from the entrance of his bedroom. Taking heed of his better judgment, he turned, deciding to head for a window instead. The fire escape would be his way out just in case police were out front watching, waiting for him to surface.

Jackson sat in his Ford Bronco just outside, waiting for Marcus to head off toward his destination. There was no need for him to follow closely, being that he had a tracking device that would lead him to Marcus's exact location. He waited, having not a clue that the man in the black ball cap was nearby spying on him as well.

Just then, Marcus climbed out of the window. He closed it behind him before proceeding to climb down the fire escape.

The alley was dark. Only one streetlamp lit the way to his vehicle. The nervous clerk looked around, searching the scene for prying eyes. Jackson went completely undetected beyond the cover of his tinted windows. Marcus climbed into his vehicle, then headed off down the alleyway. He traveled it for three blocks before driving out on to the main road.

Jackson didn't follow, intent on maintaining some distance between them as to remain undiscovered. The former marine concentrated on the device in his hand, mapping Marcus's every motion.

Not far from there, Mr. Sobieski was ready to head out as well.

"Shelby?" he called out to his stepdaughter from the opposite side of her closed bedroom door. After receiving no answer, he knocked lightly a few times, attempting to force her reply, his intuition telling him that she was ignoring him. "Shelby?" the deviant stepfather calmly called out once more, giving her the benefit of the doubt.

Dressed in pajamas and ready for bed, his stepdaughter lay there with her back rested against the wooden headboard, only one side of the headphones covering her ear. She had heard him knocking but chose not to reply. And she didn't. That was, not until he called her name a third time and much louder than the last.

"What do you want? I'm not dressed!"

"I'm going out for a moment. I'll be back in about an hour or so."

"Okay! Whatever," she replied, rolling her eyes as she pulled the headphones over her opposite ear to drown out further conversation.

Mr. Sobieski walked to the front door, then hopped into his truck parked in the driveway. Once he'd gotten inside, he took a deep breath, ready to get it over with. He hoped that everything would go as planned. Everything Mr. Sobieski needed he saw in the center console once he popped it open to ensure the money was there. It was time to face his extortioner.

***

Andre and Lydia finally arrived at their destination. "You can drop us off right up here," Andre
said to the taxi driver, instructing him to drop
them off at the apartment building next to Lake
Callis. The driver complied, putting on the brakes.
Lydia stepped out, heading for the trunk to grab
their bags, while Andre paid for the ride.

"Thanks, man," he remarked, handing over
the money. When Andre hopped out, Lydia had
already grabbed their bags from the trunk. "I'll
carry the bags," he said, grabbing her suitcase
along with his bag.

"Why are we here?"

"I didn't want the cab driver to know where
we're going. The carnival is closed, and it would
look kinda suspicious if we got dropped off there,"
Andre explained.

"Good idea. I didn't think about that."

"Don't worry. I'm gonna take care of us."

The teens traveled on foot from there to get to
the carnival. It was dark. None of the rides were
being operated, so there were no lights to assist
in guiding their way. Andre and Lydia would have
to depend on the light of the moon to travel its
fog-coated grounds.

"What do we do now?" Lydia inquired as they
navigated Lake Callis's property.

"Right over there." He pointed toward the balloon-and-dart stand. "We can hide behind that booth. We'll be able to see from the small holes in the wood. Here's the trash can where they'll deposit the money," Andre stated as they came upon it.

Chapter 38

The Final Chapter

Marcus was first to arrive. Andre and Lydia peeked out at him through holes in the wood as they ducked behind a booth, patiently waiting for him to drop the cash.

He came upon the trash can, leering in every direction, attempting to catch a glimpse of his extortioner. To his dismay, there was no one in sight. In no way did Marcus plan on willingly giving up thousands of dollars he earned free and clear. His plan was to wait to see who had lured him there. Marcus pulled the envelope of money from the back pocket of his jeans, tossing it into the trash can. He looked around once more. Not a person in sight. That was when he came up with the idea to light up the place. He walked over to the merry-go-round, flipping a switch to turn it on. The lights illuminated. Its melody sounded. "That's better," Marcus mumbled.

Fifteen minutes later, Marcus caught sight of Mr. Sobieski traveling the grounds as he hid alongside the ball-and-bucket-toss booth. The pervy principal peered left, right, then all around him as he approached where he was to deposit the money. Yet before he had the opportunity to take out his payment, Marcus attacked from behind. Wielding the small throwing knife he nabbed from one of the other booths, he stabbed the blade into Mr. Sobieski's head. The knife pierced his cheek, knocking one of the molars from his gums as the blade exited the other side of his face. His muffled screams spewed blood from his mouth, painting his lips then the bottom of his face. Marcus yanked out the knife. "Give me back my money, you motherfucker," he demanded, shoving him from behind. Mr. Sobieski's body plowed into the bottle-stand booth, smashing part of its wood structure. Marcus charged forward, ready to deliver more punishment. He leaned over Mr. Sobieski's still body, turning him over with a tight grasp on his shirt. The wounded principal swung a Coke bottle, cracking his attacker over the head. The glass shattered, leaving the jagged tip in his fist. Mr. Sobieski held tight to Marcus with one hand, then jammed the sharp glass into the side of his face, returning the favor before pulling him down alongside him. Marcus was stunned. His eyes lit up at the sight of blood leaking from his face.

"Oh, my God. He's going to kill him. What are we gonna do?" Lydia whispered as she and Andre peered at the chaotic scene from small holes drilled into the booth they'd taken cover behind.

"We're not going to do anything. If he sees us here, he'll kill us too," Andre revealed.

Mr. Sobieski got up, staggering as he spit gushing blood from his mouth down onto the grass. Attempting to flee Marcus's wrath, he rushed toward the carousel for cover, broken bottle clutched in his grasp.

The outraged clerk regained his composure quickly. "Try as you might, you're not getting away with my money," he uttered. Marcus rose to his feet, tearing off after him.

Mr. Sobieski hopped up onto the running ride, hiding behind carriages and horses abounding it.

The stone-cold stare on Marcus's face seemed as if he weren't affected by his injury in the slightest. He was intent on leaving the fairgrounds carrying the money with which he'd arrived. He wasn't scared of Mr. Sobieski, and quite frankly, he was relieved it wasn't Jackson he'd be dealing with, feeling he had a much better chance at defeating his son's former principal. Marcus searched, peeking behind then inside one of the carriages. That was when Mr. Sobieski grabbed him from behind, wrapping his arm tight around his throat in a headlock. Marcus's face burned red as the lack of oxygen began to debilitate him. The choke hold was working. That was, until he swung the knife up over his shoulder, plunging it into Mr. Sobieski's eye socket.

"Ahhhh!" he screamed, releasing the death grip he'd garnered. Marcus pulled out the knife, turned, then jammed it into the other. Mr. Sobieski fell backward, the bottom half of his body on the carousel, the other being dragged across the ground by the running merry-go-round.

That was when Jackson arrived, just in time to witness Marcus dragging Mr. Sobieski's body to the lake's edge. He trekked over to the boat lodge, grabbing one of the canoes that sat on the sand. There was a rope nearby, which he figured would be of use. His intentions were to get rid of the dead body and fast. With his eyes trained on a row of cinder blocks alongside the wooden structure, he devised a plan. Marcus tossed a few of the cinder blocks along with the rope into the canoe, then dragged it over to Mr. Sobieski's corpse. He pushed the canoe to the shoreline, then lifted the body onto the boat.

"Well, look what we have here." Jackson watched, eyes bulging from their sockets.

"Who the fuck is that?" Lydia asked once she noticed Jackson.

Andre squinted to see. "I think that's my neighbor."

"What the hell is he doing here?"

"I don't know, but we're sure not gonna ask him. Just keep quiet. Hopefully, this will all be over soon," he whispered.

Marcus yanked the knife from the eye socket of the corpse, using it to cut the long rope into three sections. He tied each cinder block to a separate extremity. One of the blocks he tied around Mr. Sobieski's neck, another to his wrists, which were bound together, then the last to his bound ankles. He tossed the blocks over first, then pushed the body over into the water, unintentionally flipping the canoe, forcing himself over into the lake with the corpse. "Fuck," Marcus yelped as he toppled overboard. Lucky for him, he could swim and, moreover, no blocks bound his extremities. The corpse sank to the bottom of the lake while Marcus managed to tread water. He flipped the canoe over, tossed its oar back aboard, then climbed back into the boat, lying flat on his back to catch his breath.

He'd successfully killed Mr. Sobieski and gotten rid of the evidence. Yet Marcus had no idea of the impending danger he would face once he reached the beach.

Back in North Carolina, Buddy's cell phone illuminated, vibrating on a coffee table in front of him.

"Who is that?" Sue inquired as she lifted her head from his lap, taking her attention away from the movie they were watching.

"It's no one. I'll handle it. Just give me a second," he replied, grabbing the phone to answer the call.

The man in the black ball cap watched as Jackson spied on Marcus, all the while relaying his findings to Buddy over the phone. "He's not alone. There's two of them here," he said. "What do you want me to do?"

Buddy replied, "No witnesses."

"Not a problem." He disconnected the call, then slid the cell phone into the front pocket of his jeans. The stranger pulled out a silencer and proceeded to screw it onto the tip of a 9 mm pistol in his opposite hand.

As Marcus approached the sand, he stepped out of the boat into the shallow water, pulling the canoe the rest of the way out. That was when he noticed the envelope on the ground. Marcus bent over, retrieving it, his pupils expanding once he realized it was full of cash. He studied the bills, surmising it was nearly double the amount he'd been bribed to bring along. "Looks like you've been busy," he uttered before stuffing the cash into his pocket. It wasn't until he'd dragged the canoe back over to the cabin that Jackson stepped out of the darkness.

"Did you think you would get away with it?" he asked the drenched clerk. Jackson had already seen him shoving an envelope into his pocket. "Tell me, Marcus, what do you have in your pocket?"

"It's none of your business what's in my pocket," Marcus countered calmly.

"Aww, come on. Show me. I won't rat you out."

"You want to see what I have?"

Jackson inched toward him. "I do. Why don't you hand it over?" he instructed, holding his hand out to receive whatever it was Marcus had tucked away.

Marcus pulled the blade from his pocket, wielding it at Jackson, aiming directly at his heart. Once he realized the knife didn't penetrate, it was already too late. Jackson grabbed his hand, bending his wrist back until his fingers snapped. "Ahhhh!"

The knife dropped to the sand as Marcus's face took blow after blow from Jackson's closed fist. He staggered backward, unable to create distance between himself and Jackson due to a hold he maintained on his broken hand. Jackson repeatedly slammed his fist into Marcus's face. Blood streamed from his broken nose. It oozed from his battered mouth. Jackson was intent on ending him right there by way of blunt-force trauma, but the bullet that pierced his back caused him to pause. His eyes bulged. He had no idea what happened. Another bullet ripped through his vest. The impact caused him to fall forward, releasing his grip. The next bullet went into Marcus's skull, right between the eyes.

His business there had been concluded. The man in the black ball cap turned, then headed back to his vehicle.

Andre and Lydia heard the car start before the stranger pulled off into the darkness. "He's gone." Andre peeked over the counter. Once he surmised no one was left, he hopped over, helping Lydia out from behind immediately after. "Let's get the money and go."

The teens darted over to the trash can, pulled off its top, and there it was: an envelope full of cash. They would settle for one stack as opposed to the entire amount. Andre pulled it out. "We gotta go before the police show up."

"Ahhh. Fuck." Jackson winced from the aching he felt as he rolled over onto his back. Bullets had wounded him yet not fully pierced his vest. He sat up looking around to see who was there. Everyone was gone, all except the dead body lying next to him. Jackson yanked at the pocket of Marcus's jeans, pulling the envelope out. "Jackpot," he remarked, flipping through the cash. That's when a canoe, cinder blocks, and rope caught his eye.

Moments later, it was Marcus's body that was being rolled into the lake. His corpse sank to its bottom alongside Mr. Sobieski's, right where it belonged.

***

Andre and Lydia boarded a Greyhound bus not more than an hour later. They'd get as far away from Clarkston as they could. "What about your dad? Don't you want to know what happened to him?" Lydia asked.

"No. I don't. I don't ever want to hear his name again," he replied, staring out of the window of a Greyhound bus as it pulled off, destination: Nashville, Tennessee.

Epilogue

The Aftermath

When the sun rose, Erick sat at Evelyn's bedside, his hand clutching her limp extremities. Bandages wrapped her head wound, and gauze covered bruises on her face. Seventy-two hours had gone by since she was last conscious. A team of medical staff huddled in the corner, discussing Evelyn's recent CAT scan. Her husband's belief in the fact that she would wake remained resolute, despite the pessimistic attitude of the surgeon who'd closed a wound at the front of her skull.

Erick whispered to her, "Wake up, my love. It's time to wake up now. I can't do this without you. I need you. The kids need you. You've gotta fight this thing. You're stronger than this, baby. Please, just wake up. Just open your eyes for me."

Evelyn didn't move a muscle. A tube protruding from her mouth, steeped into the depths of her esophagus, looked more painful than helpful. It weakened Erick at his very core to see her in such a feeble state. The fact that there was nothing he could do to save her made him feel useless. He was her protector. At least, he fancied himself being as much. His will to be strong crumbled before faith ultimately became the victor. He'd been there by her side for three days, waiting for her to wake.

Wanting had turned to wishing, but only for a day or two, at which point the doting husband was in the hospital chapel on his knees, praying at the alter for God to give her back. He vowed that no hell would be worse than losing his companion for life.

Colin peeked into Evelyn's hospital room. It was nearly empty, the doctors having all dispersed. He pushed past the door, approaching with a small bouquet of yellow lilies attached to a teddy bear. Colin had hung the postal arm badge Evelyn dropped in the ambulance around the teddy bear's neck. "I know you don't know me, but I just wanted to check on you. Make sure you made it. I, ah, also wanted to bring this back to you." He set the gift atop of the white blanket covering her legs. "You dropped it in the ambulance. You probably can't even hear me, can you? I had an aunt who was in a coma once. She swore up and down she could hear the family when they came to visit. My mom didn't believe her. She would always say, 'Aunt Raye sure can weave a tale.'"

Colin placed his hand atop hers. "Well, whether you can or can't hear me, I'm sorry this happened to you, and I hope you wake up soon."

As he turned away, Evelyn's hand clutched Colin's. He turned back, looking directly into her wild, wide-eyed stare. "You're awake."

One month later and thousands of miles away

The doorbell chimed, sending the already-flustered woman with the cordless phone pressed to her ear into even more of a frenzy. "Honey, I've got to call you back. I have twenty-five centerpieces to finish, I haven't started dinner, and the doorbell is ringing. I love you. I'll see you when you get home. Don't forget to pick your suit up from the dry cleaner," the 30-something African American woman with the Coke-bottle shape rattled on before disconnecting the call.

"I'm coming." She rushed from the living room, surrounded by flowers and crystal vases, out into the foyer to answer the door.

She opened it to the sight of a tall, handsome dark-complected bald man with a full beard. "Ohhh, how can I help you?" she said, all the while drowning in his deep brown eyes.

"Hi. My name is Jackson. I'm your new FedEx driver. I have a package for you."

"Do I need to sign for it?"

"Yes, and it's pretty heavy. Would you like for me to bring it inside?"

"Please do. I wouldn't want to break a nail." She turned, twisting her hips from side to side as she walked toward the living room. Her firm rump looked inviting under the silk red robe. "You can put it in here," she continued, her long brown dreadlocks brushing across the center of her back.

Jackson lifted the big brown box, carrying it inside with one arm. The maleficent deliveryman was sure to search the scene for prying eyes before shutting the front door, then twisting the deadbolt to lock them both inside.

The End